Flight of the Blackbird Part I
Copyright © 2023 Catrina J. Sparkman
Published by:

The Ironer's Press
Madison, WI 53713

FLIGHT OF THE

Blackbird

PART I

A LOVE STORY TOLD
IN TWO PARTS

CATRINA J. SPARKMAN

Dedication

This Book is Dedicated to Fatherless Boys everywhere: every color, every hue & every creed.

A Demand

He will cover you with His
feathers, and under His wings
you will find refuge;

Psalms 91: 4 (NIV)

CHAPTER 1

NEW YORK CITY, 2010
PRESENT DAY

Tonya sat in Ted Mitchell's office, gripping the arms of the chair. She was sitting across from Ted and his fiancée, which was impossible because he was the senior pastor of Now Faith International and also *her* fiancé.

"I've put this decision to prayer." That was Ted speaking. "As a founding member of Now Faith, you are an integral cog in this machine. This ministry doesn't work without you. We'd like for you to stay on. What you've done with the children's ministry has been nothing short of phenomenal."

"What we don't want is a church split over this." That was the new fiancée. A model turned actress that only went professionally by her first name, Tatiana. Would she still be just Tatiana after she and Ted were married? Or would she be Mrs. Tatiana Mitchell? First Lady?

"Tonya, things haven't been good between us for a while. With you studying for your boards—and I get it — your career is very important to you. I just wished being my wife and the First Lady of this church would have been more important." Ted sighed. "Tonya, don't you have anything to say at all?"

He was probably wondering why she wasn't fighting. He was probably asking himself why she hadn't raised her voice, not one time during this exchange? Tonya hadn't said a word. She just stared at their interlaced fingers and Tatiana's engagement ring. The one Tonya had seen the former model sporting two weeks ago on her right hand. It looked to be about a carat. Her Aunt Katie had been right. Tonya's Uncle Earl, Aunt Katie's late husband, had been a shoe man all his life. Her aunt had insisted that Ted did not love her. She'd taken one look at the small, murky diamond Ted had placed on Tonya's finger and said, "Throw him back. His shoes cost more than your ring."

"Well, this is a lot to absorb at once. Perhaps I shouldn't expect you to say anything."

Tonya looked at Ted, and her lips curled up into a pleasant smile. He shifted uneasily in his chair. Yeah, definitely not the reaction he expected. Tonya knew her silence had to be unsettling, but she wanted him to think—no, scratch that, she needed him to understand just how unfazed she was by his dismissal.

"Listen, the people love you. They expected you to be their First Lady. So, I need for us to be Christ-centered about this and present a united front. I propose we make an announcement to the congregation this Sunday. We can tell them we sought the counsel of the Lord and will remain partners in ministry and friends."

Tonya tuned Ted out and played back the tape in her own head. She had relocated for this man. Had turned down graduate school at John Hopkins to help build his ministry. And, when she graduated with her doctorate, he couldn't be there to celebrate with her because he was at the Oscars with the woman sitting beside him. Then there was the part she didn't dare think about. The most important thing she had given up. Tonya forced the thought from her mind. She couldn't think of that now. She would not think of the man she had walked away from, or what she thought she had heard from God because if she did, she would fall to the floor and weep bitterly, and Ted would think she was weeping for him. No, she would leave this place with her dignity intact.

"Just so you know, we plan to marry quickly." Tatiana said.

Ted's free hand stroked Tatiana's neck and his eyes studied Tonya like she was a ticking bomb. "I wouldn't want that to be an additional shock to you. And, since the three of us are now a team of sorts, and I know how much you care about this ministry, for the sake of full disclosure, I will also tell you that Tatiana is pregnant. Of course, that was never my intention for that to happen, but—"

"When two people love each other as much as we do, it's impossible to wait." Tatiana said, staring brazenly at Tonya. Translation: you didn't love him no way, Boo-Boo. If you had, you would have dropped the panties a long time ago.

Thank God for a revelation of holiness.

"Tonya, I want you to know that I've repented for this. I've cried out to God. He has shown me the error of my ways. He has also shown me I am a David. Tatiana is my Bathsheba, and this baby will be my heir, my Solomon."

Wow, way to misappropriate the Bible. "Anything else?"

"Only that I know how much you care for the people of this flock. In some ways, you've been more of a pastor to them than I have. And, well, frankly, if something like this were to get out, it would break their hearts."

Tonya stood to leave. "My lips are sealed."

Relief spread across Ted's face. "I'll walk you out."

Ted followed Tonya into the outer office where his secretary, Martha, usually sat, but today was conspicuously absent.

"Tonya." He had spoken her name barely above a whisper. When she didn't respond, Ted cleared his throat and spoke louder.

Tonya turned and faced him.

"I'll need the ring back, just so there's no confusion."

Tonya handed him the tiny, murky diamond. As he took it, he grabbed her hand.

"I want you to know that I really did love you. A part of me always will. I don't want you to think I'm going back on what God said, it's just ... I believe God gives us choices. You are the perfect woman to help me reach my destiny, but Tatiana is the perfect woman for me."

With that, Ted released her hand; and Tonya walked out of Now Faith International Church for the last time. She went back to her apartment, loaded up her car, and hit the road. All the while thanking God for an avenue of escape. On a whim, Tonya had applied for a job at an elementary school in Texas several weeks ago. She had gotten the news just that morning. They wanted her as their new full-time Child Development Psychologist. Even if Houston was the last place on Earth she wanted to run to, Tonya was grateful for a way of escape.

CHAPTER 2

HOUSTON, TEXAS, ONE WEEK LATER

THE PLAN WAS SIMPLE, work maybe three, at the most six months. Then apply like crazy and get the heck out of dodge, or rather in this case, Houston. Texas was the place where she had been born and raised. It was where most of her family still called home, except for her jet-setting Aunt Katie, who declared herself to be a citizen of the world. Most importantly, Houston, was where Michael lived. Tonya hadn't thought about how she was going to get in and out of Houston without her family knowing her whereabouts. Especially since Tonya talked to someone in her family at least once a week. She had, however, been unreachable during her move and she knew that if she didn't start leaving messages with the quickness, they would send a search party after her. Tonya continued unpacking her new office and rehearsing aloud what she would say to her mother.

"I took a temporary job somewhere, but I'm not at liberty to reveal my location." *Nah, that won't work.* "I'm back in Houston, just for a minute, so please don't tell Michael. Or anybody connected to Michael. Don't tell his mother, your best friend, who is also my godmother." *Okay, I guess that won't work either.* "I broke up with Ted. I need some time to disappear. I'm fine. Don't call me, I'll call you." *They would send a search party for sure.* A knock on her office door interrupted Tonya's thoughts. "Come in."

Julie, the school nurse, peeked her head in. "I know this is your first day, but are you ready to get your feet wet?"

"Sure, what's up?"

Julie took in the entire room. "Wow, you work fast, Tonya. I like what you've done to the place. Okay, so this is a special case. She's five-years-old. Cute as a button, but a fighter. Her dad's a high-profile celebrity. She got into another fight today, and Headmistress Tatum is calling for a three-day suspension."

"I thought you said the child was five."

"Her teacher thinks the child may have anger issues. When I tell you who her father is, you'll see why."

God, please, out of all the schools in Houston, don't let this be Serenity's school.

"Her father is Bad Boy Joshua Keys." Julie said, measuring Tonya's response.

Tonya knew all the rumors that had circulated about her godbrother and his wife, Bella, but she kept her face as neutral as possible. "Julie, are you suggesting that the dad is violent towards the child?"

"Oh gosh, no. Nobody would dare say anything like that. Anybody with a pair of eyes can see that he loves that little girl to pieces. First, let me say, I'm one of his biggest fans. I don't believe any of those rumors. I think he is one of the sexiest men on the planet."

"Good, because he's also a pastor now. So, I'm guessing he doesn't advocate violent behavior in his children. But even if that wasn't the case, it's unfair to target the child because of her father's profession."

"I know, and I totally agree. I just think Cindy, that's Serenity's teacher, may think that this anger thing may be genetic. Do you think that's even possible?"

"If her father were Charles Manson, maybe that theory would hold water, but since he's just a retired basketball player, I don't think so. Serenity will have to be judged on her own performance, not her father's."

"Would you be willing to see Serenity before her father gets here?"

"Sure. Let me have a look at her files."

Little Serenity's eyes lit up when she saw Tonya. Tonya winked and held her finger to her lips to silence her. After the teaching aid who had delivered Serenity closed the door, Tonya scooped the child up into a warm hug.

"Auntie Tonya, what are you doing here?"

"I'm going to be working at your school for a while. At school, I'm not Auntie Tonya, okay? You must remember to call me Dr. Malone, especially in front of other staff."

"Okay." Serenity said.

So much for her quiet entry and escape plan.

CHAPTER 3

Michael Dutton sat in a meeting with the senior members of his team at Home Court Advantage. The company he and his brother Joshua started together after their retirement from pro basketball. His secretary, Vernice Berry, leaned across the table and whispered to him.

"You're going to be late for your lunch date with Selena if you don't leave now."

"I thought you rescheduled that?"

"This is the reschedule."

"It's getting increasingly harder to see you these days. I talk to your secretary more than I do you." Selena said as she looked up from her salad.

Mike flashed her a debonair grin. "Sorry, baby. You remember what it was like breaking ground on a new development site?"

"Yes, I remember." She wiped her mouth with her napkin. "That's why I'm hoping that maybe you could cancel the rest of your afternoon and hang with me for a while. I mean, you are the boss, right?"

"I am."

"The boss should be able to take off from time to time. Besides, who knows when we'll have an opportunity like this again?"

"What about you? Don't you have to get back to work?"

"Actually, no I'm—"

Mike's cellphone rang. He glanced down at the screen and picked up, "Talk to me, Bella baby, what's up?"

Selena resisted the impulse to roll her eyes.

"Did she win?"

Bella said something that Selena couldn't hear. Mike responded with a hearty laugh. "I'm just playing. I'll run through there now and pick her up. Yes, I will also have a talk with her. Yeah. Don't worry. We'll hang out for a while. I'll drop her back off tonight around six. Cool."

Mike ended the call. "Suri's school called. She got into a little scrimmage today. Josh is out of town, so I gotta pick her up. I won't be able to play hooky with you today, but ..." Mike reached into his breast pocket and removed his wallet. He pulled out ten bills and set them on the table in front of her. "I want you to have a slamming spa day on me." At the sight of the stack of crisp $100 bills, Selena smiled, placated. Mike leaned in and kissed her cheek. He signaled the server, paid, and made his way out of the restaurant.

Selena sighed. It wasn't even noon. Vernice had told her she would have to meet him for an early lunch if they were going to meet at all. His plate was that full. And yet, just as Selena had witnessed many times before, in the five years since they'd been dating, Mike's full plate could be wiped clean in a millisecond at a request from one of his family members. This time, it was Bella. Selena had come here today prepared to make her play-hooky-with-me-request, but Bella had beaten her to it. Selena retrieved her cell phone from her Hermes bag, another consolation prize from Mike, and dialed her cousin's number. "Hey girl, it's me. I'm coming over."

CHAPTER 4

"So, are you ready to tell me what happened on the playground today?"

Serenity shrugged. "This dumb boy kissed me after I told him not to. He didn't listen, so I gave him a knuckle sandwich. Now my daddy's coming to pick me up. We'll go to lunch and then someplace special, just the two of us."

Serenity gets sent home from school and Daddy rewards her with a playdate. *Really, Josh?*

"You enjoy spending one-on-one time with your daddy, don't you?"

"Yes. No Jabari, and no stupid babies."

Ah, the babies.

A knock on the door interrupted Tonya's thoughts. The school nurse stuck her head inside. "I'm here to collect Serenity, Dr. Malone."

Serenity hopped up, leaving the dolls she was playing with on the floor. "My daddy's here!" She sang. "See you later, Doc. Gotta go."

Tonya held out her hand to Serenity and shook it. "Very nice talking to you today, Serenity."

Serenity skipped out of the office and Julie turned to address Tonya.

"It's not her dad, it's her uncle. He wants to talk to Serenity about the incident first. Then he wants to talk to you."

"Talk to me about what?"

"Serenity, of course. Tonya, are you okay?"

Heck no. "Actually, can you let him know I can't discuss Serenity's case with an extended relative?"

Julie shook her head. "The parents have granted him full disclosure. He's down on all the paperwork as the emergency contact person."

Of course he is. Michael was Suri's godfather. And she would know because she was Suri's godmother.

"Hey, are you nervous? He's a really nice guy. Handsome, and very personable. Dad's sexy in a dangerous sort of way, but the uncle is sexy in a come-hither sort of way."

"Okay, Julie, thank you. Can you give me five minutes before you send him in?"

"I'll do you one better. You look like you could use ten."

CHAPTER 5

Leslie was sitting on the couch smoking a joint when Selena walked through the front door.

"What happened? I thought you were spending the day with your man."

"His family happened, that's what. The little Bad Seed got into a fight. Precious Bella has the twins to deal with. Joshua is traveling, so you know the rest of the story. Hero Mike to the rescue." Selena plopped down on the couch next to her cousin.

"So why didn't you just go back to work?"

Because she hated her job. She had only applied to law school in the first place because it was the first thing that had popped into her mind when Mike asked her what she wanted to do with the rest of her life.

"I've always wanted to be an attorney." She'd told him during her Homecourt exit interview.

Joshua had fired her after walking in on an argument between her and Bella. Mike, being the gentleman that he was, had come to her rescue. She blurted out 'attorney' because she thought the answer would impress him.

She had guessed correctly. He was impressed. Mike made some calls on her behalf. Got her admitted into a top Houston law program. He also fully funded her degree, complete with her own condo and car.

"I hate my job." Selena voiced out loud to Leslie.

"Maybe you'd like your job more if you buckled down and studied and actually passed the bar this time."

Selena had passed the bar. Every single section with flying colors, except for that one very ridiculous section on moral character and mental fitness. Now the Texas State bar licensure department was hounding her to submit to a psychological evaluation. *Whatever. Like that was ever going to happen.*

"Mike was supposed to marry me by now. His family keeps getting in my way."

Leslie took a pull from the joint and passed it to Selena. "You only got two options. You either pass the bar and make your way in the world as an attorney, or you give him a baby."

Selena took a hit from the joint and held the smoke in her lungs, savoring the flavor. "I don't even like kids." She admitted on an exhale.

"Yeah, but if you had his baby, you'd have that ring, though."

Selena considered this for a moment. She shook her head. "I can't. I despise children. I even tried to break myself into the idea of having one by tagging along on a Suri Day."

Leslie scrunched up her nose. "What the hell is a Suri Day?"

Selena snorted. "A frigging national holiday. Serenity is not adjusting well to the new babies. So, Joshua and Mike take turns each week doing one-on-one activities with her."

Leslie rolled her eyes. "Rich folks are a trip. They need to beat that little girl's behind."

"That little monster has Mike wrapped around her tiny finger. It's like she's got her own brand of magic. Suri magic." Selena took another pull from the joint. This time blowing perfect circles. "I sacrificed my whole day hanging out with that little brat. Miniature golf, the state fair, the whole nine. I'm hoping that after we drop the kid off, I can have a little one-on-one time with my man. Do you know what that little monster had the nerve to say?"

"What?"

"Drop her off first, Uncle Mike."

Leslie laughed. "What did Mike say?"

"It is Suri Day, baby. Do you mind?"

"Which brings me back to my original point. You need to give him a child."

"How? We are never alone."

Leslie choked out a cough. "You telling me you haven't hit that yet?"

Selena rolled her eyes. "Joshua lived celibate for five years when he and Bella separated. Apparently, it inspired Mike so much that he made a vow to the Lord."

"Shut the front door!"

"Yep. He's made it painfully clear. He will remain celibate until he is married."

Selena stood from her seat on the couch and stretched. Her eyes shifted to the makeshift altar in her cousin's living room. Strapped to the altar was a naked Barbie doll with pins sticking into its' forehead and eyes.

"Leslie, what the hell are you up to?"

"One of my clients caught her man cheating. She's paying me to curse the chick."

"Can you press pause on this little insanity spell you got going for a minute?"

"Why, what's up?"

"I stopped by to see if you wanted to join me for a spa day, compliments of Mike Dutton."

"Hell, yeah I do."

CHAPTER 6

Julie rapped lightly on the door before ushering Mike into Tonya's office. "Dr. Malone, this is Serenity's uncle, Mike Dutton. Mr. Dutton, this is Dr. Tonya Malone, our new child development specialist. I'll keep Serenity occupied while the two of you talk."

"Thank you, Julie." Tonya said.

If Mike was surprised to see her, Tonya would never know it. He waited patiently for the door to close before he spoke.

"So, how long have you been back?"

"I just got here." Tonya held her hands up, "Look, Michael, I know you have a ton of questions for me, but can we focus on Serenity right now, please?"

"Of course." Mike unbuttoned the bottom button of his double-breasted suit coat and took a seat in a chair in front of her desk.

Tonya sat down as well and opened Serenity's file. "I've read through Serenity's record and the recommendation from her teacher is a behavior modification program."

"That's ridiculous. She's five."

"I know."

"She also has two new babies living in the house."

"I know that too."

"She told that kid Dillon to stop, and he kept going. That's sexual harassment."

"Okay, no. He's five, Michael. He didn't sexually harass her. He kissed her."

"And she responded like a five-year-old-girl who didn't want to be kissed. Bottom line, she doesn't have a behavior problem. I won't let you or anyone else stick a label on her."

"Now you wait a minute. I'm Team Suri too, or maybe you've forgotten. My assessment will have some bearing on what the school ultimately decides, but please understand, I just got here. I'm letting you know what the school nurse told me. Suri is one of the few black kids in this school and her father is Bad Boy Joshua Keys. So, like it or not, Josh's past is factoring into the teacher's perception of Serenity."

"What about a private assessment?"

"If the school presses this any further, that's exactly where we'll go next."

"And are you qualified to do such an assessment?"

"As a licensed child psychologist, I am. I've done some pre-liminary stuff with her today. From what I can tell, she just needs a little more wraparound care and support. Friends and family members who love her."

"Good. We've got all of that. Now, tell me why you're here? Last I checked, you were engaged to be married to the mega preacher." Mike stared down at her ring-less finger.

"Things didn't work out and I think you should go. Suri's waiting for you."

"Have dinner with me tonight."

"I can't."

"Can't or won't?"

"Michael, I have just gotten back into town. I've literally been living out of a suitcase for the last four days. My budget can't afford that for too much longer. I'm apartment hunting after work. If you must know."

"You could have called Josh."

"What?"

"If you needed help and thought for some reason that you couldn't call me."

Tonya stared down at the file in front of her. Mike rose from his seat and buttoned his suit jacket. "I'm going to chalk Suri's little scrimmage today up to Divine Intervention. Check out of your hotel and meet me at the house tonight at seven. You can move back into your old spot. We'll drop off your things and go grab a bite to eat."

He said it like it was settled. Like this was a done deal. Tonya wanted to object. If it had been any other man on the planet, she would have objected. But it was futile to do so with Michael. Even when she wanted to keep things formal between them, he wouldn't allow it. Besides, Harold and Barbara Malone hadn't raised no fool. It was either live in a 3000 square foot luxury cottage on his estate, or, on her salary, live in a hut. She needed his help, desperately, but he couldn't make her eat.

"Michael, I am interested in renting the apartment from you, but not dinner. I'm just not up for a public scene right now." Even though Michael was retired from pro-ball, he was still Houston's favorite son. It was nothing to see his picture splashed across the celebrity pages of some magazine. Most times, if Tonya were to be honest about it, it's how she kept up with what he was doing and who he was dating.

"We'll dine privately then." His liquid brown eyes drew hers up to meet his, and Tonya felt her face go flush as he unabashedly took in every single inch of her frame.

"You look thin, Blackbird. You need to eat."

FALL 1993

CHAPTER 7

DALLAS, TEXAS, RIGHT BEFORE SUNSET

TONYA WAS IN THE barn brushing down the golden mare when she heard the ranch hands honking their horns furiously. Their signal to her that Michael was home. Tonya cupped her hand over her eyes to block out the setting sun. In the distance, she could see the silver Lamborghini with the trademark Man of Steel emblem slowly climbing the hill toward the Kennedy ranch.

Tonya turned to Maria. "Finish up for me, please."

Maria rolled her eyes and muttered something in Spanish.

"Please, please with sugar on top." Tonya said, hopping from one foot to the next.

"Go, chica. Go greet your man."

Tonya kissed Maria's cheek and took off, like the wind.

CHAPTER 8

Melissa and Jack were outside, standing in the driveway, when their boys pulled up. They had heard the honking horns of the ranch hands, too. Melissa was so giddy with excitement she looked like she was going to jump out of her skin. When Michael and Joshua emerged from the car, they greeted their father with handshakes. Then they descended upon their mother with bear hugs and kisses. Mike popped the trunk of the Steelmobile. Melissa looked on wistfully as he and Joshua grabbed their overnight bags from the trunk.

Joshua searched his mother's cornflower blue eyes. "What?"

"I just wished you boys were staying for more than one night. That's all."

"We talked about this, remember? Mike's got a game and coach will have my head if I don't show up for practice tomorrow."

Melissa rolled her eyes. "That coach of yours is a godless man. Who schedules practice on Christmas Eve?"

Joshua grinned down at her. "You're never going to let that go, are you?"

"And Mikey, you've been working so hard since you signed with the Rockets. Can't they survive one game without you?"

"Not if they want to win, they can't." Jack said.

Melissa stared up at her oldest son. "Sweetheart, why don't you talk to the coach? Ask him for a couple of days off. You've played in every single game this season."

"I appreciate the concern, Mom. But it doesn't really work like that. They expect me to play in every game. It's what I signed up for, and it's what the fans come out to see." Mike winked at his dad, "Besides, I can't request time off from the NBA because my mom thinks they're working me too hard."

Joshua and Jack both laughed.

Melissa patted his hand. "Of course, you know best, Mikey. I think I'm just holding on so tightly because of everything that's happened this past year."

All the mirth left Mike's eyes. "Did something else happen with Unc?"

"Don't you worry about your uncle. Harold's a tough old bird. In fact, I'd say he's been doing a lot better since the doctors took him off that damn chemo." Jack said.

Joshua and Mike shared a look.

"When did the doctors take him off chemo?" Mike asked.

Jack rubbed the back of his neck. "Oh, I'd say it's been about two weeks now."

"Josh and I had a talk on the way out here. We know that things have been hard lately for everyone. We both plan to be around a lot more during the off season. Even still, I want you to know that if anything serious were to happen before then. Game or not. I'd be there."

"We know, Mikey." Jack said.

Melissa took a deep breath and rubbed her hands together. "So, did you boys bring me any dirty laundry?"

The brothers traded another look.

"Mom, you sure you're alright?" Mike asked.

"Of course, honey, why wouldn't I be?"

"Because you haven't washed our clothes since the Summer Breeze incident of 85." Joshua said, looking at his mother pointedly.

"I—well, yes, I know, but that was only one time, Joshie. And, Cally, over at The General, is always bragging about how her boys come home from college and bring her boatloads of dirty laundry. What do I have to brag about?" Melissa complained.

Mike smiled at his mother. "Cars and jewelry don't do it for you, huh? You don't feel loved unless we bring you a bunch of dirty clothes?"

"I don't know what the hell your mother is talking about." Jack said. He removed the keys to the brand-new pickup truck Mike had purchased for his birthday a couple of months ago and dangled them in the air. "You boys are old enough to wash your own damn drawers. I feel plenty loved."

Melissa frowned at her husband. "Jack, language. Mikey, you, I can understand. You hire people to do that sort of thing for you now. But Joshie, you're still in college. And that awful coach has you working day and night. I just want to help where I can."

"You help me plenty. Just keep the prayers coming. Besides, Dad is right, I'm a grown man who is fully capable of—"

"Dropping his laundry off at my place every week." Mike finished for him. "My cleaning lady does his laundry, Mom. Relax, I ain't gon have the boy, running around Houston stankin, and embarrassing the family."

Jack broke out in a fit of laughter as the two brothers tussled playfully.

CHAPTER 9

THEY WERE JUST ABOUT to walk into the house when Mike saw her running barefoot across the fields that divided their families' properties. His Blackbird. She wore a white cotton dress with a yellow flower in her hair. Mike dropped his overnight bag at the threshold of the door, hopped over the porch railing, and took off running to meet her. His long legs quickly covered the distance between them. In a matter of seconds, he was swooping her up in his arms. He peppered her face with kisses and spun her around and around until she was breathless.

"Meet me at our spot after midnight?" she whispered after he had sat her back down on the ground.

"How bout I take you to the Four Seasons instead?"

"We have to stay nearby. What if Daddy wakes in the middle of the night and Mama needs me? Besides, Auntie Mel's been talking about your visit all week. She'd be so disappointed if you didn't stay at the house." She stood on her tiptoes and encircled her arms around his neck. "You know what I think?"

He leaned his forehead against hers and stole a kiss from her lips. "I'm pretty sure you're going to tell me."

"I think you can forgo living like a king for one night."

"You're right. I can sleep anywhere, Blackbird. Even in a pile of hay. So long as you're beside me."

"I think the hayloft is romantic. I thought you did too."

"Yeah, when we were kids, maybe. But I'm the Man of Steel. What I look like sneaking off to make love to my woman in a barn?"

"Like a man who loves his family. Like a man who understands that they really need him to stay close right now."

Mike sighed. He pulled her arms from around his neck, turned her hands over gently, and kissed her palms. "Can I at least take you to dinner off site?"

Tonya shook her head, "Didn't Auntie Mel tell you? Dinner is at our place tonight. Daddy has some big important announcement he wants to make."

CHAPTER 10

HarOLD MALONE TAPPED HIS fork against his water goblet until all the side conversations at the dinner table stopped. Around that table sat the most important people in the world to him, his family. His sweet, beautiful wife of thirty-five years, Barbara. He couldn't have asked for a better mate to spend his life with. His best friend of over forty years, Jack Kennedy. Jack's wife, Melissa. Their sons, who were also his godsons, Mike and Joshua, and, of course, his baby girl, Tonya. The only one missing tonight was his sister, Katie. Harold saw no reason to interrupt her trip. He'd call her when she returned from Lagos to tell her his news. Barbara wasn't fully on board with Operation Throw Birdie from the Nest. But in time, Harold was certain she would see the wisdom in it.

"I'm glad you're all here so that I only have to have this conversation once. I am officially cancer free. So, there you have it." Harold pushed a button on his wristwatch. "I will entertain questions on the topic for the next five minutes. After that, we will never mention the big C again. Deal?"

A table full of stung faces stared back at him. The only person who didn't seem to be fazed by Harold's revelation was his godson, Mike. No surprise there. Mike was never one to show an excess of any type of emotion. A firebomb could hit the house right now. The kid still wouldn't panic. He'd just quietly and quickly usher everyone to safety.

His godson, Joshua — the one who wore his emotions on his sleeve — was the first to speak. No surprise there either.

"When did this miracle occur?"

The expression on the boy's face said he wasn't buying it, and Harold chose, for the moment anyway, to ignore the obvious sarcasm dripping from his godson's voice. "The doctor told me today. Next question." Harold said, firmly.

"Daddy, I-I want to believe it, but you just had a really bad episode last week. Are you sure the doctor really said the cancer was gone?" Tonya asked gently.

"I'm in remission, kiddo. Believe it. Can we have another question that isn't a variation of the same question?"

Melissa looked from Harold then to Barbara. "Are my ears deceiving me, or is this really true? Have our prayers really been answered?"

Harold beamed at his best friend's wife. "Mel, doll, it's as real as rain."

"Thank you, Lord!" Melissa said.

"Yes, in all things, give Him thanks." Barbara muttered as she wiped her mouth with her linen napkin.

Jack released a shout of exultation. "So, you mean to tell me I've got my drinking buddy back?"

"I'm back, baby!" Harold said, grinning from ear to ear.

Barbara shot Harold a death glare.

"I mean, I still gotta lay off the hard stuff, but I can have a beer every now and again. Everything in moderation." Harold cleared his throat, carefully avoiding his wife's gaze. "In light of this recent development, some things are about to change around here."

"What kind of changes we talkin bout, Unc?" Mike said.

"Well, for starters, Tonya is going away to college. And once the doctor clears it, Barb and I may even take a trip around the world." Harold set a stack of brochures down on the table in front of Tonya. "I've researched the psychology programs at each of these universities. They are all excellent."

Tonya stared down at the brochures. She made no motion to pick them up. "You can't just decide something like this for me."

"It's decided." Harold said. "You're going."

Tonya folded her arms across her chest, "No, I'm not."

"You seem to have forgotten that this was the original plan. You just got sidetracked playing nursemaid to me. Well, I'm healed, and it's time for you to move on with your life. New York, Chicago or Houston. Take your pick, but you are going."

A small beeping noise replaced the somewhat awkward silence that had settled around the dinner table. Harold looked down at his watch and smiled. "Well, what do you know? Looks like our five minutes are up. Who wants some pie?"

CHAPTER 11

Lᴀᴛᴇʀ ᴛʜᴀᴛ ᴇᴠᴇɴɪɴɢ, ᴡʜɪʟᴇ the women cleared away the dinner dishes, and the men sat around the television watching the game, Harold caught Mike's attention and motioned for him to join him in his study. Mike took a seat on the leather sofa. Harold sat at his desk, signing documents.

"What's up, Unc? What did you want to see me about?"

"I want you to talk to that daughter of mine and make her go to Houston."

Mike raised an eyebrow. "Are we talking about the same girl? Because I can't *make* Tonya do anything."

Harold sat his pen down and stared at Mike. "Do you want my daughter's hand in marriage or not?"

"You already know the answer to that."

"Then do me this one solid. Convince her that being in Houston with you is the best choice she could make."

"Why do I get the feeling that you're really not in remission?"

"Because he's not." Joshua said as he pushed the door of the study open and strolled into the room.

"Tonya, why don't you go take a load off your feet? Your Auntie Mel and I can finish up in here."

"It's okay, Mama. I don't mind helping."

Melissa smiled at her goddaughter. "Joshie and Mikey will be gone in the morning. You may as well spend as much time with them while they're here. Your mom's right. We can handle this."

Tonya dropped the dish towel down on the counter. "Fine, I can take a hint. I know when people just want to talk about me behind my back."

Melissa's mouth fell open. "Talk about you behind your back. Why in the world would we do that?"

"Mel, don't pay this girl no mind. She's just upset with Harold and trying to take it out on the rest of us. Don't nobody care about you being mad. You need to be looking through those brochures your daddy gave you." Barbara called to Tonya's departing back.

Harold glared at Joshua. "How the hell do you know? Were you at the doctor's appointment with me?"

Joshua took a seat on the sofa next to his brother. "No, I wasn't."

"Okay then. Did I ask you to barge into my study and put your two cents into this very personal and private conversation between me and my future son-in-law?"

"Naw, I just figured I'd follow along for the hell of it. For the record, you not doing Tonya any favors by keeping her in the dark. It's only going to make things worse for her in the end."

Harold rose from his seat at the desk. He walked over to the door, snuck a furtive glance out at Jack, who was busy yelling at the TV screen, then closed the door. "This is none of your got damn business."

"Really? When you're gone, who do you think is going to be left to pick up the pieces?"

"Shut your face. You hear me? Don't you breathe one word to her, or anybody else, about what you think you know."

"Unc, Josh is right. If something happens to you and she's not here, Tonya will never forgive herself."

"Doesn't anybody listen around here anymore? I'm not dying."

Joshua and Mike both stared at their uncle.

"Come here, boys. Bring it in." Harold held out his arms. Joshua and Mike both stood and walked into a huddle with the older man.

"I'm your godfather. Well, Mike, technically not yours anymore, but Joshua, I'm still yours. Both of you are like sons to me. I practiced law for fifteen years. When my best friend called to tell me he had adopted two black boys, and that he needed me to help raise them, I gave all that up. I laid it all down and moved to Texas to become a cattle rancher for you."

"We know the story, Unc. What's your point?" Joshua said, the anger and agitation clearly building in his voice.

"My point is this, son. If I would lay my life down for you, do you really think that I would lie to you?" Joshua met his godfather's gaze square on.

"If you felt like it was in our best interest, yeah, you'd lie. You'd do it in a heartbeat."

Harold squeezed the back of Joshua's neck, "Fair. That's fair. Well, know this. I will live to see you play in the NBA. That is no lie. I promise you. I want good seats too. I want you to get me one of those fancy suites. When Michael here fulfills his mission, I'll need you to look out for our girl on campus. Can you do that for me?"

"You know I will. You don't even have to ask."

Every now and again, Melissa wiped away an errant tear as she helped her best friend finish up in the kitchen.

"I'm so happy for you and Harold. All of us, really. This is just a dream come true." Melissa said, as she dried and stacked the wet dishes Barbara handed to her. "And you already know you don't have to worry about a thing around here. Jack and I will take care of the ranch while the two of you are on your world tour."

Barbara's hands stopped moving in the suds.

"Barb, what's wrong?"

"It's not true, Mel."

"What?"

"None of it is true. The doctor didn't tell Harold he was in remission. That stubborn, beautiful man just decided to be in remission."

"So, all of this is for Tonya's sake?"

Barbara nodded. "Harold calls it, 'Operation Throw Birdie from the Nest'. He's right about one thing. If he doesn't force her to go, she'll be here trying to take care of us for the rest of her life."

CHAPTER 12

"The nerve of that man!" Tonya fumed as she paced back and forth in the hayloft. It was after midnight, and she had snuck off to meet Michael after she'd been assured that her parents were asleep. "I cannot believe this! The audacity of him to-to- just decide my future and then announce it over dinner to the whole family like it's no big deal!"

"Blackbird, I know you don't like the way he went about this. But he does have a point."

"What point?"

"Baby—"

"No, Michael, what point?" She stopped pacing and stood directly in front of Mike. "Are you siding with him on this? Because he is dead wrong and you know it."

"Are you going to keep cutting me off, or are you going to let me finish a thought?"

Tonya closed her eyes for a moment and exhaled. When she opened them again, they were wet with tears. "I'm just so angry with him right now. But I know that doesn't give me the right to take it out on you. I'm sorry."

"C'mere." Mike pulled her down onto his lap. He kissed her lips tenderly. "How you feel is how you feel. So, there's nothing to apologize for. But when you come up out of your feelings, all I'm asking is that you consider the wisdom behind what he's saying to you."

"So, you agree with my dad?"

"I don't appreciate the way he's going about this, but I do think it's time for you to focus on your own life. You were there for them through the most difficult parts of all of this. Every day, holding it down for the last three years 24/7. You delayed your admission to HU. And now, according to him, he's out of the woods. So yeah, I agree. It's time for you to start living for you. For us."

Her eyes met his. "Us? Is that your way of telling me you want me to choose Houston?"

Mike laced his fingers through hers. With his other hand, he made small circles on her back. "First and foremost, I want you to be happy. Ever since we were kids, you've always dreamed of being a child psychologist. So yeah, I really want that for you. If you decide that Chicago or New York is the best place to make that happen, then I'll wait. I ain't gon lie, it'll be hard. Because the truth is, I need you too. It's killing me not to be able to see you every day. Not to be able to hold you every night."

"Michael, you have no idea how much I want and need that, too. I really want to say yes... but I'm just not comfortable being so many miles away from my parents yet. What if Daddy relapses?"

"What if I told you that you'd still be able to have dinner with them every Sunday night? And that anytime you wanted to go home, for any reason at all, there would be a car ready to take you. Even if you just wanted to come look at them for a few minutes."

"That wouldn't be necessary, Michael. I've made the drive between here and Houston plenty of times before."

"No, that's six hours, there and back. I don't want you on the road like that. Not every weekend."

"Josh drives back and forth all the time. You never complain about him."

"Not every weekend he doesn't. Besides, he's already agreed to come home for Sunday dinners. He's going to be taking the car service, too."

"Okay, well, in that case, I guess I could take the car service, too."

Mike's face broke out into a grin. "Seriously?"

Tonya nodded. "I'll start next semester."

CHAPTER 13

Joshua was sitting on the back porch the next morning eating an apple when Mike came back from the hayloft. Mike took a seat next to his brother. Together, the two of them watched the sunrise. "Tonya?"

"HU in the fall."

Joshua held out his fist. Mike bumped it.

"Congrats, man. I know that's what you wanted."

"Yeah, I just wish it wasn't like this, though." Mike muttered.

"You mean Uncle Harold lying about being in remission?"

"How you know he lying, Josh?"

Joshua stared at his brother until Mike looked away.

"Listen, I kind of told Tonya that you would come home for Sunday dinner on the weekends. I said we both would when I'm in town."

"That's not a bad idea. I don't mind driving her."

"The thing is, I told her you already agreed to take the private car service I'm hiring to drive you two. I don't want either of you driving back and forth every weekend. I figured you could chill on the way out. Study or what not?"

"This is a bad idea, man."

Mike flashed his brother a dimpled grin, "I promise you, little brother, the car will be fully stocked with whatever you need."

"You know what I'm talking about."

"What you want me to do, Josh? You heard the same thing I did. The man said he's not sick. Dad believes him. Why don't you?"

"You know as well as I do, Dad believes what he wants to believe. Uncle Harold is sick. Lying to Tonya is just going to leave her unprepared."

"It's what he wants, Josh."

Joshua stood and pitched his apple core over the porch railing. "I'll take the car service, but I won't lie. If she asks me, I'mma tell her the truth."

The screen door banged shut as Joshua walked into the house.

"Yeah, I know that too." Mike muttered into the empty morning air.

Present Day 2010

CHAPTER 14

HOUSTON, TEXAS

MIKE DROVE INTO HIS brother's driveway. He looked back at his niece Serenity, who was happily singing along with one of her favorite kid tunes. "Suri?"

Serenity opened her eyes and stopped singing. "Yes, Uncle Mike?"

"We're here."

She unbuckled herself from the booster seat and scrambled towards the door.

"Wait."

Serenity froze.

"Before you go into the house, I need you to get your game face on. Your mom got a call from the school today about you fighting. She's going to be pretty upset about that. You need to at least look remorseful."

"What's remorseful?"

"It means you're sorry for what you've done."

"You want me to be sorry for punching Dillon?"

"No. No guy ever has the right to touch you without your permission. I just mean that when you go in the house, you should be remorseful in general about the situation."

Serenity folded her arms across her chest and frowned. "I'm not."

Mike stared at the defiant five-year-old. It was hard to believe that Serenity was not his brother's biological child. Joshua could never go along just to get along, either. Not only did Serenity look like Joshua, she was a pint-sized female version of him. Serenity was Joshua, the uncut edition. Mike stared into her fiery brown eyes. He knew that this was exactly the type of attitude that would send his sister-in-law over the edge. Joshua was still in Dallas with Jabari. They wouldn't make it back to Houston until later that evening. Mike checked the clock on the dashboard. He had agreed to meet Tonya in an hour. He couldn't stick around to run interference between Bella and Serenity. He flashed the five-year-old a handsome smile. The one that usually made the ladies melt. Serenity wasn't having it. "How bout, being sorry for getting in trouble?"

Serenity shook her head. "If I hadn't gotten into trouble, you wouldn't have come and picked me up. I'd be stuck at that dumb school all day. We wouldn't have gone to House of Bounce either."

"Yeah see, you might not want to mention to your mom that I took you to House of Bounce."

"Why not? Mommy knows I love House of Bounce?"

"She does. That's why it might look like I was rewarding you for getting into trouble at school today—which I wasn't. I just thought you needed to jump around in the ballroom for a bit and blow off a little steam."

Serenity nodded her head sincerely. "You were right. I really needed that."

"I know you did, but if your mom thinks I rewarded you for getting into trouble, then she'll be mad at me."

Serenity thought about this for a moment. "Okay, Uncle Mike. I'll be re-moist-ful. I don't want you to get into trouble."

Mike held out his fist for a pound. Serenity touched her smaller fist to his. "My girl."

CHAPTER 15

"Bella, why are you grinning?"

Bella touched her face. "Am I? I just can't believe it. The thing I've been praying about is finally here." Mike sat at Bella's and Joshua's kitchen counter. He had just told his sister-in-law the news about Tonya's return.

"She's wounded, Bella. She's not the same. She didn't even want the family to know she was back. I'm pretty sure she didn't know it was Suri's school when she took the job."

"That just goes to show you how God works. Oh Mike, she's been really heavy in my spirit lately. I called her number at the church, and they told me she no longer worked there. When I called her apartment, the number said it was disconnected. We talk at least three times a month. I couldn't imagine her moving without telling me. But if things went south suddenly with Ted, then that would explain it. I can't wait to see her. When she's ready, of course. Please, please, give her my love."

"I'm sure she'll be calling soon. At the very least, she'll want to talk to you and Josh about Suri."

Bella nestled herself into her brother-in-law's arms. "Oh my gosh, Mike. Tonya's back."

Mike hugged Bella tightly and kissed the top of her head. "Do me a favor and go easy on my niece, alright?"

"I'm in such a great mood right now. Spanking somebody is the furthest thing from my mind."

CHAPTER 16

Tonya checked out of the hotel she had been staying in and drove to Michael's estate. When she pulled up to the large metal gate, she pulled out her driver's license and handed it to the security guard without being asked.

The guard smiled down at her from his position in the booth. "No identification necessary, Ms. Malone. Welcome home. Please follow the drive around back to the cottage. Mr. Dutton is expecting you."

Mike came walking up the path just as Tonya was getting out of her car.

"You got stuff in the trunk?"

"A few boxes."

"Leave your keys on the kitchen counter. The staff will unpack everything for you."

Mike reached into his pocket. He pulled out a set of keys and opened the front door to the cottage. He turned and handed the keys to Tonya. "Front door, back door, everything's still the same."

Tonya walked into the cottage and found a myriad of memories colliding into her at once. She and Michael painting the walls together, snuggling on the couch in front of the fireplace.

Paint in her hair.

Paint in her hair.

Paint in her...

Tonya closed her eyes and tried to steady herself. She took a moment to tamp down the tears she felt building behind her eyelids before turning to face him.

That beautiful, chocolate, impassive face. He was quietly watching her from his position in the doorway. Did the memories strike him the same way they did her? Michael never allowed you to see anything he didn't want you to see. Unless she asked him what he was experiencing at that moment, she would have no way of knowing. Tonya was not about to open that can of worms. So, she asked another question instead. "How much are you willing to rent it to me for? I won't stay here if I can't pay you. It's not the same as before. Nothing is."

"We'll discuss rent later, Blackbird. Right now, we eat."

CHAPTER 17

Tʜᴇʏ ᴅʀᴏᴠᴇ ɪɴ sɪʟᴇɴᴄᴇ. Not an awkward silence, a companionable one. Being with Michael was one of the most natural things in the world. When they were children, they could sit quietly for hours and watch a sunset together. When they got older and started dating, she could read a book with her head in his lap while he read the newspaper or studied post-game film. Even now, driving to wherever they were going—because she hadn't even bothered to ask him where he was taking her. Tonya realized that the hollow ache that had made its habitation in her heart from the moment Ted had called her into his office, that it didn't hurt so much. She knew that was because of Michael. He had always been a safe space for her, a cocoon.

Tonya looked up to see the passenger door of the truck open and Michael reaching out his hand to her. She glanced at the sign advertising the restaurant he'd taken her to. Sasha's was a popular who's who spot for Houston's elite. Tonya scanned the parking lot. It was empty. Odd for the most notoriously busy restaurant in the city. She knew for a fact that it took weeks, if not months, to get a reservation here.

"Michael, I think they're closed."

"They're open. Just not to the public tonight."

She stared at him.

"You said you wanted to dine privately."

"So, you called, and they just cleared their books? Just like that?" Tonya snapped her fingers to emphasize her point.

"The owner's a friend. I told him I had a friend who loved his spot but needed her privacy. He was happy to accommodate me."

Tonya could hear the Maitre d's shoes echoing across the marble floor before his face came into view.

"Ah, Mr. Dutton, welcome. Come right this way, sir."

He led them into a large, almost completely empty candle lit dining hall. A jazz quartet waited on stage. "Anything in particular you'd like to hear tonight, sir." The bandleader asked.

Mike looked at Tonya.

Tonya shrugged. "I don't know. Surprise me."

"You heard the lady. Surprise her."

Tonya watched him watching her. No doubt he was remembering all the times she had practically begged him to bring her here. She didn't have the courage to tell him it was never about the food. The food was okay. What she had really wanted was for the world to see her in this place with her man, Michael Dutton. But that would never happen because Michael was a public figure by then. One who was dead set on keeping his personal life private. The few times he had surprised her with reservations here, Joshua, not Michael, accompanied her.

"I haven't had much of an appetite." She said, answering his unasked question.

"Doesn't look like you've been sleeping too well either. What happened between you and the preacher?"

"Tatiana."

"The model?"

"He needed a certain type of woman to take his ministry to the next level. Apparently, I'm not it." Tonya sat back in her chair and used her fork to drag her food across her plate. "Actually, that's not exactly true. What he said was, 'Tonya, you are the perfect woman to help me reach my destiny, and Tatiana is the perfect woman for me.' He called me into his office and the two of them told me together. Tatiana's pregnant, because, apparently, when two people love each other as much as they do, it's impossible to wait."

"Guess he never heard of a cold shower, huh?"

Tonya looked up from her art project and met his eyes. "I guess not."

A small smile played at the corners of Mike's mouth, and Tonya knew they were both experiencing the same excruciatingly painful, beautiful memories.

"I drove home, loaded up my car and left. I didn't plan it out. I had sent my resume to a bunch of places before everything happened. So, I took the first job offer. That job happened to be in Houston at Serenity's school."

"So, if Suri hadn't gotten into that fight today, we never would have known you were here?"

"I was trying to fly under the radar for a while. My plan was to work here for three months or until I could find something else."

The quartet played the theme song from the movie, *Mo Better Blues*.

Mike rose from the table. He extended his hand towards Tonya. "Dance with me."

Tonya looked momentarily startled, but she stood and took his hand.

Mike led her across the dance floor. "Did you really think you could go three months without the family finding out about this?"

"It was a plan, Michael. I never said it was a brilliant plan. I just leapt first. I needed to go someplace quiet for a while to lick my wounds."

"I guess I should be thankful that kid Dillon got fresh." Mike pulled her close, and Tonya felt his breath brush against the contours of her neck. "But don't ever try anything like this again."

"I wasn't trying anything Michael. My world blew up. I didn't want to come home and blow up anybody else's life, too."

Mike stopped dancing mid-stride. He stared down at Tonya, willing her to speak words, she knew she had neither the courage nor the right to speak.

"Whose life are we talking about here, Blackbird? Your mom's or my parents? Because they have all been praying for your return since the moment you left. So, you can't be talking about blowing up any of their worlds. If you're worried about Aunt Katie, don't. I'm pretty sure she wants your preacher dead. Every chance she gets; she's bending my ear with the latest BS happening between you two. If it were not for the power of God restraining me, I would have flown to New York and choked your boy out years ago. So, it's gotta be Josh, right? That who you are worried about? Is he the reason you wanted to run and hide instead of coming home to me? You afraid Bad Boy would come out of early retirement over this?"

Tonya felt Mike's unrelenting gaze pressing her to look at him, urging her to speak.

"Michael—"

"Answer me."

"You. Okay?" She whispered. "I didn't want to come back here and blow up your world."

Mike released a breath that sounded more like a drowning man taking the first snatches of air. He rested his forehead against Tonya's. "We're way past all that, Blackbird. The first time I laid eyes on you, you blew up my world. We made a promise. Do you remember the promise we made to each other, baby?"

She nodded. The tears she could no longer contain wet the front of his shirt.

"I need to hear you say it, Tonya." A sob broke free from her chest. "Tell me." he said when she had finally quieted in his arms.

"Before there was us, there was us." She croaked.

"And as long as there is breath in my body, what will there be, Blackbird?"

"Us."

"That's right. Don't ever forget." Mike pulled her close and led her across the dance floor for the rest of the song.

FALL 1993

CHAPTER 18

HOUSTON, TEXAS, EVENING

SHANNON LOOKED UP AT the soaring ceilings and blew out a long, frustrated breath. When Joshua had asked her if she wanted to go to his brother's house after his game to catch the second half of the Rockets game. He really meant, 'let's go to my brother's house and watch the second half of the game.' Not 'let's go to my brother's house so that you can scream-as-loud-as-you-want-and-my-frat-brothers-won't-hear-you.' Nope. Let's watch the game. Joshua's eyes had been glued to the television from the moment they'd arrived. He'd spoken more words to the screen than he had to her the entire night. Right now, he was rubbing her thigh absentmindedly, and telling his brother's teammate to take his time, and let the clock run out. As far as Shannon was concerned, she had already gone above and beyond the girlfriend call of duty. She had positioned herself so he could always see her from the court. She had screamed until she'd damn near lost her voice, and she had worn a custom designed hoodie that read, 'Get That Junk Out of Here, Fool. This is Bad Boy's

House.' She even painted his number, 42, in their school colors across her face. And what had all her efforts gotten her tonight? He'd silently read her hoodie and mumbled, "That's what's up." Gave a crooked little half smile at his number painted on her cheek, then asked if she wanted to go to his brother's house and chill with him for a while. It wasn't like she expected him to curl her toes with a kiss right there on the spot, but she had hoped, at least, that when they were alone that there would be... something.

In the three years that they'd dated off and on, Joshua had never been down with PDA, public displays of affection. On the other hand, public displays of aggression he did do. All the time and very well. He had earned the nickname Bad Boy his freshmen year in college because Joshua's reputation for both junk talking and backing it up was on-lock.

Shannon sighed again. She had sat through one basketball game tonight, because she was all about protecting her investment, but she had an exam tomorrow and truth be told, she didn't even like this sport. She loved this man, though, and he ate, slept, and drank basketball.

"Joshua?"

"Come on, baby. We got this."

"Joshua?"

He tore his eyes away from the TV screen. "What's up?"

She wanted to tell him she was bored. Bored out of her daggone mind. But now that he was staring at her, she decided to take a different approach. Shannon stood up and walked directly in front of the television, blocking his view. "I'm hungry."

"I already fed you."

"That was over an hour ago." She straddled his lap, wrapping her arms around his neck.

His arms, as if on automatic pilot, encircled her and began an absent caress of her back. "Now that's what I'm talking about, baby, all net."

"Joshua?"

"Go downstairs. See what you can find in the fridge."

"Don't you want to come with me?" Shannon moved her head back and forth, trying to block his view of the television screen.

"The game is almost over. Let me watch my brother knock out this post-game interview."

"But it's dark down there." She whined.

Joshua pushed her off his lap. "Turn on the lights."

Shannon stalked towards the door.

"Shannon?"

"What?"

"Next time, say what you mean and mean what you say."

"What's that supposed to mean?"

"It means don't say you want to chill out with me and watch the game when what you really want to do is jump my bones."

Shannon rolled her eyes and flipped Joshua the bird.

"Adjust that attitude while you're down there, and I may decide to curl them toes when you get back."

Shannon trotted down the stairs, giggling under her breath. She walked into the kitchen and opened the huge refrigerator door. Shannon couldn't remember which came first, the voice or the knife. "Who are you and what the hell are you doing in my man's kitchen?"

CHAPTER 19

Joshua bolted down the stairs the moment he heard Shannon's screams. He ran into the kitchen just in time to see the woman who had his date hemmed up against the refrigerator with the butcher knife.

"Whoa, you don't want to do that." Joshua said, as he slid between Shannon, the woman, and the blade.

"Bad Boy, is that you?"

"It's me."

"Can you tell me what this heifer is doing in my man's house?"

Joshua wrapped Shannon protectively behind him. "She's with me."

Shannon sobbed and clutched Joshua's waist tightly.

"Relax, baby. I won't let anything happen to you." Joshua said, keeping his eyes trained on the woman. "If you're here, you must know my brother."

The woman smiled a beatific smile that lit up her entire face. "He's the love of my life." The smile disappeared. "He hasn't told you about me?"

Joshua studied the woman for a beat. "My brother's a real private person. The people he cares about most, he holds close to his chest."

Her face lit up again. "Like you. The Man of Steel loves him some you."

"That's right. What's your name, sweetheart?"

"Candace."

"Joshua, what is going on here? Is this some crazy fan?"

"Keep it up, home wrecker. I'll show you crazy." Candace growled.

"Shannon, this is Candace. You heard her, baby. She's Mike's—"

"Fiancé."

"Okay, yeah. That's what's up. Candace, Shannon is my girl. So, I'mma need you to put down the knife."

"For the love of my love? Certainly, Joshua."

Joshua motioned toward the large center island. "Have a seat. You can tell me all about how you met my brother."

Joshua pushed the silent alarm underneath the counter.

Mike had just finished showering and dressing when his phone rang.

"Mr. Dutton, this is your home security service. We just received a notification. The silent alarm has been tripped at your residence. Is someone with you? Are you free to talk?"

"This is my cellphone you've called. My brother is at my place."

"We've already notified the police, sir."

"I'm about thirty minutes out. I'll meet them there."

"Mike and I work together. That's how we met. I'm a Rocket's Power Dancer. Normally, in my line of work, nobody even notices you. Unless you are damn near white." She took her eyes off of Joshua long enough to glare at Shannon.

Anger quickly replaced the look of fear in Shannon's eyes. "Don't let the gray eyes fool you, girlfriend. I am not white."

"Candace, do you mind if I have a word with my girlfriend for a sec?"

Candace sucked her teeth. "By all means. Please put this heifer in her place."

Joshua pulled Shannon up from the stool and dragged her over to the refrigerator. He placed two large hands on her face and kissed her thoroughly. When he finally pulled away, Shannon was breathless.

Joshua leaned in and whispered into her ear, "I'm sorry. I'mma get you outta here. I promise. But until I can make that happen safely, could you please not antagonize the chick with the knife?"

Shannon nodded her head, uncurled her toes and took her seat next to Joshua at the counter.

"Mike saw me. Every day, he would go out of his way just to speak to me. If I was having a hard day, he would tell me to keep my head up."

Joshua smiled kindly at the woman. "That sounds a lot like my brother."

"Sometimes when I'm really down, he sings that song by New Edition. You know the one, *Candy Girl.*" Candace smiled that beatific smile again. "That's what he calls me, Candy Girl."

"You're a Power Dancer. That must be really fulfilling. I'm on the dance team at our university. It's really hard work, so I have a lot of respect for what you ladies do." Shannon said.

Candace rolled her eyes. "It's not. I got cut. You wanna know why? Because of bright skinned heifers like you. I always gotta worry about you bright skinned heifers either trying to steal my man or trying to steal my spot."

"Hey, relax. She didn't mean anything by that. I told you, Shannon's not a threat. She's with me."

Mike sped down the freeway, pushing the Steelmobile to its limits. He dialed his home phone. "Come on, Josh. Pick up the damn phone."

"I'm pretty sure that's my brother trying to call. You mind if I answer it?"

"Oh, no. That's fine. Tell him I said hi."

Joshua moved cautiously to the wall-mounted phone. "Hey, bro, what's up?"

"The security company called. You alright?"

"Just chilling at the spot with my girl, Shannon, when your girl stopped by."

"Hey, baby!" Candace called loudly.

"Who the hell is that?"

"Your fiancée."

"Does she have a weapon?"

"I can't call it."

Mike floored the accelerator. "Sit tight, little brother. I'm on my way."

The moment she heard the sirens racing toward the property, Candace pulled a gun from her waistband. She pointed it at Shannon's chest. "What did you do?"

Joshua quickly jumped in front of Shannon. He held his hands out in front of him, palms facing up. "Easy."

"What did she do?!"

"I didn't do anything. I've been sitting here with you this whole time. We both have." Shannon said, attempting to keep her voice measured.

"LIAR! YOU CALLED THEM!"

"Hey, what's going on here?" Mike walked into the kitchen, asking the question just as easily as if he were inquiring about the weather or the time of day. Like Joshua's, his hands were also palms out and in front of him.

"Oh, baby, thank God you're here! They didn't believe me when I told them I knew you." Mike stared at the pretty, but clearly deranged young woman holding his brother and Shannon at gunpoint. He had seen her a few times around the Astrodome. Mike's outward features remained calm. But he was frantically ransacking his mind for details. At least a name. *I gotta have a name. God, please. This could go sideways real quick if I don't remember this girl's name.*

"You tried out for the Power Dancers." Mike said, the details coming to his mind. "But you didn't make the cut. I'm real sorry about that. If you want, I could talk to someone in the front office for you. All you'd have to do is let my brother and his girl go."

She shook her head. "That's what I love about you. When I'm down, you always try to make things better. But being a

Power Dancer isn't important to me. I only tried out in the first place so that I could meet you."

Candy, her name is Candy. You found her crying in the hall-way after practice one night and you sang Candy Girl to her.

Mike smiled, "Well, mission accomplished, Candy Girl, you met me."

Candace smiled triumphantly at Joshua and Shannon. "See!" she spat. "He knows me. She said I was some crazy fan. I'm not crazy! He knows me."

"Candy, look at me." Mike said, pulling her attention away from Joshua and Shannon. "I know you, and I think you know me, too."

She nodded her head eagerly. "I do. I know everything about you."

"Okay, then you know my brother is the most important person in the world to me. If you hurt him, then you might as well hurt me."

Candace lowered the gun to her side. "I would never hurt your brother. I love you far too much to ever do that. It's not him I want. It's her." She said, glaring at Shannon. "She's the one who wants to come between us."

"No, sweetheart, Shannon is Josh's girl. She has nothing to do with us."

"She called them!"

"Who, baby?"

"Them!" Candace waved the gun towards the kitchen window.

They could all see the reflection of the flashing police lights through the window.

"They want to lock me away again and hurt me."

"My hand to God, Candy, I will not let them hurt you. Just put the gun down and come to me, baby. We'll walk out there together. You and me. I'll tell them who you are to me, and we'll clear this whole thing up." Mike crooned.

The sound of a helicopter suddenly filled the kitchen. "This is the Houston Police Department." A male voice rang out over a loudspeaker. "Drop your weapon and come out with your hands up."

Candace trembled violently.

"Candy, hold steady, baby. Just focus on me." Mike started singing the words to New Edition's *Candy Girl* as he walked towards Candace with his arms outstretched.

Tears rolled down her face. "I wish I could. I wish we had more time."

She lifted the gun and pulled the trigger.

"NO!" Joshua screamed.

CHAPTER 20

DALLAS, TEXAS, SAME NIGHT

Tonya stood in the kitchen popping corn for game night. Both Michael's and Joshua's games had aired during overlapping times. Joshua playing for HU, and Michael playing for the Houston Rockets. As was their family tradition, whenever their dads couldn't be there personally in the stands to cheer the brothers on, they always watched the brothers play together at home. Prior to her dad getting sick, he and her Uncle Jack spent a lot of time on the road.

Tonight, her dad had recorded the Rocket's game, while Uncle Jack had recorded HU's. She could hear them in the other room discussing which game they would all watch first. Her mom and Auntie Mel didn't really weigh in, seeing as how they would only watch for a while until they got bored. Besides their mutual delight of watching both Joshua and Michael stuff the ball inside the hoop, both women could really care less about the game. Tonya would watch tonight, but only until Michael's call. Tonight was their phone sleep night. They didn't do it every night because whenever they did do it, practices the next day for him were particularly grueling. But at least one time a week, the two of them would talk until the wee hours of the morning, then fall asleep together on the telephone.

Tonya walked into the living room carrying a tray of popcorn and drinks just in time to see the words, 'Breaking News' fly across the bottom of the television screen.

Harold motioned towards the screen, "Jack, turn that up."

"Houston Rockets star player, Michael Dutton, aka The Man of Steel, led his team to victory tonight only to return to a home invasion. Preliminary reports say that shots were fired at Dutton's Lakeside residence and that at least one person involved in the incident has been critically injured. We'll have more for you as the story unfolds."

Tonya released a small moan and the drinks, popcorn, and the tray all came crashing down to the floor.

CHAPTER 21

MIKE HELD THE PHONE up to his ear and tried to calm a hysterical Tonya. He hadn't accounted for this aspect of his fame. The inevitability of his family hearing about an incident like this. Before he had an opportunity to talk to them, to spin the situation for them.

"Baby, please, stop crying. I'm sorry you saw that on the news. But I'm fine and Josh is fine. Yeah, he went to take Shannon home. Yes, she's fine too. No, there was no gunman. Yes, there was an intruder. She had a gun. Just not the way the media made it seem. She was just a troubled fan. I tried to save her, but... I—"

Mike pulled the phone away from his ear and squeezed his eyes shut. The combination of hearing Tonya's sobs alongside the one constant thought tonight that had invaded his mind — *that could have been her at the other end of that gun. That could have been her coming downstairs for a snack or a drink of water in the middle of the night. That could have been Tonya.* That thought, along with hearing her sob like this, almost completely wrecked him.

"No. Definitely not. I don't want you on the road right now. Not while you're this upset. Tonya, you gotta promise me you'll stay put. I can't be worried right now, not about you. I know. I want to see you too. I'll be home in three days. Listen, I know I said we'd do the phone thing, but I can't, baby, not tonight. Do me a favor before you go, though. Stop crying and breathe for me. That's it. That's my girl. Now let me speak to my dad, please."

"Mikey, what in the Sam Hill is going on out there?"

Mike smiled when he heard his dad's voice. For the first time that evening, he felt the muscles in his body relax.

CHAPTER 22

Steve ran the surveillance film of the woman climbing through a first-floor window of Mike's home.

Mike stared at the footage but said nothing.

"If you're wondering how I got this, it was captured with your neighbor's security camera. She didn't even bother to call the police because she thought the assailant was some harmless groupie."

Mike rolled his eyes at Steve's use of the word 'assailant'.

"Your neighbor feels terrible about that, by the way."

"We already know how she got in, Steve. What's the point of all of this?"

Steve picked up the remote and paused the footage. "The point is, somebody else's security camera captured this. So this has got to end today, Mike. No more of this, I-just-want-to-be-a-normal-person-crap. You're famous. Alright? Michael Jordan famous. Michael Jackson famous. And it's high time you realize the lengths people will go to just to meet you."

"You don't think I realize that now, Steve? My brother and his girl were almost—" Mike ran his large hand over his face.

"You don't think I realize the danger they were in because of my fame?"

"Yeah, I think you realize it now, but I hope you'll also agree with me when I say it's time for you to take precautions."

Mike nodded. "I do. So, what do you have in mind?"

Steve handed Mike a picture of a tall, muscular looking white guy with a buzz cut. "I searched high and wide for this guy. He runs the best security outfit around. He's protected a few presidents and some other foreign diplomats. He's ex-military and gets the job done. Name's Caesar. He's the absolute best at what he does, but he's not cheap."

Mike handed the picture back to Steve. "Get him. I don't care how much it cost."

Steve frowned, "Really? I'd thought for sure you'd balk at the idea of having a security detail."

"First of all, nobody's going to be following me anywhere. But I also can't have the people I love put in danger again either. You feel me?"

"Yeah, Mike. I feel ya. How are you holding up? Management treating you okay?" Steve looked around the luxurious apartment. "The penthouse up to your standards?"

Since Mike's home was now an official crime scene, the Rockets' management staff had quickly sprung into action last night, supplying their star player with an all-expense paid, full-service penthouse apartment for as long as Mike would need it.

"Listen, before I forget, I want you to send a check to Candy's family. Enough to pay for the funeral. I also want you to start a memorial fund for mental illness research in her name."

"Yeah, about that... Mike, that's very noble of you, but writing checks isn't the wisest thing to do right now. You putting money behind this could be misconstrued as an acknowledgement of wrongdoing."

"I'm not acknowledging anything, Steve."

"I know, but a year or so down the line when the dust clears on this, her parents could use that as an excuse to file a civil suit against you. I say we reach out to her parents through a representative and issue a statement offering your condolences."

"I already talked to her parents this morning."

"They reached out to you? My god, I knew it, they're probably lawyering up this very moment."

"I reached out to them personally, to offer my condolences."

Mike walked over to the huge floor length picture window and stared out at the downtown Houston skyline. "She was a twenty-one-year-old straight-A student at Texas AM when she had her first psychotic break. She's been in and out of hospitals for the last two years. About a month ago, her parents saw the signs, knew she was going off the rails, but because she was legally an adult, the best they could do was wait for something to happen and hope that when that something did happen, they'd be able to get her committed on a 48-hour hold. But before they could get her that 48-hour hold, she blew her brains out, in my kitchen."

"Mike, I know where you're going with this. I can see the wheels turning in your head. But I want you to know that this was not your fault."

Mike turned and looked at his agent. "Save the pep talk, Steve. They're not going to sue. Calvin and Vivian are just two devastated people who lost their baby girl."

Steve removed his glasses and squeezed the bridge of his nose. "You mean to tell me you're on first name bases with her parents?" Steve muttered a curse under his breath.

"Just write the damn checks, Steve. Don't talk to me about liability. It's the decent thing to do."

"Okay, we'll do it your way. I'll handle everything, but are you sure you're okay?"

Steve searched his number one client's face for signs of... *heck, he didn't know what to look for.* Mike was so frickin Zen all the time. What's a guy like this supposed to look like when he's having a meltdown? "Do you need to talk to anybody, a professional or something? Because there's no shame in that if you do."

Mike waved him off with his hand. "Naw, forget all of that. Just get me that security detail. Tonya starts school out here in the fall. I want to make damn sure that nothing like this ever happens again."

CHAPTER 23

MIKE SAT AT THE conference table with his brother Joshua, his agent Steve, and the key players from Caesar's security outfit. They were all listening to Caesar's security pitch. Caesar currently had the blueprints to Mike's home up on the screen. Mike didn't even want to think about how he had obtained those.

"My first recommendation is going to be that you relocate to a property where you have more control of your access points." Caesar moved the pointer across the screen. "From a security standpoint, your property is—"

"It's a nightmare, right?" Steve interjected.

Caesar's cool blue eyes scanned the faces around the table. "It's an unpredictable situation and I don't particularly like unpredictability, Mr. Barns." Caesar's eyes met Mike's. "From a security standpoint, you're entirely too close to your neighbors. As it stands right now, random people can come onto your property anytime they please. Their claim could be that they simply got lost or are looking for a neighbor."

"Or that they just want to get a picture with The Man of Steel." Joshua added.

Steve nodded his head in agreement. "I said that when he bought the place. Joshua, didn't I say it?"

Joshua smirked. "Only like a thousand times, Steve."

"I've never liked his home from a security standpoint. But Joshua here said it was dope and Mike, you referred to it as fly. But here's the thing, I'm not famous. I'm a nobody and I've got better security at my house than you do."

"Okay, Steve, you've made your point. I get it. I'm famous now." Mike said.

Joshua leaned back in his chair and grinned at his brother. "You're Michael Jackson famous."

Mike nodded. "And that's why we're all here today. But you're not a nobody, I take exception to that." Mike looked at his brother, "Josh, if I'm Michael Jackson who we gon call Steve?"

Joshua tented his fingers together. "He gotta be the Rainmaker, man."

"You hear that, Steve? You're the Rainmaker. Now let the man finish his pitch." Mike motioned to Caesar. "Go ahead, man."

"Until you find a more suitable property, one that fits your needs and the needs of your family, my men would be on the ground monitoring those access points."

"What effect will these extra security measures have on my neighbors?"

"My men are all ex-military, Mr. Dutton. They are going to blend in. That's what they are trained to do. Your neighbors won't even know they are there. Unless, of course, there's a problem."

"And if there is a problem?" Steve asked.

Caesar's artic stare met Steve's across the table. "My men will neutralize the threat."

One of the men, a burly guy named Jake, cleared his throat and picked up the notepad in front of him. "Steve mentioned on the phone that the safety of your family is your primary goal."

Mike fixed his eyes on the man. "It's my only goal."

Jake nodded. "Understood. For training purposes, our team would need to meet and interact with your family. If someone wanted to get to you, there is always the strong possibility that they would try to go through one of them. For the time being, we'd like to assign a security detail to all the key people in your life. We would create workups for everyone in their lives, from the dental hygienist who cleans your mother's teeth to the butcher she buys her meat from. We'll pull their bank statements and check their credit histories."

Jake spoke to the unspoken question on both Joshua's and Mike's faces.

"I know that seems like overkill, but people in financial crisis do desperate things. An added benefit of these work- ups is that we will be able to detect the entrance of any new entity into your family members' lives."

Mike looked at his brother. "Well, what do you think?"

"I like it. But I can tell you right now, the fam is not going to. Especially Dad and Unc."

"As Caesar mentioned before, for the most part, they won't even know that we are there. We'll be completely hands off, unless you inform us you need us to be otherwise. We'll also try to make our entry into their lives as seamless as possible."

"For example, the car service you hired to take your brother and girlfriend back and forth to Dallas. I'd be more comfortable if my men staffed that." Caesar added.

Mike nodded. "Done."

"I'd also suggest eyes and ears inside your house."

Steve sat forward in his seat. "Who do you have in mind?"

Caesar pulled up a photograph of a distinguished looking black man on the screen. "This is, Martin Jeeves. In his everyday capacity, he would serve as your house manager."

Steve looked up at Caesar. "No offense, but this guy looks kind of old?"

"Don't let the salt and pepper hair fool you. I've fought in combat with him. He's an aristocratic-looking fellow, but a most formidable foe. He specializes in hand-to-hand combat. He's a master of ninjitsu, a highly skilled knife fighter, as well as a master of disarmament. He's also a damn good chef."

Mike leaned back in his chair and tented his hands in front of his face. "Word?"

Caesar nodded. "Word. Most importantly, if anyone were ever to breach the perimeter of your home, Martin Jeeves would put down the threat."

CHAPTER 24

As Mike had requested, the entire family was assembled at the Kennedy home when he, Joshua, Steve, and Caesar arrived the next day. Tonya, who usually made it a point to keep public displays of affection to a minimum, especially in front of their parents, ran outside the moment she heard the car drive up. Joshua was the first one to exit the vehicle and Tonya nearly knocked the wind out of him when she flew into his arms. Joshua staggered backwards a step to regain his balance, making sure that both he and Tonya wouldn't go careening to the ground.

"Don't you dare almost die on me again. Do you hear me?" she whispered.

"I won't if you promise to let go."

Tonya squeezed him tighter. "I love you so much."

"Tonya, I'm serious."

"Hum?"

"I can't breathe."

"Sorry." Tonya released him. Joshua saw tears brimming in her eyes. He glared down at her. "I'm fine. Mike's fine. We got company so, get it together. Don't go making this weird." He glanced over at the two white men who were also getting out of the car.

Tonya wiped her eyes, "Sorry, Josh. I know how much you hate tears."

"I got nothing against tears. I just don't like seeing yours. Seeing you cry makes me want to hurt somebody. And since there's nobody to hurt in this case, it just makes it weird so, stop."

"I will. It's just I was worried, you know? You're the only brother I've got."

"Nah, you can't do that either."

"What?"

"Steal my lines. You're the only sister I've got. That's my line." He called over his shoulder.

Steve and Caesar hung back a respectful distance as Mike greeted Tonya. He lifted her up off her feet and cocooned her in his arms.

"I love you, I missed you, and I adore you." She whispered as she smothered his face with kisses.

Mike chuckled. "Yeah, how much?"

"To infinity and back. This has been the longest three days of my life."

"Yeah, for me too, baby. Me too." Mike motioned for the men to follow them as he led Tonya inside the house.

CHAPTER 25

Mike leaned against the wall in the living room and stared into the waiting faces of his seated family members. "I want to try to be as transparent with you as I can. I ain't gon lie. What happened at my place the other night was a wake-up call. That's why I asked these gentlemen to join me today. Caesar is my new head of security, and you all know my agent, Steve."

Everyone around the room issued a round of polite hellos.

"I asked them to come today so that they could explain the new security measures we are putting in place to make sure what happened the other night never happens again. I'm also hoping that my family is willing to come on board with the plan my team is launching for me."

"We'll cooperate in whatever way we can, Mikey. You know that." Melissa said, as she contained her loose blonde hair into a ponytail.

Barbara also nodded in agreement.

"Thank you, Mom and Aunt Barb. I really appreciate your support. Dad, what about you?"

Jack rolled his eyes. "Mikey, what the hell kind of question is that? Don't I always support you boys?"

"Fair enough." Mike looked over at Harold. "Unc, I could really use your support."

"You already have it, Mike."

"Blackbird?"

Tonya smiled up at him, "Of course, Michael."

Mike shifted his eyes to Katie. "Aunt Katie, what do you say? Can I count on you to cooperate?"

Katie folded her arms across her chest. "This smells like a setup to me. I ain't agreeing to nothing until I hear what it is first."

Joshua's face turned up into a half smile. He and Mike had discussed the day's strategy in the car, and just as the brothers had predicted, Katie had been the last to hold out. *Definitely the sharpest knife in the drawer.*

Mike flashed Katie his most winning smile, the one that usually made the ladies swoon. "Aunt Katie—"

"No. That Pretty Boy Floyd routine won't work on me. Not today. You're gorgeous, I'll give you that, but you're also jailbait."

"Aunt Katie!" Tonya cried.

Katie shrugged. "It's true."

Harold spoke to his sister from across the room, "Sissy, the boys have driven all this way. For once in your life, can't you please just cooperate?"

"Fine." Katie huffed. "I'll cooperate."

"You heard that, Josh?"

Joshua, who was leaning against the wall directly across from Mike, nodded. "I heard it, bro. Unanimous agreement across the board." Joshua winked at Aunt Katie. "Just remember, you can't take that back later."

"I'm glad you're all willing to cooperate because, effective immediately, each of you will have your own personal security detail." Mike said.

"Dammit!" Jack said. "Katie was right. This was a setup."

"Language, Jack! Mikey, why on earth would we need security details?" Melissa said.

Jack's eyes narrowed. "What else is going on that you boys aren't telling us?"

"Yeah, you need to explain this." Harold said.

The room erupted into a frenzy as everyone began talking at once.

Joshua stuck two fingers in his mouth and whistled loudly. All conversation in the room came to a complete halt.

"Alright, let me give you the real story, without the spin." Mike said. "A member of this family was held at gunpoint because of me. A woman blew her brains out in my kitchen also because of me."

Tonya's hand flew to her mouth. Melissa released a small gasp.

"So yeah, I get it. Y'all don't like this. I don't like it too much either. But until Caesar and his team can get some basic security measures in place and assure me that the people I love are safe, then... y'all just gon have to deal. Because if I lost any of you over some BS, I wouldn't be able to deal."

"Mikey, I know this has been traumatic for you, but sweetheart, put this, all of this, in God's hands. Trust Him, ultimately, He protects us all." Melissa said softly.

Mike closed his eyes. "Mom, if I lost any of you. I wouldn't be able to deal."

"Okay, Mike. We hear you. Loud and clear, son. We will all cooperate." Harold said.

Mike ran one large hand over his face and cleared his throat. "Caesar will fill you in on the details. Then Steve is going to tell you about the re-brand of my image we are launching this spring." Mike pushed off the wall and walked towards the door.

"Michael, where are you going?"

"I'll be back in a bit, Blackbird. I just need some air."

CHAPTER 26

Exactly thirty minutes later, Caesar finished his security presentation and Steve stood staring into the silent, stone faces of Mike and Joshua's family members. He cleared his throat, loosened his tie and began.

"The fan who broke into Mike's home seemed to be fixated on causing any female near him harm. So, Mike is, of course, very adamant about making sure that, especially with Tonya starting school in Houston in the fall, this type of situation never happens again. As a result, we are re-branding the Man of Steel this spring as the consummate playboy with no one special in his life."

Steve turned his attention to Tonya. She looked momentarily stunned. "The goal is to create a juicy enough public persona that people never come looking for his real life. The goal is that they never come looking for you. We have photo shoots lined up with *GQ* and *Vanity Fair*. We also have photo shoots lined up with various female celebrities, who Mike will accompany to different awards nights, banquets, and galas."

"I don't understand. How is Mikey publicly dating other people supposed to keep Tonya safe?" Melissa said.

Katie sucked her teeth. "That's what I want to know, too."

"These aren't actual dates, Melissa. Nothing's changed about Tonya's and Mike's relationship. But for her safety, we will not make their relationship public in Houston."

"So, you're saying that Mike here is going to be going out on fake dates with singers and movie stars, celebrities and what not."

Steve nodded. "That's exactly right, Katie. The key word here is fake."

"Well, while he's fake dating, can she fake date too?"

"I seriously doubt it, Aunt Katie. Not unless those fake dates want to get their real teeth broken." Joshua said.

"I like it." Harold declared. "Anything that keeps my little girl out of harm's way. I'm all for it."

"I like it too." Jack added.

"Well, I don't." Barbara said.

"Neither do I." Melissa said. "How's Tonya supposed to feel about this?"

"You're both missing the point. The point of all of this is to keep Tonya out of the crosshairs of some psycho." Jack said.

While the elders in the room argued, Mike kept his eyes trained on Tonya. She hadn't moved from her position on the couch. She sat as still as a painted picture, staring down at her hands the entire time.

"Blackbird, what do you think?"

Silence permeated the room. A minute ticked by, then two.

"Baby, please, talk to me."

"What do you want me to say, Michael?"

"You can tell me how you really feel."

Mike bent down on one knee in front of her. "And if you can't do that yet, can you please at least look at me? I'm not playing you. I'm not ashamed of you. I certainly wouldn't ask our entire family to be a part of some elaborate scheme to deceive you. I love you. Do you hear me, Tonya? Girl, I love you. Having a camera constantly in your face changes everything. It's like living your life in a fishbowl. I don't want that for you, baby. I don't want that for us. Please, baby. Please."

Finally, Tonya looked at him. She rested her hand on his jaw. "Okay, Michael."

Present Day 2010

CHAPTER 27

HOUSTON, TEXAS

WHEN JOSHUA AND JABARI stepped into the house that evening, toddlers came racing towards them from different directions.

"Daddy! Jabaree!" The twins squealed.

Joshua dropped his bag onto the floor and scooped both twins up in his arms.

Bella pulled Jabari into a hug. "Hey sweetie, how was the game?"

"Mom, you should have seen him. Marcus is a beast! I definitely want to play for DU."

"You have time to consider your options. So just hold on. You hungry?"

Jabari shrugged. "We ate on the road, but I could eat again."

"Go put your bag up and wash up for dinner. There's a plate waiting for you on the stove."

"Thanks Mom." Jabari kissed Bella's cheek, then ran up the grand staircase, taking the steps two at a time.

Bella waited patiently as Joshua greeted Michael and Jackson, their three-year-old identical twin boys. Who everyone in the family affectionately called Mikey Jr. and Jackie. She couldn't help but smile at their riotous laughter. Only after each twin had been thoroughly tickled and zerberted, did Joshua look up and acknowledge her for the first time. He grinned sheepishly at Bella, "Oh, hey, bae."

"It's okay, Josh. You ought to know that I am thoroughly used to the sloppy seconds around here."

"Boys, let me show your mama some love." Joshua sat the twins down and pulled Bella into his arms. He kissed her gently. "Did you miss me, Bella, my beautiful Rose?"

Bella wrapped her arms around his neck. "You bet I did. Ba-by, have I got news for you."

Joshua's eyes searched the foyer. "I see my Beautiful Rose. Where's my Wildflower?"

"She's upstairs."

"Kind of strange she didn't hear the door. She asleep?"

"Oh, she heard it. She's pouting. Suri got suspended from school today."

Joshua released Bella. His features settled into a deep frown. "Why?"

Bella raised an eyebrow. "We get calls twice a week from her school. Are you seriously asking why?"

Joshua started up the stairs. "Yeah, she's five." A moment later, he stood outside of Serenity's bedroom door knocking. "Suri, can I come in, please?"

Bella folded her arms across her chest. "Really?"

Joshua put a finger to his lips, a signal for Bella to keep quiet. Bella rolled her eyes and began again. This time in a stage whisper. "Really, Josh. Are we *those* parents now?"

"That depends." Came the tiny voice on the other side of the door. "Who is it?"

"It's Daddy, baby."

"Am I in trouble?"

"Yes." Bella hissed.

"No." Joshua said firmly. "I heard you had a rough day. Can we talk about it?"

"If that was Jabari or one of the twins, you would tell them to open this door right now, cause they don't pay no bills around here." Bella said, using her stage whisper voice again.

"Bella, let me handle this. Alright?"

"Fine." Bella threw her hands up and stalked off.

CHAPTER 28

Later that night, Joshua found Bella in bed, reading. He attempted to lean over and kiss her. She blocked him.

"I don't appreciate how you handled things this evening."

"From the stiff arm you just gave me, I kind of gathered that." Joshua said dryly.

"And what was that Wildflower-may-I-come-in-mess? You would have never taken that approach with anyone of the boys."

"You're right. I wouldn't have. I treat Suri differently."

The angry look on Bella's face dissolved into one of confusion. "You're agreeing with me. Why?"

Joshua sighed deeply. "Cause it's true. Baby, the society we live in is going to tell our boys that it's okay to push through any boundary. I'm trying to teach them how to properly discern them. When they should respect the lines, and when they should tear through them. I gotta be firm sometimes to do that. And with our daughter, I'm trying to teach her how to set her own boundaries. I'm her father. She lives in my house. I pay the bills—all that is very true. And that doesn't give me the right to violate her space. If the first man who ever loved her can accept her boundaries, she'll expect every other man who comes after me to do the same. I get that you're mad, Bella, but —"

Bella pressed her palm against Joshua's cheek. "No. I get it. I'm not mad anymore. You are a good father. My life would have turned out totally different if I would have had a father who thought the way you do. I want every boy to have a father like you and I pray that every black, brown, butterscotch and beige girl in the world would have a champion in her corner that fiercely loves, values and protects her the way you do. I don't know if I can ever thank you enough for loving my babies, Joshua Keys. God couldn't have blessed me with a more amazing man."

Joshua rolled on top of Bella. "Talk is cheap. If you really want to thank me, stop flapping them jabs, woman, and put your body where my mouth is."

Bella giggled, "Boy, stop. I'm serious."

"I am too." Joshua said, nibbling the tip of her earlobe. "If I'm so amazing, why you wasting time fighting with me on my first night back, girl? I can think of so many other more productive things we could do right now. Can't you?"

Bella planted her hands firmly on top of Joshua's broad chest and pushed, "Yes, but after you tell me about your talk with Serenity."

Joshua sighed and dropped back down to his side of the bed. "Why was she even fighting in the first place?"

"Some kid named Dillon has been trying to get at her all week."

"Get at her how? Did he say something she didn't like?"

"Following her around on the playground. Being overly aggressive during gym. Just being a pest. Today, he tried to kiss her. She told him to back up. He didn't, so she popped him. Simple as that. A suspension is way too harsh for this. And if they were going to suspend anybody, it should have been Dillon for sexually harassing my daughter. I'mma follow up with the headmistress tomorrow though. You can believe that."

Bella studied her husband. He was staring up at their expansive bedroom ceiling. For the duration of this conversation, a deep scowl had taken up permanent residence on his handsome face. Bella knew that if she didn't start walking this conversation back with the quickness, Joshua would mount an all-out war against Serenity's elementary school.

"Hey, Josh."

"What?"

"Dillon is five and sexual harassment is definitely not the right word. Both he and Serenity got sent to the office for their behavior. Dillon apologized. Serenity gave Dillon a black eye, and when she was called on to apologize for it, she refused."

"Of course, she refused. She wasn't sorry. It's called honesty, Bella. It's actually a pretty good trait to have in this world these days."

"Okay, but did you at least tell her during your conversation that fighting was wrong?"

Joshua smirked. "Why would I do that? I'm the one who taught her how to throw a punch. I've been working on her jab technique since she was three. For moments, just like these."

Bella stared at Joshua incredulously. "So... what? You told her good job?"

"Pretty much. I praised her for verbally establishing and then protecting her boundaries."

"Josh, do you even hear yourself?"

"I sound great. Do you hear yourself? You need to fall back on this, Bella. I can't have random dudes rolling up thinking that it's okay to take anything from Suri."

"Baby, I feel you, but I'mma need you to dial it back, just a little because Dillon is five. Five, Josh, not fifteen."

"Five comes before fifteen, don't it? You gotta nip deviant behavior in the bud right away. Instead of punishing my daughter for exercising her right *not* to be touched, the school should have gave her an award. Suri just stopped a serial date rapist in his tracks. I bet you Dillon won't try that again."

"You're serious right now?"

Joshua folded his arms behind his head. "You'll see just how serious I am tomorrow, when I talk to the headmistress about this."

Bella grabbed his t-shirt. "Joshua Keys, you will absolutely not tell that woman this crazy mess."

Joshua rolled over and positioned his body over Bella's again. With his chin, he nuzzled her neck. "I'mma tell Headmistress Tatum that Suri deserves an award because she chose the most expedient path. Five-year-old boys don't always understand the word no, but they do understand knuckle sandwiches." Joshua planted a trail of kisses down the nape of Bella's neck.

Bella squirmed beneath him. "Okay one, we're not done talking and two, I don't remember giving you permission to kiss me either."

"You don't like this, Bella?" Joshua murmured into her neck. "I ain't Dillon, baby. Tell me you don't like it and I'll stop immediately."

Bella giggled, "Three—"

"Tell me to stop, Bella Rose and I will."

"Three, Josh, I don't know why you are trying to make our daughter out to be some type of civil rights activist. And four, when did you become a feminist?"

Joshua lifted his head and peered into Bella's eyes. "I've always been a staunch supporter of women's rights. But I became radicalized when you gave me a daughter."

Bella howled with laughter.

Joshua dipped his head low and captured Bella's lips in a lingering kiss.

"Apparently, five-year-old boys aren't the only ones who don't understand the word 'no.'"

Joshua rolled back over to his side of the bed. "Yeah, you right. Let me stop violating your rights."

Bella grabbed him. "Boy, you better get over here and finish what you started."

CHAPTER 29

Tonya awoke the next morning in her four- poster bed with the warm Houston sun beaming down upon her from the sky window. She rolled onto her side to avoid the sun's intense rays. When she did, the most enchanting scene outside her bay window greeted her. Baby ducks frolicking on her little pond and the bright yellow buds in the rose garden Michael had the grounds crew plant right outside her window, rising to greet the sun in full bloom.

Tonya smiled to herself, remembering the day Michael had called to tell her he had purchased this place. He had chosen this property because of the guest cottage for her, and the various outbuildings for all his toys already on the property. For one amazing year, this cottage had been her dream home.

Tonya spied a little card propped up on the table beside her bed. She opened the envelope and found a handwritten note on Dutton House stationery from Jeeves, the Steward of the House, letting her know that the few belongings she had brought with her had already been unpacked, and that when she was ready, he would send for the rest of her things.

Tonya sat the card back down on the table and sighed contently.

After living in land locked New York for the past ten years, returning to her dream cottage was like having her very own slice of Heaven on Earth. For the first time ever, Tonya found herself thanking God for Michael's stubbornness. He had been right. This was exactly where she needed to be to heal, to mend her bruised heart. Or had it really just been her ego? Whatever it was. She couldn't think of a better place in the whole wide world to get over Ted.

CHAPTER 30

Tonya slipped into a dark pants suit and pulled her straightened hair back into a tight bun. She heard the doorbell ring. She opened the door to the cottage to see Pearl, who was Michael's grandmother and her Aunt Katie's best friend, holding a basket of muffins in her hand.

Pearl's eyes lit up when she saw Tonya. "It's you. The answer to my prayers. You're back this time to stay."

Pearl said this not like a question but like a statement. Like she was making a declaration.

"For the time being. Yes, ma'am."

Pearl waved Tonya off with her hand, "Oh don't ma'am me. I can't take it. Do you mind if I come in?"

Tonya stepped out of the doorway. "Sorry, of course. Please."

Pearl took a seat on the sofa.

"People call me Pearl, you know. Or Grandma Pearl. Mike likes to call me Granny P. He adopted me."

Tonya knew this. She had heard this same story from Pearl's own lips a few times before. But this seemed to be the way of elders. They often told the same stories more than once.

So Tonya sat down on the couch beside Pearl, prayed she wouldn't be late for work, and listened.

Pearl, and her teenaged grandson, Marcus, and six other people had come from New Orleans after Hurricane Katrina with Bella and Jabari. Michael, grateful to Marcus for hot-wiring a school bus and driving Bella and Jabari to safety, had taken Marcus into his home on what was, at the time, supposed to be a temporary basis. After ten months of living with the young man, Michael decided to adopt Marcus and make him a son.

"Me and Marcus both. Up and adopted. A teenager, and you know they never get adopted. Right? And a 60-year-old woman. Can you believe that?"

Tonya smiled. She could. It was very Michael.

"The first thing my grandson did was retire me. But I've been working my whole life, so I like to stay busy. I'm the den mother at Hope House."

"Do you live here in the Mansion then?"

"I go back and forth. Do one week here, one week there. I like to give the young girls over there some encouragement and what not. Normally, this would be my week there, but Marcus is coming home this weekend. It's time for me to prep the boys' dinner. If I don't cook something, ain't no telling what they gon be around here eating. Mike eats out a lot. I keep telling that boy you can't eat out every night. That ain't good for nobody. Especially nowadays with everything they're putting in the food."

"What happened to Penny?"

Pearl waved her hand. "She was getting up there in years. Mike retired her about a year ago. A lot of the old staff is gone, except Jeeves. Jeeves still manages the house and all the staff. And now that Penny is gone, he calls himself fixing the food on most days, too."

Pearl sniffed and rolled her eyes. "He can do a lot of things, but if you ask me, cooking ain't really one of his areas of gifting."

There was obviously a little jealousy there, so Tonya resisted the urge to blurt out the obvious. She didn't doubt that Pearl could burn as she came from a generation of black women who knew how to throw down in the kitchen. But when it came to preparing the finest cuisine from around the world—*Jeeves was a frigging rock star*. After all, Michael had only hired Penny in the first place because Jeeves had responsibilities in so many other areas and he didn't want his Steward of the House stretched too thin. After Penny was hired, when Jeeves cooked, much to everyone's delight, including Penny's, it was because he wanted to.

"I mean, who ever heard of a black man who couldn't cook collard greens?"

"He's Moroccan. And I've had his greens, they're vegan and—"

"Exactly. Who ever heard of vegan greens?"

Tonya was going to say that them vegan collard greens were melt in your mouth good. What she said instead was that Michael was so lucky to have both Pearl and Jeeves looking out for him. This seemed to please the older woman tremendously.

"Say, do you like fried chicken, black-eyed peas, and cornbread?"

"Yes, I do, but don't worry about preparing food for me. I won't be taking dinner with the family."

Pearl stood from the couch and shoved the basket of muffins into Tonya's hand. "Dinner is at six tonight. Don't be late. I'm not gon hold you. I know you got to get to work. I just stopped by to see this secret visitor, who Mike says really needs their privacy."

"Yeah, about that privacy thing. Have you... spoken to my Aunt Katie lately?" It was probably pointless trying to get Pearl to conceal her whereabouts, but Tonya could try.

"We talk on the phone every day. Why, you got a message you want me to give her?"

Tonya shook her head. "Oh, no, no. It's just that my family doesn't know that I'm back in Houston yet."

"If you don't mind my asking, what happened with you and the preacher man?"

"It didn't work out."

"Well, thank the Lord Jesus! I never believed he was the one."

Tonya nodded her head politely. "Yes, Ma'am. I know." The family had met Ted at Joshua and Bella's vow renewal ceremony five years ago. Neither Pearl nor her Aunt Katie had been able to contain their disdain for him.

"Don't worry. I won't say nothing to Katie about you're being here. That's your business to tell. But tell it quick cause I can't be holding critical information from my best friend."

"I will. I promise." Tonya said quickly.

Pearl pointed to the basket of muffins Tonya still held in her hands, "Had I knew you were coming, I would have had a proper breakfast waiting for you this morning."

"Thank you, ma'am, but this is more than enough."

"Now that's the third time in this conversation that you've called me, ma'am." Pearl stared pointedly at Tonya.

Tonya leaned over and kissed the older woman on the cheek, "Really? Because what I meant to say was, thank you, Grandma Pearl."

CHAPTER 31

Joshua Keys strolled down the long corridor leading to his brother's division of their shared company, Home Court Advantage. He greeted his brother's secretary, Vernice, warmly. "Hello Mother Berry."

The older woman smiled up at Joshua from her work. "Morning, Just Joshua. How was your trip?"

Vernice Berry and Joshua both attended the same church. She was just as adamant about being called Mother Berry at work as he was about not being referred to as Pastor Josh while they were on the clock.

"It was great." Joshua pulled out his phone and took a seat on the edge of the older woman's desk. He showed her picture after picture of Marcus shooting three pointers during a game. "My nephew's a beast, Mother B!"

"That's an awful turn of phrase, but I suppose it means that you are very proud of him."

Joshua motioned towards Mike's door. "Is my brother here?"

"He's in there. He made it in about an hour ago."

"Cool." Joshua walked towards Mike's closed office door.

"Joshua, wait."

"What's up, Mother B?"

"He's in a very unusual mood. I don't believe I've ever seen him quite like this before."

"What do you mean?"

"Dalton Enterprises."

Joshua nodded, "That's today."

"Yes, but your brother just texted me thirty minutes ago and told me to cancel the meet and greet."

"Did he say cancel or reschedule?"

"That's just it. I went in there to clarify. He said he wasn't up for all of that today. When I asked him about a reschedule, he said I should do whatever I thought was best. Joshua, these people are flying in this afternoon from Italy. They are scheduled to visit Home Court development sites all week."

"It's cool, Mother B. They can still do all of that. That's why we have a stellar management team in place."

"Everyone has their days. I'm not concerned about that, but I know your brother and something is wrong. He just doesn't handle business this way."

"Have you contacted the agency yet?"

"No, I'm still trying to figure out what to say."

"This is what you do. Have a bottle of wine waiting for them inside their hotel suite. Make sure they have a car available for the entire week and send some tickets compliments of us. Let them know that we've had a family emergency that needs to be attended to."

Vernice looked up from her notepad in alarm.

"Nothing serious, Mother B. It's Tonya, my sister, Mike's..." Joshua let his words trail off. He cleared his throat. "Well, anyway, she's back."

Vernice's lips formed a small 'o'. She turned her attention back to her notebook. "You were saying?"

"Let them know that we'd like for them to enjoy the city — on us, of course. And that we'd be happy to hear their proposal at the end of the week. How does that sound to you?"

The older woman looked relieved. "That sounds much better, Joshua. Thank you."

"Good." Joshua started towards his brother's door.

"Joshua, one more thing. I know you don't like to wear your clergy cap while you're at work, but perhaps you should say something to encourage him."

CHAPTER 32

"I hope I didn't interrupt your study time?" Joshua said, eyeing the open Bible on the couch.

Mike closed the Bible and set it down on the coffee table. "Naw, you good. What's up, little brother?"

"Just stopped by to check on you. Bella told me Tonya was back."

"He hurt her, Josh. Broke her heart for some flyby. It's taking everything in me not to call downstairs, tell them to fire up the jet, so that I can fly out there and beat the hell out of him."

Joshua took a seat on the couch next to his brother. "I feel you, man."

"Josh, you good. You ain't had an altercation like that in years, man."

"Man, that doesn't mean I don't still get angry. A part of me wants to say, let's do it. Let's fire up the jet and both go. When Tonya first brought that cat home, I knew something like this was gon happen. He never was good enough."

"Thank you. That's exactly what I said. Not good enough."

"That's all the more reason Tonya needs you to be here for her right now. Not wrapped up in any lawsuits or media frenzy that an action like the one you're considering might cause."

Mike smirked at his brother.

"Come on, man. It's not like I ain't speaking from experience. Had I known what I know now, when all that stuff went down with the Rev, I would have just walked away. I wouldn't have put Bella, Mom and Dad, or you through that. But anger had a hold on me. I just didn't stop to think about how, in the long run, my actions would cause more pain. I ain't gon lie. It felt real good to beat the hell out of LeBlanc. But it didn't make my woman's pain go away. And it was only by grace that I didn't kill him."

"You know what I don't get, Josh? If God is real, and I ain't tripping about that, cause I know He is. Why does He allow a man like that to stand up in the pulpit and preach?"

"It's a gift, man. The gifts of God are without repentance. God is so honorable to His word that, whether we are honorable or not, He'll never take them back. After I found out about Bella, I asked that same question, on the daily. I kept waiting for God to do something biblical to him. When it seemed like nothing was happening, I grew bitter, and I walked away. But you know what? LeBlanc died broke and alone in a nursing home, supported by the same person he ran down in the media all those months. I'm not saying that was justice. But God has a way of dealing with people far better than you or I ever could. Concentrate on Tonya. Make sure she doesn't get locked in a prison of bitterness over this."

CHAPTER 33

Mike returned home from work that evening to find Pearl in the kitchen jamming to the oldies station while she prepared the evening meal.

Mike kissed her cheek. "Smells good in here. You getting an early start?"

"Oh, this isn't for Marcus."

"Who's it for?" Mike reached over and dipped his finger into one of her pots.

"Us. We are going to have a nice, quiet dinner at home. You, me, and Tonya."

"You went over to the cottage."

"You knew I would. Honey, I can't tell you how happy I am for you. I feel like it's my own birthday."

"Don't do it, Granny P."

"Do what?"

"Don't go getting any ideas. Tonya's just a friend in need right now. Nothing else."

Pearl pushed Mike from the kitchen. "Well, go tell your friend that dinner is ready. And hurry back before my black-eyed peas get cold."

Mike knocked lightly on the opened door before stepping into the kitchen.

Tonya was leaning against the kitchen counter, reading. She was just about to bite into the rest of her lunch sandwich when she was startled by his knock. Tonya nearly jumped out of her skin. Her book went flying in one direction, her sandwich in the other.

Mike's face clouded over in anger. "You mean to tell me I made it all the way up that path, up these stairs, and inside this kitchen and you didn't hear me?"

Tonya shrugged. "I was reading."

"I could have been anyone, Tonya. You need to be more alert. I know you're in the middle of your little pity party, but you can't be walking around the streets of Houston with your head in the clouds."

Tonya picked her book up off the floor. "First of all, Michael. I am not having a pity party. Secondly, I'm not walking around the city with my head in the clouds. I'm here in my cottage on your estate, which is tighter than the Pentagon. So, what's your problem?"

"You got the door wide open."

Tonya sighed, "What do you want, Michael?"

"Granny P sent me to tell you dinner is ready."

"Tell her I'm your tenant and that I don't take my meals with your family. By the way, we need to talk about rent."

"Whatever, tell her yourself, shot caller." Mike turned and stalked down the stairs.

"Michael, get back here. I'm not playing with you!" Tonya stamped her foot and screamed after him, "You-you, big baby!"

"Yeah, right back at you!"

FALL 1994

CHAPTER 34

Fall Semester, Houston Texas

On move in day, Joshua loaded up his brother's truck with Tonya's belongings and drove her to campus. HU was bustling with new and returning students and Joshua had to park behind a long line of cars that were already in front of Trident Hall, the apartment style dormitory where Tonya would be staying. Joshua jumped out of the truck and walked around to the passenger side and opened the door for her.

"Go check in and get your room key. I'll start unloading your things."

"Okay."

Joshua was opening the hatch when he heard someone call his name. He turned and greeted the two students approaching him. "What up, frat. What up wannabe, frat."

The first guy, Terry, greeted Joshua with their secret fraternal handshake, "Bad Boy."

The one known as Brown Nose bowed low to Joshua and began a soliloquy, "Greetings Big Brother Dean All Might—" Joshua shook his head. "No need for all that today. What y'all up to?"

Terry grinned, "Checking out the new honeys in Trident Hall. I swear this dorm has the finest girls on campus."

Tonya walked out of the building with two other girls. Terry spotted her immediately. "*Dayamum*. Like that beauty right there."

Brown Nose craned his neck to see. "I see three Nubian Princesses, which one are you referring to, Big Brother?"

"The one in the middle, of course. She's radiant. Watch the Master at work, Brown Nose. I'm about to get those digits." Terry said.

"Slow your role, Romeo. That girl in the middle, her name is Tonya Malone. She doesn't exist to you."

"Oh, so you saying that's you?"

Tonya waved at Joshua.

He smiled and waved back. "Yeah, that's me."

"Oh, okay, cause see, I thought you and Shannon were..." Terry's voice trailed off.

Joshua took his eyes off Tonya and turned his full attention to Terry. He raised an eyebrow. "You thought what?"

"I thought Shannon was you."

"That's right. That's me too."

Terry shrugged, his eyes following Tonya. "Alright, man. If you say so. But a girl that fine does not belong on the side. No disrespect to Shannon. She's banging, but if that girl right there was mine, I'd make her my main dish."

"That's my sister, fool, and she ain't nobody's side piece. So put your eyes back inside your head, before you lose them. You feel me?"

Terry held his hands up in surrender. "My bad, Bad Boy. That's all you had to say, man. I didn't know she was fam."

"Now you know. Make sure everybody else knows it, too."

"I got my keys, and I met my new roommates." Tonya said, as she approached Joshua and the two guys. "Josh, this is Carrie, and this is Nisha."

Joshua smiled at the two women. "Hi Carrie and Nisha."

"Hi Joshua." They both said together.

Tonya looked back and forth between her roommates and Joshua. "Oh, so you already know each other?"

"We've never officially met." Carrie said. A deep blush covered her face and neck. "But everybody knows Bad Boy."

Joshua grinned at Tonya. "I told you, you are in my house now, girl."

"Whatever." Tonya looked at the two men standing beside Joshua. "Aren't you going to introduce me to your friends?"

"Naw, they're not important."

Tonya pushed his shoulder playfully.

"This here is my frat, Terry, and this right here is, Brown Nose. While you're on campus, they both gon help me look out for you."

Tonya extended her hand to Terry first. "Tonya Malone."

"Terrence Masters the third, at your service. My friends call me Terry."

The one called Brown Nose stuck his hand out to Tonya next. "It has not yet appeared what my new name will be, but for now, my big brothers call me Brown Nose."

Tonya raised an eyebrow at the young man, "Okay then." She turned her attention back to Joshua. "I couldn't find any carts. It looks like it will be awhile before any become available."

"I can call my line brothers if you like, Big Brother. We can carry this beautiful young lady's things on our backs."

Joshua nodded. "I like your initiative. Go, do that." To Tonya he said, "What room are you in?"

"411."

Joshua kissed her cheek. "Chill with your girls for a minute and I'll handle everything here."

"Thanks."

"Girl, how in the world did you manage that?" Nisha said once they were out of earshot of the guys.

"I know! She just got here, right?" Carrie said.

"Manage what?"

"Are you serious? You pulled the finest man on this campus."

"Who, Joshua? No, we are not dating."

"You sure bout that? He was awfully protective of you and I'm not trying to throw shade, but he's been dating this girl named Shannon off and on for a few years now and He ain't never moved her into her dorm."

"I know Shannon."

"You do?"

"Yeah, she's cool."

Carrie and Nisha shared a look.

Tonya laughed, "Oh, my goodness, it's not like that, you two. Joshua and I grew up together. He's my godbrother. Technically, I'm an only child, so he's the closest thing to a sibling that I have."

"Oh, wow, that's too bad."

"Why?"

"Because your dating life on this campus is officially over. I'm pretty sure he just A-LISTED you."

"What?"

"Joshua's frat runs the social scene on this campus. If he says hands off, it's like the kiss of death around here. No guys will even look at you."

"Remember the guy Terry who was with him?"

"Yeah."

"He is a notorious hound. Normally he would have tried to get your number, right there on the spot, but he didn't, because Bad Boy already put you on the list."

"Dee's our other roommate. You'll meet her tomorrow. Her brother is in the same fraternity as Bad Boy. She hasn't had one date since she got here. That was two years ago. The guys from the other fraternities won't even date her. Trust me, hands off means, hands off."

Tonya shrugged. "Doesn't really matter to me. I came here to get an education, not a man. Besides, I already know the man I'm going to marry."

Present Day 2010

CHAPTER 35

HOUSTON, TEXAS

"TONYA, CAN I INTEREST you in more sweet potatoes?" Pearl asked.

"Yes, please."

Mike smiled. "I take you to one of the hottest restaurants in Houston. You don't eat. I take you home and you devour Granny P's cooking like it's going out of style."

Pearl pointed the serving spoon in Mike's direction, "Tonya, I keep telling my grandson here that a body can't eat out all the time. It's not healthy. Home cooking is what's best for you."

"Well, especially your food, Grandma Pearl. It's made with love. I think that's what my belly's been missing for a very long time."

"I like her." Pearl declared. "I don't know why this girl is talking about staying a year or two. I decree and declare that we are keeping her."

Mike laughed. "Amen to that, Granny P."

Tonya sat her napkin down on her plate. "I appreciate dinner, Grandma Pearl. Really. You fed my body and my soul, but despite Michael's and my history, I am only a tenant. I don't expect to take my dinner with your family every night. Michael and I are going to be sitting down and discussing the details of my rent soon. Isn't that right, Michael?"

"Whatever, Tonya."

Pearl placed a hand on Tonya's arm, "Baby, if you're here, then you must be family, otherwise Mike wouldn't have it any other way. Now that other one, Sister Satan, she's had her eye on that cottage since the first day. She sees it all painted and done up nicely and she wants to know why she can't stay there. And you know why that is? Cause it wasn't for her. It was for you."

Tonya turned to Michael, "Who's Sister Satan?"

"Nobody."

"So why couldn't she stay in the cottage? I thought you told me you were in between tenants?"

"I am."

"Who's the last tenant who stayed in the cottage, Michael?"

"You."

Mike stood from the table and kissed Granny P's forehead. "Dinner was delicious. I'll be in my study."

Tonya folded her arms across her chest, "Michael, we still need to talk about this."

"There's nothing to talk about."

"We need to talk about my rent."

"Are you deaf? I said later."

Pearl and Tonya watched him stalk out of the kitchen.

CHAPTER 39

IT WAS HER FIRST Saturday morning in Houston and Tonya was on her way to the kitchen to make a cup of tea when the doorbell rang.

She opened her front door to see a carbon copy of Michael standing in her doorway.

"Hello, Ms. Tonya. I'm Marcus Dutton. I don't know if you remember me."

Everything about the young man, from his smile to his mannerism, to the way he casually leaned his tall lanky body against the doorframe, was familiar. Tonya ignored Marcus's out-stretched hand and pulled him into a tight embrace.

"Of course I remember you, Marcus. It's good to see you again. Please, come in."

"Actually, I can't stay. I just stopped by to tell you——"

"Marcus!" Pearl's voice carried across the courtyard.

"That breakfast is ready."

"I guess there's no point resisting her, huh?"

Marcus smiled down at Tonya, "No, none whatsoever."

Tonya, Mike, Marcus and Pearl all sat around the kitchen table talking after breakfast. "Once again, Grandma Pearl, the food was spectacular. You really outdid yourself. I haven't had shrimp and grits this good since I left my mama's house. Thank you." Tonya said.

Mike and Marcus both echoed their agreements on how wonderful everything was.

"You're all welcome. Tonya, don't let me have to send any-one to come get you to eat no more. Breakfast is at 8 on week-days. 9 on the weekends. Dinner is the same time every night, and that's 6 pm. Now, I ain't trying to get in your business, but you look like you lost a lot of weight since I last saw you. I don't know how they were treating you in New York, but now that you're home, I intend to feed you well."

"I'll be on time from now on and I'll call whenever I can't make it."

Pearl locked eyes with Tonya.

Mike chuckled.

Tonya continued, "I mean, it's not like I'm anticipating not being able to be here, it's just that sometimes... things come up."

Pearl continued to stare at her blankly.

"You know what? I'll be here from now on." Tonya said.

"Good, that's exactly what I want to hear." Pearl patted Tonya's hand, then rose from the table and began clearing away the breakfast dishes.

"Grandma Pearl, sit. We'll get the dishes."

Mike looked around the room. "We who?"

"You and me. I can wash, you can rinse, and Marcus can dry."

"I would, but the staff really doesn't like it when we do their jobs." Marcus said.

"He's right, they don't." Mike said.

Tonya stood. She took a bowl from Grandma Pearl's hand and kissed her cheek. "If I'm going to be taking all my meals here, then we are going old school."

"What's old school?" Marcus asked.

"The chef never cleans after she cooks. Cleaning is everyone else's job."

"Oh goody. What a treat. I like old school." Pearl declared.

"Granny P, what are you talking about? You know you don't have to clean a thing in here." Mike said.

"Yeah, my dad and I keep telling her to go sit down somewhere. But she likes doing stuff."

Mike shrugged. "So, we let her."

"Grandma Pearl, you go enjoy your down time. We'll take care of everything here."

"Thank you, sweetie. I will. I think I'll take myself a nap. Wake me up if anything interesting happens."

Pearl leaned over and kissed Mike and Marcus. She walked out of the kitchen.

Mike stood up from the table and stretched. "A nap sounds pretty nice right about now."

Marcus faked a yawn. "Oh yeah. Sure does."

"So, the two of you are just going to bail on me? Leave me here to do all the dishes by myself?"

"Of course not. That's why I pay Doreen, baby. So nobody has to do this."

Tonya pushed a towel into Mike's hand. She threw another across the kitchen to Marcus, who caught it easily. "How about I wash and you boys dry?"

Exactly one hour later, Tonya removed the large rubber gloves and cut the water off. "See, that wasn't so bad, was it?"

Mike leaned in and kissed the tip of her nose. "With you, no."

Tonya smiled up at him, wondering how such an insignificant gesture had made her stomach grow wings and take flight. She turned to Marcus. "So, Marcus, how do you like DU?"

"It's pretty cool."

"I bet Mel and Jack love having you so close."

Mike laughed. "Boy, do they ever." Mike started humming the song, *Summer Breeze*.

"Is there an inside joke that I'm missing here?" Tonya said, when Mike began playing air guitar on the chords part of the song.

"He's tripping, Ms. Tonya. Ignore him." To his dad, Marcus said, "See, you laughing now, but it wasn't so funny to you when it happened."

"Of course not. I thought you were dying."

"What happened?"

"Ms. Tonya, you don't want to hear this story."

"Marcus, everyone wants to hear this story. I cannot wait to tell your future wife, and your firstborn child, this story."

Marcus groaned.

"Tonya, freshman year this boy wakes up, goes to the bathroom, takes a piss, gets in his car and drives all the way back to Houston. No call or nothing. Just comes straight to my office. I'm in a meeting. I look up and see him standing outside the conference room, looking scared. So me and Josh both jump up. We don't know what's happened. We take a walk back to my office and he says, 'Yo, Dad. Yo, Unc, my junk don't look right.'"

Tonya's hand flew to her mouth.

"That's not how it went. I didn't say —— I said I had a rash in the general vicinity and that I was concerned."

"Bull! So now I'm scared, right? So I tell him, 'Drop your drawers, let me see it.' He all like, 'Dad, ain't you gonna close the curtains? How you just gonna ask me to drop my pants with the windows all open?' My office is on the nineteenth floor, right? Can't nobody see nothing."

Marcus pointed to his dad. "Mr. GQ Smooth himself, the Man of Steel right here, goes totally off. 'Boy, if you don't drop your pants right now, I will rip them off of you! I got a lot of money, Marcus, but I can't buy new balls! So, I need to know, right here and now, have you been with anybody! Anybody at all!' So I say, 'No, Dad. No girls.' 'No girls?! What the hell does that mean?! What are you trying to tell me, Marcus?!' 'I ain't trying to tell you nothing, Dad. Except that I haven't been with nobody!'"

Tonya laughed till tears came into her eyes and her gut hurt. "So what, what did you do?!"

"If the Man of Steel and Bad Boy Joshua Keys were standing over you, threatening to rip your pants off of you, what would you do? I dropped my pants."

Tonya laughed even louder.

"They just stood there staring at it. Unc like, you sure you ain't caught nothing from some little honey? Cause your dad is right. We can't replace the family jewels, but we can get you a shot. I'm like, I ain't been with nobody, Unc, I swear. Then my dad starts sniffing the air around me—"

"Tonya, this boy came up into my office smelling like Summer Breeze."

Tonya's eyes widened. "That cleaning stuff Auntie Mel used to get from those shady distributors?"

Mike nodded, "Still gets. Josh was like, 'Yo man, that's what's up. Mom's been washing this boy's drawers.'"

Tonya shook her head. "Ya'll ain't right for that, Michael. You should have told him. Don't you remember that time Joshua broke out in those giant hives?"

Marcus threw his hands up in the air. "Thank you! That's what I'm saying!"

Mike shook his head, "I told him. I said never let my mother wash your clothes."

"Yeah, but you didn't tell me my junk could fall off if she did."

The house phone rang. "Who dat?" Mike said.

Marcus leaned over and checked the caller ID. "It's Auntie." Marcus's cell phone rang next. Mike's cell phone rang, too.

Marcus looked at his phone. "That's Jabari."

Mike looked down at his phone. "Josh. They gon keep calling like this until somebody answers. Everybody's dying to see you."

Tonya wrinkled her nose. "Everybody like who?"

"Josh, Bella and the kids."

"Oh, now that I can do. It's just my mom still doesn't know that I'm here yet."

Mike groaned. "Tonya, we talked about this."

"I know. I called and left a message. She knows I'm fine. She just doesn't know that I'm in Texas."

"Handle your business. If she asks me about it, I'm not lying for you."

Tonya stared at Mike, "Why would my mom call you?"

"Who, Auntie Barb? She calls and visits all the time." Marcus said.

"Really?"

"Yeah."

"So, if my mom is Auntie Barb, why am I still Ms. Tonya?"

"My bad. What would you like for me to call you?"

"How bout we start with just Tonya?"

"Alright, I can do that." Marcus said.

Tonya turned to Mike, "I didn't know you and my mom were so chummy."

"There are a lot of things you don't know about me."

"So, I take it you two have known each other for a long time?" Marcus said.

"Ever since she was in her playpen. Outside of your uncle, there is nobody that I've known longer."

Mike's cell phone beeped. He looked down to see a text message from Joshua.

Where r u? Why r u not picking up?

Mike texted him back. *I'm washing dishes.*

Joshua's response was immediate. *Why?*

Mike chuckled and showed Tonya his phone.

"Let me see that." Tonya took the phone and replied to Joshua's text. *Because rich people gotta eat too.* She typed.

Mike's phone beeped as Joshua's text came across the screen. *Tonya! What's up, girl!!!*

"Unbelievable! How did he know it was me?" The house phone rang again.

"That's Auntie again." Marcus said.

Mike looked at Tonya. "You gonna answer? I'm pretty sure she's not calling for me."

Tonya picked up the phone. She pushed the talk button and immediately squealed into the receiver.

"I know me too! Today? Let me check with Michael."

"I'm all yours, Blackbird. Whatever you decide is fine."

"Okay, Bella, yes, today. We can come to you. Hang on for a moment, okay?" Tonya removed the phone from her ear. "Marcus, what about you? Are you free today too?"

Marcus looked momentarily shocked by the invitation, but quickly recovered with a smile. "Uh, yeah sure."

"Marcus will be there, too. Grandma Pearl is napping, but I'll ask her when she wakes up. Bella, you have to kiss all of my God-babies for me. What am I talking about? I'll see them in a couple of hours. I'll smother them with kisses myself!"

CHAPTER 37

AT SERENITY'S INSISTENCE, THE whole family stood outside on the front lawn, awaiting Tonya's arrival. Serenity and the twins, Jackie and Mikey Jr., began jumping up and down screaming with excitement the moment they saw one of their Uncle Mike's many cars drive up.

"Where's Auntie Tonya?" Serenity said, when only Mike and Marcus got out of the Beamer.

"What, no love for Uncle Mike?"

Serenity and the boys took off, running at breakneck speed. All three leapt into his arms at the same time.

"What about your big cuz? Where's my love?" Marcus said.

Serenity and the twins released their uncle and turned to attack Marcus next.

Jabari, now sixteen, and much too cool for all of that, sauntered over to his uncle and cousin. While his younger siblings led the charge with hugs, kisses, and sloppy face farts, he offered both his uncle and his cousin a simple fist bump.

Marcus smiled wryly and took Jabari's pre-offered bump, but Mike ignored Jabari's fist completely and pulled him into a crushing hug. Because according to him, "Only a fool gets so cool that he can't properly greet his family."

And then, as if to re-emphasize his uncle's point, Jabari's dad greeted his brother and nephew with big, crushing hugs and his mom followed suit and did the same.

"Where is Tonya?" Bella asked.

"She should be here shortly. Her and Granny P stopped off to get a few things for the kiddos." Mike said.

Serenity's eyes lit up. "Auntie Tonya went to get presents for me?"

"Yep, you and your brothers."

"I made a banner for her. Jabari helped a little, but the babies mostly drooled on it."

Marcus studied Serenity's banner with admiration. "That's really nice work, Lil Bit."

"Marcus, did I tell you that Auntie Tonya works at my school?"

Jabari rolled his eyes. "Only like a thousand times."

"I wasn't talking to you, Doofus!"

"Hey!" Bella scolded, "No name calling."

Marcus pointed to an old jalopy inching down the street. "Lil Bit. Here she comes. Look alive."

Serenity shouted orders to her brothers, "Hold the banner! Hold the banner! Nice and tall, so she can see it!"

The twins held the banner as high as their little bodies would allow while Tonya's car, sounding like it was in the throes of an asthma attack, wheezed its way slowly up the hilly street.

Joshua stared, "Is that——"

Mike nodded, "Yep."

When the car did finally stop at their house. Pearl flew out from the passenger seat, thanking Jesus for their safe arrival. Tonya had to brace her foot against the car then yank once, twice, no three times before she could get the back door open to retrieve the gifts she had purchased for the children.

Joshua continued to stare. "She got on the freeway in that?"

Mike nodded, "Yep."

"Drove 1600 miles?"

"Yep."

Serenity and her brothers ran to greet Tonya and Pearl as they came up the walk.

"Hello, hello, oh my, aren't you all getting so big!" Tonya hugged Serenity, then Jabari, and then each one of the twins. She turned next to greet her friend. "Oh, Bella, it's so good to see you!" The two women laughed and rocked in each other's arms.

Joshua tilted his head to the side, checking out the car's exterior, which was decidedly more rust than paint. "What do you think it runs on?"

"If I had to take a guess right off the top of my head, I'd say, God's breath." Mike said.

Joshua tore his eyes away from the monstrosity parked in his driveway. His critical gaze now landed on his brother.

Mike returned his brother's stare. "What?"

"You slippin."

"Please. I ain't slippin."

"Yeah, you are."

"My game is tight, little brother. Trust and believe. No slippage."

"You telling me you're cool with the woman you love driving around in that thing?"

"I'm telling you I'm straight up breezy with it, brother."

Joshua pointed to Mike's face. Like always, Mike's facial features remained smooth and impassive. "Naw, see, this here is some reverse psychology stuff. I know you, bro. On a fundamental level, you can't be cool with this."

"You're forgetting one thing, Josh. Tonya's not my woman. She can drive whatever she wants."

"He's right, Joshua." Tonya walked over to the two brothers. She stood on her tippy toes and kissed Joshua on the cheek. "Michael and I are just friends. He has no say in what I drive."

Mike shrugged. "See."

Joshua pulled Tonya into a tight embrace. "He might not be your man, but you will always be my little sister. Let me retire that thing for you. Please. We can go down to the dealership right now and pick out whatever car you want."

Bella nodded her head in agreement. "Girlfriend, you really need a new whip."

"Why does everyone keep doggin my car? Grandma Pearl spoke in tongues the whole way over here."

"I had too, otherwise we wouldn't have made it. That thing went into cardiac arrest twice on the freeway." Pearl said.

Tonya waved her hand, "Oh, that wasn't cardiac arrest. I need a new muffler, is all."

Bella pursed her lips. "What you need is a new car. I'm thinking one that runs on something other than faith."

"You know what, Bella? I really don't appreciate y'all talking about Beauty that way."

"What did you just call that thing?" Mike asked.

"Her name is Beauty." Tonya said, proudly.

Everyone roared with laughter.

"Go ahead. Yuck it up, all of you. Me and this car have been through a lot together. I'm not about to trade her in for some younger, hotter model."

SPRING 1995

CHAPTER 38

SPRING SEMESTER, HOUSTON TEXAS

"For your own safety, Tonya, you need to tell us."

"We know he's rich. We've been watching the Bentley pick you up now for months."

"Is he old?"

"You're not carrying on with a married man, are you?"

Tonya had been in her room packing an overnight bag for her weekly staycation with Michael when her roommates had barged into her bedroom for this little... intervention.

This semester, Tonya had registered for 18-course credits and scheduled all her classes on Mondays, Tuesdays and Wednesdays. Such a hectic schedule meant that she was bone tired when she finished her official school week. But it also meant she got to spend three days a week with Michael. Sundays they reserved for their folks. Just as he'd promised, Tonya had been home every Sunday for dinner this school year. When Michael wasn't traveling for an away game, so had he. He still wouldn't budge on the car service, though. Per his stupid, I-have-to-keep-you-safe-at-all-cost edict; the couple never traveled publically together.

"You think the president and the first lady travel together?" Michael had said to her one morning at breakfast, it was just one of many times that they'd had this same argument.

Tonya sat her fork down and smiled triumphantly up at him, "Yes, all the time, actually. They do."

"I'm not talking about in the States, Blackbird. I'm talking about heads of states in other parts of the world, say, war-torn countries."

"Michael, how should I know? I don't know the travel protocols of foreign dignitaries in other countries."

"Fair enough. What about the president and the vice president here in the US? Do they ever ride together in the same vehicle?"

"No."

"Do you know why that is?"

Tonya sighed, "If something were to happen to the president, the vice president still needs to be alive to run the country."

Mike had leaned back in his chair and lifted the glass of OJ smugly to his lips. "I rest my case."

"You rest your case? Michael, your case makes absolutely no sense at all. You're driving to Dallas today. I'm riding to Dallas today, albeit in the stupid car service you hired for me—"

"It's a reinforced vehicle. If anything foul were to pop off, Parker would protect you."

"Are you saying that you can't protect me?"

That was a low blow. Tonya had struck a nerve, and she knew it. She had seen it, an almost imperceptible tightening of his jaw muscle. Still, when he spoke, his voice remained annoyingly unaffected.

"This is my way of protecting you."

Tonya closed her eyes. She shook her head, attempting to stave off impending tears. Because, although he was calm, she was completely livid.

"Michael, this... this is an obscene waste of resources. I don't need it, but all over this world children are—"

"Stop. Don't start with the starving kids bit again."

Now he was angry. Now they were a perfect pair.

"I'm just trying to get you to see reason, Michael." Tonya said quietly.

"Naw, what you're trying to do is guilt trip me. The car and the driver are here to stay, Blackbird. That's our new normal. The sooner you come to grips with this, the better."

"Tonya, you can't weasel out of this. I see the car parked outside for you. So, before you jet off to God knows where again, with God knows who, we need to have this conversation." That was her roommate, Nisha. The attitudinal one. Her voice was just the catalyst needed to shift Tonya out of the past and right back into the drama that was unfolding in her bedroom today. Tonya zipped up her overnight bag and looked into the anxious faces of her three roommates. Two anxious faces, actually. Carrie and Dee looked genuinely concerned for her. Nisha just looked like she always did, one moment away from pissed.

"He's not old, and he's not married. Unfortunately, that's all I'm at liberty to say."

Nisha sucked her teeth, "Unfortunately, that's not going to be enough."

"What Nisha means is that you're good people, Tonya. You come from a wonderful family and we don't want to see you get hurt." That was Dee, the sweet one.

"We also don't want to see the finest dude on this campus, who is also your godbrother, get arrested, because you got hurt by some mystery Negro and he did something stupid to that mystery Negro." Nisha said.

"That's sweet, ladies. Really, but I don't want you worried about me, okay?" Tonya looked at Nisha, "Or Joshua. I'm not in any danger. I'm not having an illicit affair. I'm good." Tonya smiled brightly at her roommates.

"If everything is as good as you say, you shouldn't have a problem being honest with your friends." Carrie said. Carrie had given her life to Christ last semester. These days, her conversation was all about truth and honesty.

Tonya sat her bag on the floor and took a seat on her bed. "Okay, but what I am about to tell you must stay between the four of us. Deal?"

The three women scurried up on top of Tonya's bed.

"Scout's honor." Dee said.

"We won't say a word." Carrie said.

"Remember when I told you I didn't care whether Joshua placed me on some stupid list?"

"Yeah." All three girls spoke in unison, even though Dee hadn't actually been there for that conversation.

"Remember how I told you I had already met the man I was going to marry? Well, his name is Michael."

The three women stared at her blankly.

"Dutton."

Nisha's eyes bucked. Carrie let out a soft gasp.

"You're dating The Man of Steel?"

Tonya nodded. "The one and only."

Dee's face crinkled in confusion. "But that's Joshua's brother. Doesn't that make him your godbrother?"

"No. Well—yes, sort of. He used to be, but not anymore. Michael divorced my parents when he was nine. He told them that having them as his godparents was kind of creepy because he was going to marry me when we grew up."

"That was a long time ago. You sure he still feeling you that way?"

Carrie elbowed Nisha. The look on her face demanded that, for once in her life, their roommate keep quiet.

Nisha glared at Carrie. "Oh no, Ms. Holy Ghost in Effect. You're the one who wanted to come in here and have this little, come-to-Jesus-moment with her. We're all being honest here. So she needs to know the truth." Nisha turned her attention back to Tonya. "You're obviously the girl he left back home. But you need to be careful. In Houston, the Man of Steel has a reputation of being a player."

Tonya bit her bottom lip. "So it's working?"

"What?"

"I mean, is that what people really think?"

"Honey, please. It's what we know. The Man of Steel goes through women, especially celebrities, faster than you can change your panties."

CHAPTER 39

Tonya returned to her apartment after a long morning run. She took a seat on the couch and undid the laces on her cross trainers.

"So, are you celebrating Valentine's Day with Michael?"
Dee cut her eyes at Nisha.

"He's traveling tonight. We'll probably celebrate sometime next weekend."

"He's traveling alright."

"Nisha, stop. Just give Tonya her mail, please." Carrie said.
Nisha set the February issue of *Essence* magazine on top of the coffee table in front of Tonya.

Tonya looked down at the cover to see Michael in a passionate embrace with Brandala, a Houston native, and chart-topping popstar. The magazine cover promised that the two mega stars were finally coming clean about their love life.

"This my copy?" Tonya said, glancing up at Nisha, fully aware that all three of her roommates were studying her face.

"Yep, came in the mail this morning. Just in time for Valentine's Day."

"Any other mail come for me?"

"A delivery guy dropped these off a few minutes after you left." Carrie said hopefully. She was pointing to the large crystal vase filled with what looked to be two dozen yellow roses.

"Thanks." Tonya picked up the magazine, walked into her bedroom, and closed the door.

"Yo, Bad Boy, you better get in here. We got a major problem."

Joshua walked into his frat house's den to see his entire line of pledges in the plank position on the floor. His frat brothers circled them like a horde of angry sharks. From the glistening beads of perspiration dripping off the recruits' faces, he could tell that they'd been frozen in position for a very long time.

"Somebody care to tell me what's going on?" Joshua said.

"Go ahead, tell him!" Kevin barked, "Tell your Dean how you had one job and you screwed it up!"

"I take full responsibility." The recruit known as Butterfingers sputtered. "I and I alone, not my line brothers, are responsible for this Valentine's Day debacle, sir!"

"Do you realize I had to listen to my girl crying and screaming for three straight hours on the phone this morning?" Another frat brother called Ghost said.

"Brown Nose, what do you have to say for yourself? You're the anchor. How did you manage not to hold things down?" Kevin said.

"I-I don't know, Big Brother. We purchased two gifts, one for each of our illustrious Big Brothers' special ladies. Just as we were instructed. A major gift for the main girl, a minor gift for the side girl. Somehow things must have somehow gotten switched around." Brown Nose said.

"You sent my side piece, pearls and my main girl, candy!" Tank bellowed. "My fiancée just broke up with me over email this morning because, to make matters worse, not only did you send her a trifling gift, you put my side piece's name on my main girl's card! Now, not only do I have to figure out how to get my girl back. I got to figure out how to get my grandmother's pearls back too!"

Joshua laid a hand on the man's shoulder. "Calm down, Tank. How many girls got the wrong gifts?"

"All of them."

Brothers all around the room began to groan and curse.

Joshua stooped down, so that he was eye level with the sweaty recruits. "What'd y'all send my girl?"

"I wish we could say that we got that right, Big Brother, but she received candy."

"What kind of candy?"

"Chocolate candy, sir."

Joshua rubbed one large hand over his face. "Did we not have a conversation about this? Did I not specifically tell you that Shannon is allergic to chocolate? Are you trying to kill my girl?"

"No, Big Brother, never that!" All the pledges answered at once.

"Are you trying to send her into anaphylactic shock?"

"No, Big Brother!"

One of Joshua's frat brothers approached, holding a decorated wooden paddle. "Josh, it's time. You've been protecting them long enough. These fools got to eat wood today."

Joshua raised up off his hunches to a standing position. When he stood, he towered a full head and shoulders above the man holding the paddle. "Did you eat wood when I brought you over, Sultan?"

"Naw, but—"

"Then put that up." Joshua turned his glare onto the recruits. "Drop to the floor!"

The pledges collapsed to the floor, groaning in relief.

"Give me two hundred and fifty pushups." Joshua said. The pledges cried out again, this time in agony.

"While you're down there, you had better think of a way to fix this mess." Joshua said.

"They had better fix this." Tank fumed as he paced around the room. "If you fools don't fix this, you won't have to worry about crossing the burning sands. I'm going to kill every single one of you pledges myself! And bury you together in an unmarked grave!"

"Permission to speak, big brother!"

"Speak." Joshua said.

"All the side chicks were supposed to get candy and all the main chicks were supposed to get either flowers or jewelry. Shannon should have gotten flowers, because that is what you requested. Your other girl was supposed to get the candy, but somehow their names and addresses got switched."

"What other girl?"

"Lucinda Adams."

Joshua froze. He hadn't messed with that girl in a minute. "You sent Lucinda a gift, in my name? Who told you to do that?" Unlike many of his fraternity brothers, Joshua didn't keep a girl on the side. One girl was problematic enough. Even if he were to keep a side chick, he'd never be stupid enough to acknowledge her with a gift.

"Her name was on the list Big Brother Terry gave us. We followed that list precisely."

"Where's Terry now?"

"He went to get supplies for tonight's party."

CHAPTER 40

Terry was in the grocery store purchasing supplies for his fraternity's epic Valentine's Day bash when he saw Tonya staring at a wall of canned goods in aisle three. Terry walked up behind her. As he leaned in, he caught the alluring fragrance of lavender wafting off of her skin. "Cheer up, pretty lady."

Tonya, startled at the sound of Terry's voice. "Oh, Terry, I didn't notice you."

"I didn't mean to scare you. I saw you from across the store. You looked sad. I just wanted to come over and say hi."

Tonya fixed him with a polite smile, "I'm fine, really. Thank you."

Terry tilted his head to the side. "You sure about that? I'm a fantastic listener if you ever want to talk."

Tonya shook her head. "No, thank you."

"Okay then. Lucky for you, I have something in my pocket guaranteed to cheer up any beautiful lady." Terry pulled out a flyer and handed it to Tonya. "There is a party at my place tonight. And you're invited. Only the best-looking girls on campus can attend."

Tonya laughed, "Is that so?"

"It is. That's why you have to come."

"This says here that there is a dress code."

"Jeans and a t-shirt. But your t-shirt needs to be one of the three Valentines day featured colors. Wear a white tee if you're feeling nice, pink if you're feeling sweet and red if you're feeling..." Terry paused for a moment, thinking of just the right word. "Dangerous. I think you'd look good in red."

Tonya smiled. "Can I bring my roommates?"

Terry pretended to think about this for a moment. He rolled his eyes playfully. "I guess they can come. Just be sure to bring this flyer. This is your access pass. Give the brothers my name if you run into any problems at the door. So, will I see you tonight?"

"I'll think about it."

"Dude, what the hell is wrong with you?" Andre said when Terry met him in the check-out line.

"Chill out, man. I got the stuff for the jello shots right here." Terry said, holding up seven boxes of jello in one large hand.

"I saw you talking to that girl. Please tell me you did not do what I think you just did."

"Hell yeah, I did. We are supposed to have only the finest girls at our party. That's the tradition, and that girl is arguably one of the finest, if not the finest, girl on this campus."

"Naw bro, that girl is an A-lister. You violating the code. The bros already on edge about this side chick main chick stuff too. You must want to get messed up seven types of ways. You know who she is, right?"

Terry waved him off. "Yeah, Bad Boy put her on the list, I know. I ain't scared of him."

"The word around the yard is she's dating The Man of Steel. If you not scared, frat, maybe you should be."

Terry pointed to the *Essence* magazine on the rack in front of him. "Looks like there's trouble in paradise to me. It's all good though. I'll be there to wipe those pretty eyes."

Andre emptied the contents of the cart onto the checkout counter. "I know one thing. You are going to take the heat for this one, not me."

CHAPTER 41

JOSHUA SAT AT THE makeshift bar on the third floor of his frat house, nursing a beer. For big parties like this one, their annual Valentine's Day Bash, they always turned the third floor into the VIP room. Unlike the seam busting, house shaking affair happening on the first floor, in the VIP section, the crowd was smaller, the lights dimmer, and the music, though popular, would be much more low-key.

Tonight, the pledges had been charged by their dean to find the best-looking girls at the party. Of those beautiful ones identified, only the ladies who knew how to conduct themselves were to be invited upstairs to the VIP lounge. Joshua stared at the side profile of the mocha skinned sister who had just walked through the door. She had a head full of naturally curly hair. Hair that looked like it normally lived a life of confinement inside of a braid or a bun but had, just for tonight, been allowed to come out to play. It was the hair that drew Joshua's attention. It was also the hair that caused him not to get a clear, unrestricted view of her face. She wore tight fitted jeans that screamed curves for days and she wore a chest hugging red tee, signaling that she was down for whatever.

Joshua took a swig of his beer, was just about to introduce himself, when she moved a tendril of hair behind her ear, and he got an unobstructed view of her face. Joshua choked on a cough and beer flew everywhere.

Tonya looked up to see Joshua staring down at her. She had figured that if what her roommate said about this so-called list was true, then he'd be majorly pissed to see her here. He was. Anger was rolling off her godbrother in waves. Too bad she didn't care.

"Oh hey, Josh."

"You have two options. Option one, you can put on my jacket, walk out that door and go home. Option two, we walk out together, and I take you home. What's it going to be? You gonna handle this on your own, or do you need an escort?"

Tonya rolled her eyes, "I'm not leaving. I was invited."

"Oh yeah, by who?"

Tonya lifted her chin defiantly. "Terry."

"Did he tell you to wear that t-shirt, too?"

"Actually, yeah he did."

Joshua's expression went from angry to murderous.

That probably wasn't the best thing to say.

"Do you even know what walking up into this house with that shirt on means?" Joshua took his jacket off and held it out for her. "Put it on, now."

"No, if I put on your jacket, guys are going to think that I'm unavailable."

Joshua lifted an eyebrow at her. "Aren't you?"

Tonya looked away from him. She bobbed her head to the music.

"There is a third option. I can start busting heads. Starting with Terry's. I owe him a beat down anyway."

"Okay, so let me get this straight. Michael can do whatever he wants with whomever he wants, and I'm just supposed to roll with it?"

"What are you talking about?"

Tonya pulled the copy of the *Essence* magazine cover out of her back pocket and handed it to Joshua.

He stared at the crumbled cover. Tonya had given the pop singer a mustache and a beard. She had also drawn pointy ears, a pitchfork and a tail onto Mike's photo.

Joshua sighed. "I thought you were cool with this?"

"Getting played? Nah, I'll never be cool with something like that."

Joshua noticed Tonya's roommates for the first time. They were standing across the room gawking at him like he was a god. Tonya was sure he made their entire semester when he smiled at both Nisha and Dee and offered a little wave. "You told your little roomies, didn't you? When this article came out, you looked played. I'm sorry that happened to you. But he's not playing you."

Tonya cut her eyes at him.

Joshua shrugged. "Break up, or stay together. That's entirely up to you. But it's true he's not."

"Whatever, Josh, like you wouldn't lie for him."

"I would, in a heartbeat, but never to you. If you ask me anything, I'mma always tell you the truth."

Tonya's eyes went soft. "Look at her Josh, she's every man's fantasy. I can't compete with that."

"I think you've got her faded right now, especially with the beard."

"Josh, do me one favor, please. Take my name off your list, just for tonight."

Joshua smirked. "Just like you rolled up in here with a screw-my-brains-out-t-shirt on, I'm sure you have no idea what you're talking about."

Mortification spread across Tonya's face. "Okay... so, I obviously misunderstood the t-shirt thing. But what I do know is that my roommate over there hasn't had a date since she got to this campus. Her brother is a member of your fraternity. That horrible list has totally ruined her self-esteem."

Joshua's eyes followed Tonya's gaze to the thick, cute girl wearing a tight baby pink tee. "What's your roommate's name?"

"The one in the pink that's Dee."

Joshua's eyes bucked. "Is that Kev's little sister?"

"Yes."

Joshua shook his head.

"Josh, hear me out. She's super cute. One of the nicest people you'll ever meet, but she can't get a date to save her life and it's all because of that stupid list."

"You'll get no sympathy from me. She should be happy she has family looking out for her. She came to college to get an education. Not to be pissed on by some dog. And trust me, my frat brothers are all dogs."

"Even you?"

"Don't get it twisted, little sister, I'm the Alpha dog. Go get your girls. I'll take y'all home."

Tonya folded her arms across her chest. "No, I'm not leaving, Josh. It's Valentine's Day. If Mike can be on a fricking cover kissing Brandala, I can at least have one night of fun."

Joshua lifted his hand in the air. One of his pledges came running.

"Where's Terry?"

"Big brother Terry is downstairs about to host a wet t-shirt contest, sir."

"Naw, shut that down. Tell him I said we got fam in the house. Ain't nobody getting wet tonight. You know what, on second thought, I'll tell him my damn self."

Tonya grabbed his arm, "Joshua, no, wait! Please don't make a scene. I'll take the jacket."

Joshua spoke to the pledge. "Go handle that for me."

Tonya released a small sigh of relief when the young man ran from the room.

Joshua helped Tonya into his fraternity jacket. It swallowed her petite frame, making her look like a child.

"This is probably the smartest decision you've made all night." Joshua said as he zipped the jacket up so high it looked like a turtleneck on her. "But you're only delaying the inevitable. I'm still going to kick his a#$."

"Yeah, Josh about that. I don't want to come between you and your fraternity brother. I know we got our wires crossed about the t-shirt, but I'm sure Terry didn't mean anything malicious by it."

"I'll keep that you think that in mind while I'm rearranging his face."

"No really. He saw me in the store today, right after the magazine came out, and it was just nice to know that some guy thought I was pretty."

Joshua massaged his temple. "I swear you are hurting my head right now. Are you serious?"

Tonya stared up at him.

"You don't need a jackass like Terry to tell you that you're beautiful. Any man with a pair of eyes can see that."

"Even you?"

"Yes, even me."

"For real? You're not just saying that to make me feel better?"

"Yeah, I was on my way over to holler until I realized it was you."

"Really?" Tonya screeched with excitement.

Joshua rolled his eyes. "Look, you and your roomies can stay."

Tonya beamed and motioned to her roommates to join them.

"You can stay as long as you agree to stay up here. Use the bathroom up here. Don't go to any other rooms in the house."

"We can agree to that, can't we, ladies?" Tonya said to Dee and Nisha. Both women agreed they could.

"And when you're ready to bounce, you don't leave with anyone. You have someone come and find me."

Tonya nodded, "Agreed."

Joshua motioned to another recruit, who came running.

"This is my sister, Tonya. These two ladies are her roommates. Dee and — remind me of your name again, sweetheart?"

Nisha, who was usually loud and brash with everyone else, spoke softly, "Nisha."

Joshua spoke to the recruit, "Make sure Tonya, Dee, and Nisha have a good time, but not too good of a time. You feel me?"

"I got you, Big Brother."

"Can I interest any of you ladies in a club soda?" The recruit asked after Joshua walked away.

Nisha sucked her teeth. "A club soda. Is that the best you can offer us?"

"Yes, I'm afraid so."

Tonya waved her hand happily in the air. "I'll take a club soda."

CHAPTER 42

ONE WEEK LATER

JOSHUA WAS WAITING OUTSIDE the psychology building when Tonya finished her last class of the day. A sense of panic spread through her body the moment she saw him. Joshua, who had been leaning casually against his car, reacted immediately. He moved quickly, closed the distance between them, and pulled her into his arms. Tonya's heart was beating a mile a minute. He pulled away and searched her face. "What's wrong?"

Tonya shook her head, "No, I'm—it's stupid."

Joshua stared down at her. "How bout you tell me what's bothering you and like always I decide whether or not it's stupid."

"When I saw you waiting for me just now, I thought you came to tell me something bad." Tonya's voice faltered. "I thought you came to tell me Daddy was gone."

No matter how much she knew Joshua wanted her to, she couldn't keep the tears from falling from her eyes. "See, stupid, right?"

Joshua sighed deeply and pulled her into another tight hug. "Naw, not stupid at all. I feel stupid though. I thought I'd surprise you and take you to dinner. I see now that I should have called."

CHAPTER 43

TONYA BEGAN SHAKING HER head the moment they pulled up in front of Mike's place. "Joshua, no."

"Didn't you just tell me you were hungry? Where else are we gon get gourmet food this good for free? You know Jeeves can burn."

Tonya bit her lip, "Jeeves can burn. But no."

"How long you gon ignore him?"

"I don't know what you're talking about. I'm not ignoring anybody."

"Listen, there's nothing wrong with being angry. You got a right to feel the way you feel. Just be an adult about it and talk to him."

"Oh, you mean like the way you're being an adult with Shannon. She told me about how you sent your little recruits to clean up your Valentine's Day screw up. Seriously, Josh?"

Joshua shrugged. "They made the mess. Why shouldn't they fix it?"

"Well, you should know that it didn't work and that she's even more hurt that you didn't come personally and apologize to her yourself."

"And yet she tells you all this instead of me. I'mma deal with Shannon when I'm ready. But you should know that the stakes aren't as high for us as they are for you and Mike."

"And why is that?"

"Shannon and I are temporary. You and Mike, that's forever. So do yourself a favor and talk to him."

Joshua opened the passenger door for her and grabbed a duffel bag off the back seat.

Tonya eyed the bag suspiciously. "What's that for?"

"I'm spending the night."

"What if I don't want to spend the night?"

"Then I'll take you back to campus. Or, here's a thought: the driver you've been ignoring for the past week can take you back to campus. How does that sound?"

Tonya rolled her eyes and stomped ahead of him up the walk.

Michael's house manager opened the door the moment Joshua and Tonya stepped onto the threshold. He held out his hand first to Joshua and then to Tonya.

"Master Keys. Mademoiselle Malone. please come in."

"Jeeves, it would really make me happy if you would just call me Tonya."

Jeeves bowed low, "Of course, Mademoiselle. Your wish is my command."

Tonya took in Michael, who was standing behind Jeeves, and tried not to think about how handsome he looked in something as simple as a t-shirt and a pair of jeans. *Do not cave. You are furious at him.* She scolded herself.

Michael greeted Joshua with their customary combination hug and handshake. All the while, he never took his eyes off Tonya,

"Thanks for bringing her, bro."

"No problem. I'll be out by the pool if anybody needs me. Jeeves, what you got to eat around here?"

"That depends on what you are in the mood for, sir. I can throw a few burgers and or steaks on the grill."

"That'll work. Tonya, give a holler when you're ready to bounce."

"You're not staying?" Michael asked.

"Why should I, Michael?"

"Because we need to talk."

Michael stared at her and Tonya found herself drawn into his dark liquid brown eyes.

Not caving. Not caving. Not —

"Please. Take a ride with me? No driver, no armored car, just you and me."

CHAPTER 44

MIKE AND TONYA DROVE for a good twenty minutes in complete silence. Finally, they turned onto a winding side lane that looked to Tonya to be some type of private access road. Two large iron gates opened automatically.

"Michael, where are we?"

Mike looked over at her, but said nothing. When they pulled up to the front of the enormous house, the singer, Brandala, came walking out the front door. Mike jumped out of the car and opened the door for Tonya just as the singer ran down the stairs to embrace her.

"You must be Tonya! Mike has told me so much about you." Brandala said, hugging Tonya like she was a long-lost friend.

"She's absolutely breathtaking, Mike. I can see why she's the love of your life."

Brandala grabbed Tonya by the hand and pulled her into the house. "Come on. I want you to meet my sweetheart."

Brandala took Tonya on a whirlwind tour of her home and introduced Tonya to her fiancé, Derick. Now, the couples were relaxing in the den, waiting for dinner to be served. Brandala and Tonya sat curled up on the couch enjoying a glass of wine, while Derek and Mike were deep in conversation at the bar.
***

"Mike tells me you two didn't get to celebrate Valentine's Day together. Derek and I didn't either. I hope you don't mind, but I put together a little something special, just for the four of us."

"Seriously, Brandala, you inviting me into your home like this is already special enough."

Brandala shooed Tonya with her hand. "This is nothing. This is just a couple of friends getting together for wine and dinner."

Derek and Michael's baritone laughs drew both women's attention across the room. Brandala smiled at Tonya, "See, our beaus get along, and you, my friend, are the bomb digiddy, so trust me, we're going to be doing this a lot more often." Brandala's eyes twinkled playfully. "But tonight, I have something special in mind. Should I tell you, or should I keep it a surprise?"

"Actually, I hate surprises."

Brandala laughed. "Hey, that's why I asked. I'm the same way. I love to give surprises. I just don't like to be surprised."

"Same." Tonya laughed.

"Okay, so I won't keep you in suspense. There is this new group that I'm thinking about managing. It's a girl group. They kind of have this TLC/SWV vibe going on, but their songs are all about women's empowerment. And I am all about girl power, so I figured, what better way to check them out than to have them perform for the four of us at our Valentine's Day celebration tonight?"

"That's really thoughtful of you, Brandala, and it sounds like so much fun. Thank you."

"No, I should be the one thanking you. I'm so glad that Mike did the spread in *Essence* magazine with me. In my line of work, you must have media exposure, but on the flip side, the media has just about destroyed every relationship I've ever had. So, I want you to know that Mike's agreeing to do the cover shoot with me means everything. I know from experience how hard it is to date someone who is constantly in the public eye. Derek is the only man I've ever been with who's been able to deal with all of this." Brandala sat her hand on top of Tonya's. "From the bottom of my heart, I want to say that I'm sorry the *Essence* article hurt you."

Tonya shook her head, "It shouldn't have. Mike and his agent told me what to expect, it's just..."

"Different when you see pictures, right?"

"Yeah."

"If it makes you feel any better, that was a stage kiss." Brandala held her hand up in the air. "Scouts honor. Absolutely no tongue."

Derek laughed.

Brandala threw a look over her shoulders at the men. "Hey, are you two listening to our conversation over there?"

Mike smiled tentatively at Tonya. "It's kind of hard not to, B." When she returned his smile, Mike walked across the room and sat down on the couch beside Tonya.

Derek also walked across the room and sat beside Brandala. "Guilty as charged."

Brandala looked up into Derek's eyes. "So tell her why you were laughing at what I just said. Tonya, did I mention that Derek is also in the business?"

"No. You didn't. What do you do?"

"I'm an actor. Nothing big, just daytime television." Derek pulled Brandala into his arms. "Tonya, I was laughing because what my baby here said is true. There is nothing sexy about shooting sex scenes. It's all a very technical, awkward dance made to look romantic."

The chef stood in the doorway, beckoning them to dinner.

When the two couples walked outside, Tonya took in the erected stage, the fragrant blossom filled garden, the white linen cloth-covered table set for four, and the lit candelabras surrounding the space that gave everything an ethereal glow. She released a tiny gasp.

"Do you like it, Blackbird?"

Tonya nodded, "I do. It's beautiful."

Brandala smiled up at Mike. "I think that means she forgives you.

Later that night, Brandala handed Tonya a gift bag as she and Derek walked Tonya and Mike to the front door.

"Brandala, you've already been too kind. I don't think I can take anymore gifts from you tonight without crying."

"This isn't exactly a gift. Mike told me you were a big fan of my music and that you had all of my CDs. I figured you *had* all of my CDs until that *Essence* issue came out."

Tonya's mouth fell open, and Mike and Derek both roared with laughter.

It was true. After she had completed her little coloring project on the Essence magazine cover, she had taken a hammer to all of her Brandala CD's. "Well, what had happened was—"

Brandala shook her head. "No need to explain. I thought I could replace them for you."

CHAPTER 45

Tonya was unpacking her overnight bag. Thanks to Jeeves it was filled with freshly laundered clothes. She was grooving along with Brandala's newest CD when her roommates descended upon her like a tsunami.

Nisha turned Tonya's stereo system off and pointed to the stack of Brandala CDs sitting on Tonya's desk. "You took him back, didn't you? And since you already crushed these with a hammer last week, I guess this means you're still her number one fan too?"

"Nisha, it's complicated and I really don't want to talk about this with you. All I can say is that... it's not what you think."

Dee sat down on the edge of Tonya's bed and smiled in relief. "So he's not playing you? I knew it. The eyes can tell you a lot about a person's character and his eyes say he's too kind to do anything like that."

"I'm really not at liberty to discuss the details, but no, he's not."

"Tonya, has Mike ever taken you to Sasha's?" Carrie asked.

"Exactly. Has he taken you to Sasha's!" Nisha clapped her hands on every syllable to—what? Other than being just plain rude and annoying, Tonya didn't know why her roommate was clapping her hands in her face to emphasize her point.

Tonya looked back and forth between Dee and Carrie. Choosing, for the moment, to completely ignore Nisha. "What's Sasha's?"

"Are you kidding me? It's only 'The Spot' to be seen in Houston. Tons of celebrities take their significant others there. And the food." Dee groaned and fell back onto Tonya's bed, and collapsed. "I've never been there, of course, but I hear the food is amaz-balls."

Tonya bit her lip, "Really?"

"Exactly, so if he's not playing you and this is all just a misunderstanding, he shouldn't have any problem taking you there."

Present Day 2010

CHAPTER 46

HOUSTON, TEXAS

MIKE, TONYA, PEARL, AND Marcus joined Bella, Joshua, and the children in the Keys' family backyard for dinner. They sat around the table enjoying delicious creole cuisine prepared by Bella. They laughed and caught up on old times. And for Tonya, even though she had been gone for five years, it was like no time had passed between them at all.

"Tonya, your timing couldn't be more perfect. The boys need to be dedicated to the Lord." Bella said.

Tonya took a bite of her fish and smiled across the table at Bella. She wanted to tell her she could thank Ted and his baby's mama drama for the timing part, that in fact, they should all raise a glass to the perfect timing of her trifling ex. They had been doing that all night, raising glasses of sparkling apple juice in a toast for either one thing or another. Apple juice, for the sake of the children. But of course, Tonya held her tongue because her cheating ex wouldn't be appropriate dinner conversation in front of her precious godbabies.

"Mike has already agreed to stand in as godfather for the twins. Josh and I are hoping you'd agree to be their godmother too."

"Are you kidding? Of course, I will. They're already mine." Tonya smiled proudly at Mikey Jr. and Jackie, who were busy finger painting with the food on their dinner plates.

Tonya listened intently as her family filled her in on all the parts she had missed. She marveled at how things were so completely different now, but also the same.

She heard about Home Court Advantage, the company that Michael and Joshua had formed together after retirement from pro ball, and the latest urban renewal project the brothers were working on.

She learned everything there was to know about the children's activities, from high school basketball for Jabari, to Little League for Serenity, and t-ball for the twins. Marcus was looking for a good workout in the off-season, so Tonya offered to give him ballet lessons. He and Jabari both liked to have fallen out of their seats with laughter.

Joshua pointed his fork at Marcus and Jabari. "Don't laugh. It's a seriously intense workout."

"My dad, Bad Boy Joshua Keys, did ballet?" Jabari asked incredulously.

Mike nodded, "Yep."

"Your dad and your uncle both. Why do you think they were both so graceful on the court?" Tonya said.

"Yo, Josh, you hear that?"

"I did. Tonya, we make it a point to use correct grammar around the children." Joshua nodded toward the toddlers, "Especially in front of the twins since they're still learning language."

"Oh, I'm sorry. What did I say?"

"You used the wrong tense." Joshua said.

Pearl chuckled.

Bella rolled her eyes. "Here we go."

Mike spoke to the confused look on Tonya's face, "What you should have said, Blackbird, is, 'that's why your father and uncle are so graceful on the court.'"

Tonya bowed her head reverently, "Excuse me O' Great Ones. I didn't know you two were still on the court."

"Every day." Mike and Joshua said in unison.

"You mean you haven't seen the full regulation size court and locker room at Home Court yet?" Bella said.

"I've seen it. I just didn't know that you guys played that much anymore. Aren't you supposed to slow down in retirement?"

Joshua smirked. "Please, we hash most of our deals out on the court. Speaking of court action, I want to raise a glass to my nephew here, who just finished an amazing season at DU. I see a championship ring in your future." Joshua held his glass up in the air.

"Here, here!" Mike said, lifting his glass.

"I'll put my agreement to that." Pearl chimed in.

"Thanks Unc, coming from you, that means everything."

"You worked hard, hard work pays off."

"What about your academics, Marcus? Have you chosen a major yet?" Bella asked.

"No, not yet." Marcus said, dropping his eyes to his plate.

"It's only his second year, Bella. He's got time." Joshua said.

"Your Unc didn't choose his major until his junior year." Mike said.

"Actually, I hadn't planned on discussing this right now, but one reason I haven't chosen a major yet is because I was thinking about dropping out and entering the draft this summer."

Silence fell over the table as everyone took Marcus's words in.

"Is this a joke?" Mike finally asked.

"No, sir. I spoke to Unc about it when he came out to my last game, but he wasn't trying to hear it."

"I'm still not." Joshua said. "I told you, in a couple of years after you finish college, if you still want to go pro, I'll do everything I can to help you accomplish that goal. The right way."

Marcus looked at Bella, "Auntie, you said yourself college isn't for everyone."

Joshua and Mike's eyes flew to Bella.

Bella shook her head. "No, sir. You are not about to drag me into this. What I said was that college was not for me. It's for every one of y'all sitting around this table. So you better make it do what it do." Bella pointed her finger at each of her children and then at Marcus.

Marcus's eyes fell on Pearl.

Pearl shook her head. "Don't look at me. I stay in my lane. This conversation is between you, your dad, and your uncle. But it would seem to me that a body ought to keep their options open. What if you were to blow out your knee or something? I rebuke that in the name of Jesus. But, still, I'm just saying. You got to have some skills and purpose in your life. I've never been to college myself, but that seems to me to be the purpose of school."

"That's a whole lot to say for somebody staying in their own lane."

Mike stared at his son across the dinner table. "Hey man, check your tone."

Marcus muttered an apology to his grandmother, and the family continued to eat their meal in awkward silence.

"We can vote on it." Jabari said.

"No." Joshua said.

"That's not fair, Daddy. You said we're a family. That everybody is important, and that we all have an equal say." Serenity said.

"You did say that, Dad." Jabari quipped.

"That's not what Daddy meant, baby." Joshua glared at Jabari. "Equal is relative. We may let y'all weigh in on a family vacation from time to time, but college is non-negotiable."

Marcus shot his father a pleading look. "Dad, tell me I'm not good enough right now. If you say I'm not good enough, I swear I'll let this go."

Pearl, who was sitting beside Tonya, leaned in and whispered to her, "This boy has been playing the two best players that ever played in the NBA for the last five years. So you know he's good, right? Shoot, all these kids are good. Heck, I'd put my money on Suri over that boy. What's that boy's name, LeBron? Any day."

"Your skill level is not the point, Marcus. This is not the plan. Your reality isn't the same as it used to be. You don't need ball, but you do need an education." Mike said quietly.

Too quietly, Tonya thought. The slight hardening of his jaw muscle, his measured tone, were sure signs that Michael was very angry.

Marcus polled the table. Obviously not picking up on his father's this-conversation-is-over-cue. "Okay, so how many people at this table think my game is cold enough for the NBA right now?"

Serenity, Jabari, and both the twins' hands all shot up in the air.

"How many people think I should stay in school and graduate?"

Bella sighed, "I can't believe we are actually voting on this."

Mike, Bella, Pearl, and Joshua all raised their hands.

"It's a tie." Serenity said. "Auntie Tonya, vote. We need a tiebreaker."

"No, sweetie, I'm going to abstain."

Mike wiped his mouth and set the linen napkin down on his plate. "There's no tie. You're not dropping out of school. That's final."

CHAPTER 47

Per Pearl's edict, Tonya arrived on time for breakfast the next day. When she walked into the kitchen, Mike looked up from his morning paper. He took in her appearance, then quickly hid his displeasure with a smile. This was the fifth day in a row he had seen her dressed entirely in black.

"Morning, Blackbird."

"Good morning, Michael."

Tonya walked over to the large center island, fixed herself a plate of food, then took a seat at the table across from him.

"So, where is everyone this morning?"

"Granny P had an early meeting at the church and Marcus is worshiping with his girl and her folks today."

"Church with the family. Sounds serious."

"What about you? You feel up to going to church with me this morning?"

Tonya studied her plate. "I think I'm going to hang back for a while. It really sounds like a great ministry you all are a part of, but I'm kind of churched out at the moment."

Mike leaned back in his chair and studied her for a beat. "That's fair."

"Besides, I don't really want to answer the 'what are you doing here?' question if I run into people that I know. But please, don't think you have to babysit me, Michael. I don't want to stop you from worshiping."

"I can worship anywhere, Blackbird. In fact, I know the perfect place. I'll take you there after breakfast."

Tonya looked down at her slacks and sweater. "Am I dressed okay?"

"Nah, that won't work for where we are going. Put on a pair of sweats and some kicks."

CHAPTER 48

MIKE GRABBED A BLANKET out of the trunk of his car and led Tonya through a thicket of grass and trees. When they had finally emerged through the clearing, they arrived at a small, secluded lake. Tonya looked out over the water. "It's pretty. Do you come here often?"

"Every now and again."

"Thank you."

"You're welcome."

"You know, there was a time when, if the church doors were open, I'd be there. But the way I feel today... feels like I may never go back."

Mike picked up a rock and skipped it across the water. "You'll go when you're ready. Nothing wrong with taking some time off, getting a little balance and perspective."

"There's that word again, balance. You used to tell me that all the time. That I needed to be balanced. Too bad I didn't listen. Maybe if I'd been more balanced, I wouldn't have found myself in this predicament with Ted."

Mike turned and looked at her.

"You know what the scariest part about all of this is? I keep thinking, what if he's right? What if waiting is outdated and archaic? I mean, I've been trying to follow God's word all these years and look where it's got me."

Mike sat down beside her, and Tonya busied herself picking invisible lint balls off the blanket.

"Look at me, Blackbird."

Tonya turned to face him.

"Man regrets. God redeems. Take it from a man who has had a lot of sex with a lot of different women. You did the right thing. I'm glad you didn't compromise in that area. You'd feel even worse than you do right now had you given yourself to him in that way. It took me a long time to understand that. And ultimately, I have you to thank for it."

"Me?"

"You do realize the unique position you hold in my life, don't you? You're the only woman who has ever said no to me."

"Seriously?" Tonya rolled her eyes. "Yeah, no, I don't believe it."

Mike smirked, "I'm the Man of Steel, trust me, baby. No woman in her right mind is turning me down. Present company excluded; I mean."

"Well, those were all worldly women so..."

"Naw, I've had them all. Church girls too."

Mike stretched his long body out on the blanket and looked up at the sky. "I'm glad you ended our sexual relationship all those years ago. I know I gave you a hard time initially, but—ow!"

Tonya had balled up her fist and punched him as hard as she could in the stomach.

Mike sat up quickly. "What was that for?"

"What do you mean, you gave me a hard time? Michael, you broke up with me!"

"I know—"

"You shattered my heart into a million tiny pieces." Tonya balled up her fist to hit him again, but Mike lifted her up off the blanket and sat her in his lap.

"And then I came to myself and I apologized because I realized we were so much more than that. I'm sorry I hurt you. I'm sorry if it still hurts you now. My point in bringing up all this old stuff is that it had to happen like that for us. You helped me to see your value."

Mike leaned his forehead against hers. "Tonya, if a man can't wait for you, then he's not worthy of you. And baby, trust me when I tell you that you are every bit worth the wait. I wish I could tell the woman I marry one day that she was my one and only. I wish I could give her the assurance that there has never been anyone more perfect than her. I won't be able to do that. At least not in that respect. Even so, I can't regret my past."

"That's just it, Michael. Society says you don't have to. You drop your drawers and the world sees you as a god, a sex symbol. If I give it up, I'm a whore. If I don't give it up, even worse, I'm a prude."

"God doesn't see it that way. In His eyes, you're a daughter of Zion and I'm the damaged goods. I thank God that He redeems." Mike grabbed his cellphone out of his back pocket and pulled up a scripture verse. "Check this out right here. Read that verse for me real quick."

Tonya took the phone from his hand and read, "Proverbs 16:25. There is a way that seems right to a man, but the end thereof is death."

Mike nodded. "Yep, all day long, that was me. I was young, dumb and—"

Tonya smiled wickedly at him, "And full of—"

Mike touched his fingers to her lips gently. "I didn't understand covenant." He said quietly.

Something broke inside of Tonya at that moment and she dissolved into a puddle of tears right there on his lap. She sobbed hard, deep, bitter tears. Mike pulled her close and let her body racking cries wet the front of his shirt.

"What's wrong, Blackbird? Tell me what's hurting you right now."

But she couldn't. She couldn't tell him that despite everything he had said about God's redemption plan and man regretting, she was filled with so much regret. Him and her together like this, it was the one thing she had prayed for, that she had asked for. No, scratch that, it was what she had begged God for. And at God's command, when Michael wouldn't answer the call, she walked away into the arms of a man who wore the title of minister with none of the honor that went along with it. *For what?* So that some other woman could come along and reap the benefit of her tears? Her prayers? Her reward?

"Blackbird, talk to me. Why are you crying right now, baby?"

Tonya took a deep breath, swallowed all the pain and the regret. "I'm okay. God, I'm so sorry. I hit you. I don't know what came over me."

"Relax, Blackbird, it's okay."

"No Michael, it's not okay. Violence is never okay. Did I hurt you?"

He looked like he wanted to laugh. Like he wanted to throw his head back and release a gut busting chuckle right now, but also like he wouldn't because she was crying and it would be impolite in this moment to laugh.

"You said ow, when I hit you. I heard you." Tonya said flatly, as she wiped away her tears.

Mike's lips turned up into a sexy half smile. "That was more like, ow, a mosquito just bit me. I'm fine. Josh is going to be pissed, though."

Tonya bit her lip. "Now that he's in the ministry, I'm guessing Josh has zero tolerance for violence of any type, huh?"

Mike snorted, "Please, he'll love that you tried to swing on me. What he'll be pissed to know is that after all those boxing lessons we gave you, you still can't throw a proper punch."

Mike lifted Tonya off his lap and stood up. "You ready to go?"

"Bible study over already?" She said, because she wasn't quite ready to break their connection yet.

"What? You want to sit here and talk about the Bible all day?"

Actually, she kind of did. The words he has spoken over her had filled her heart with an incredibly soothing balm. "I enjoyed it. I guess I didn't know that you knew the Word like that. You surprised me."

"I keep telling you, Blackbird, there are a whole lot of things you don't know about me. Anyway, haven't you ever read the verse that says, works without faith is dead?"

"Huh no, sir. That's faith without works is dead."

Mike grinned and reached out his hand to help her up from the ground. "I know. Just testing you. Come on, there's one more spot I want to show you."

"Michael, what is this place?" They were in the heart of the city. That much she could tell, but what confused her now were the large metal gates they'd driven up to.

"This is Hebron. This is one of the urban renewal projects that Josh was telling you about at dinner the other night. Hebron is a community for recovering addicts and their families."

Upon seeing Michael, the guard at the gate happily waved him through.

Tonya took in her surroundings. There was literally a whole different world behind the gates. It was like a city within a city. They drove past multiple outdoor basketball courts, some newly constructed houses and newly constructed apartment buildings. As they drove through Hebron, Michael explained the process to her. Each resident who came through Hebron was first assigned to a group home. After they successfully completed their stay in group living, they were issued an apartment. From there, they could meet with a financial coach to reach other goals such as credit repair and eventually home ownership.

As they drove, Michael pointed out the on-site clinic, the daycare, the community center, and the senior center.

Tonya pointed to a building. "Is that a grocery store?"

"It's more of a co-op, but yeah."

"Who runs it?"

"The people who live here. We have some paid staff working in specialized areas, like the daycare, the clinic, and the elementary school, but everything else you see here is community owned and operated."

"Wow, Michael, this is incredible. This is it. This is your ministry." Tonya said, in awe.

"Nah, Blackbird. This is my service."

Tonya grinned. "Still not comfortable with the title of minister, huh?"

Mike grunted.

"Well, like it or not, this is exactly what this is. It's like you're doing the thing that you were meant to do. You have always loved to give. Even when we were kids. It wasn't until I met Ted that I realized that giving was an actual gift to the body of Christ. This is beautiful."

Mike pulled up into the parking lot of a small nondescript building.

"I know you weren't really feeling the church thing today, but this is a special little spot. When I don't feel like dealing with the crowds, I come here."

Mike grabbed Tonya's hand and led her into the building. They slipped into the back row, next to a small lemon colored woman. The woman's face lit up like Christmas morning when she saw Mike. That's when Tonya recognized the resemblance. She was staring into the face of Brenda Dutton, Mike's birth mother.

CHAPTER 49

MIKE REINTRODUCED THE TWO women to each other after the service had ended. "Mama, you remember Tonya?"

Brenda nodded. "I remember."

"It's nice to see you again, Ms. Dutton." Tonya said, pulling the woman into a tight hug.

Brenda seemed both pleasantly surprised and equally embarrassed at Tonya's greeting. "I'm nobody's Ms. Please, just call me Brenda. It's nice to see you too."

Brenda tugged at her sleeves, and self-consciously wrapped her arms around her torso in a protective hug.

"Why are you fidgeting?" Mike asked quietly.

"I just wish I would have worn something nicer today. I didn't know ya'll were coming."

A small smile played at the corner of his mouth. "I'm the one wearing a sweatsuit in church today. How is it you feel underdressed?"

"It doesn't matter what you wear. You could walk in here with a loincloth on and everybody else would still feel underdressed next to you."

Tonya snorted and laughed out loud. Mike shot her a look.

"What? I happen to agree with her."

Mike turned his attention back to his birth mother. "Are you clean, healthy, and sober today?"

"Yes." There was a note of pride in Brenda's voice. "Three years, two months, and seventeen days."

"Then it doesn't matter what you wear to me, either. You couldn't be more beautiful right now."

Brenda blushed deeply and stared down at the floor. "Can you stay? I made lunch."

"Blackbird, is that alright with you?"

Tonya beamed. "I would love to stay for lunch."

Mike shook a few hands, making sure to greet the pastor. Then he led Tonya and Brenda both out of the church and to his car. And even though Brenda insisted that she was perfectly fine sitting in the back, Tonya practically forced her bodily into the front seat of Mike's car.

"Smells good in here." Mike said, the moment they stepped inside of Brenda's tiny, but neat apartment.

"I got some northern beans and oxtails waiting on the stove. Collards and cornbread too. How does that suit you?"

Mike kissed the top of her head. "That suits me just fine. Why don't you fix me a plate while I go wash up?"

Tonya surveyed the small feast Brenda had prepared. "Ms. Brenda, this is a lot of food. Were you expecting company?"

"I cook like this every Sunday. Just in case Mike stops by."

Tonya reached across the table and squeezed her hand. "Thank you."

"What for?"

Being clean for the last three years. Making him Sunday dinners. "I know this time is very special for you and Michael. Thank you for allowing me to share it with the two of you today."

"I'm glad you're back. I'm glad the two of you are together again. There's been a hole in his heart since you left."

Tonya didn't bother to contradict her.

Mike pulled up in front of Tonya's cottage and killed the engine. "I hope you're not too full, because in a couple more hours, Granny P is going to expect us to do that again."

"Thank you for taking me to Hebron today."

"No problem. When you feel down about your own situation, it's good to be reminded that there are a lot of people who have it far worse than you."

"Ms. Brenda looks great." She offered tentatively.

Mike stared straight ahead, not meeting her gaze.

Tonya touched the side of his face, drawing his eyes to meet hers. "I can tell that you're very proud of her. You should be. Three years clean, Michael, that is no small feat."

"The fam doesn't know my mom is there. Nobody does. Not even Josh."

"I would never betray your trust, Michael."

Tonya felt her heart take a long drive off a short cliff when Mike leaned in to kiss her. His mouth hovered over her lips just for a moment before he redirected and planted a soft kiss on her cheek instead.

SUMMER 1996

CHAPTER 50

HOUSTON, TEXAS

TONYA HAD BEEN THROWING out hints to Michael about Sasha's literally for months. So here she was sitting inside Sasha's, the premier restaurant in Houston with... drumroll please, none other than Joshua.

Mike had gotten them reservations to celebrate Joshua's induction into the NBA. Joshua had just been named the number one draft pick of the season and people all over the city of Houston, the State of Texas, really, had lost their cotton-picking minds. Case in point, the standing ovation Joshua received when he and Tonya walked into Sasha's that evening.

Tonya resisted the urge to roll her eyes when yet another person approached their table and asked for her godbrother's autograph.

"Congrats on the draft. Do you think I can get a picture with you before you become famous?"

"Absolutely." Joshua said, signing the man's napkin, then posing for a picture snapped by the man's girlfriend.

"I was really hoping you and your brother would play on the same team."

Joshua nodded. "That would be dope."

"I'll follow you to New Orleans, though."

"Thank you, I appreciate that."

Joshua turned his attention back to Tonya. "Dang girl, as long as you been talking about this place, I would have thought you'd have that menu memorized before we got here. Hurry up and choose something. I'm ready to eat."

"Excuse me for not having a chance to read my menu. I didn't know this was going to be Joshua Keys' Fan Club Night."

"It ain't complicated. They got beef, chicken and fish. Pick one." Joshua leaned into the table and grinned at her. "All this attention is crazy, though, right?"

Tonya rolled her eyes, "It's ridiculous."

"It's a good thing you're here with me and not the Man of Steel, huh?" Joshua stared at her pointedly until Tonya looked away.

"Yeah, you ain't slick. You need to stop listening to your little friends."

"I don't. I mean... I'm trying not to, but sometimes it gets hard." Tonya fiddled with her silverware. "I guess if you figured it out, then that means that Michael did, too."

Joshua snorted, "Tonya, please. You're so transparent Ray Charles and Stevie Wonder saw you."

"Fine. So why didn't he call me on it? For something like this, if he thought my intentions weren't genuine, he usually would."

"I think he understands how hard things have been for the two of you since you moved to Houston. He's trying to let you find your way. My brother loves you. Never doubt that. Everybody who means anything to him in this world knows it."

"I know."

Joshua lifted his hand in the air and flagged the server over to their table. "Good, then it shouldn't matter what anybody else thinks."

CHAPTER 51

Tonya awoke from a fitful dream and sat up in bed. Immediately, she picked up the phone and dialed home.

Her mother answered the phone on the second ring. "Tonya, what's wrong?"

"Nothing Mama, I was just thinking about you and Daddy."

"We are fine, baby." Barbara said, pulling the wet sheets from her and Harold's bed and rolling them into a ball.

"Mama, is Daddy... is Daddy still in remission?"

"Don't worry about your daddy, baby. He's in God's hands. You hear me?"

"Yes, ma'am."

"You live your life and focus on your studies. That's what we both want. Speaking of studies, don't you have a class in the morning?"

"Yes, ma'am."

"Didn't you tell me just the other day that summer classes were brutal?"

"Yes, ma'am."

"Well, it's after midnight. I think a certain somebody ought to get herself some sleep. Warm milk."

"What?"

"That's what I used to give you when you were little and couldn't sleep. You warm yourself some milk."

"Okay, mama, I will. I love you."

"Love you too, baby. We'll see you this weekend."

Harold sat on the edge of the tub in the master bathroom, thinking about cancer. The worst part about cancer wasn't the chemo, it wasn't the pain, the lack of energy or even the shortness of breath he was experiencing right now. The worst thing about cancer had been the night sweats. Harold pulled the sopping wet t-shirt over his head and threw it into the tub. He looked up to see Barb standing in the doorway. God, he would miss this woman when he was gone.

"The sheets are ready. You can come back to bed."

"Was that Tonya I heard you talking to on the phone?"

Barbara came into the bathroom and set down beside Harold on the edge of the tub. She stared straight ahead, never meeting his gaze. "Yes."

"It's after midnight. What did she want?"

"She wants the same thing I want, Harold." Barbara said, finally daring to look at him, "For you to tell our daughter the truth. I think she can feel what's coming."

"Barb, we talked about this."

She laid her head on his shoulder. "I know."

"Death sentence or not, I'm still the head of this house. It's my duty to decide what's best for each member of this family."

"I know that too."

Harold took her hand in his. "She's got to have a life when I'm gone. A routine that will keep her head above water, something she can lean into. This is me giving that to her."

Tonya sat at the kitchen table staring down at her mug of warm milk. She looked up when Carrie walked into the room. "I hope I didn't wake you."

"No, I was working on some stuff for church." Carrie stared at Tonya's untouched milk. "You okay?"

Tonya attempted a smile but came up short. "I'm fine, just thinking about my daddy."

"It must be hard for you being away from them right now, what with the cancer."

"My dad says he's in remission, so it shouldn't be this hard, I guess, but I can't seem to shake this awful sense of dread."

"You know, Tonya, we're having a woman's retreat at our church this weekend. That's what I was working on tonight. I've been feeling God's leading now for a while to invite you, but every time I've gotten up the courage to ask you, Nisha was around. It's not that I have anything against Nisha, and it's not like I'm ashamed of my faith. It's just she makes such a mockery of everything."

Tonya shook her head, "Say no more. I completely understand."

"Anyway, if you're free this weekend, I'd love for you to come?"

Tonya laid her hand over Carrie's. "Thank you so much for inviting me. Under normal circumstances, I would love to come, but I'm going home this weekend. Our family is celebrating Joshua's induction into the NBA. But I'd be really grateful if you would remember to say a prayer for me?"

Carrie smiled. "I will. But if you don't mind, I'd like to pray with you now."

Tonya nodded, "I'd like that."

CHAPTER 52

Tonya threw her psychology book onto the leather seat and sighed in frustration. She shot an annoyed glance over at Joshua. He was relaxing beside her inside the limousine Michael had hired to take them back and forth to Dallas. Joshua's long legs stretched out in the car's roomy interior and his attention was 100% focused on the video game he was playing. They were already an hour into their three-hour trip, and other than muttering a greeting to her when she had first climbed into the car, he hadn't said a single word to her.

"Josh?"

"What?"

"Are you going to play that stupid thing the whole way?"

"I've muted the sound, Tonya. It's not like it's bothering you."

"I thought you were taking a summer course?"

"So?"

"So, now that you've been drafted into the NBA, you don't have to study?"

"I study. I just don't have to do it every waking moment. I'm not struggling like you."

"I have a 3.5 GPA. I'd hardly call that struggling."

"It is compared to my 4.0."

Tonya rolled her eyes. "Does the university pay people to take your exams too?"

"Please, I'm brilliant and you know it. Why you buggin' today?"

"I hardly see you as it is now, and in a few more weeks, you're going to be moving six hours away." She said, because this was the truth that she felt most comfortable expressing at the moment.

The hitch in her voice must have told Joshua that she was dangerously close to tears because he sat his controller down and turned off the game.

"Are you having female problems? Is this that time of the month for you?"

Tonya frowned, "No."

"I'm just checking cause it's a 48-minute flight, and you love Cajun food. And before you say you can't afford the ticket, you already know I got you. I'll send for you whenever you want me to. So why don't you tell me what's really bothering you?"

Tonya stared out the window. "You ever get the feeling that everyone you love is lying to you?"

"No, but I'm guessing you do. So, talk."

"I don't think Daddy is in remission."

It was something about finally saying those words out loud, words she had been carrying around for so long in her head, her spirit, and her heart, that caused a deep well of pain to unfurl inside of Tonya.

"Daddy would never tell me that. Mama won't go against his wishes. M-Michael thinks I'm not strong enough, but you—" A sob caught in her throat. "Y-you promised to always tell me the t-truth. And even though I'm crying right now, I c-c-can handle it."

Joshua wiped her face with the edge of his t-shirt. "You kidding me? I know better than anyone just how strong you are."

And for the first time in their lives, Joshua didn't tell her not to cry. This time, he pulled her close and told her to let it out.

They stayed that way for a while, her head on his chest, his chin on top of her head, watching the landscape pass by. After her tears had stopped and her breathing had finally calmed, Joshua spoke.

"The cancer is progressing. He promised to see me play my first game in the NBA. I don't think he can last much longer than that. Get your heart ready. Brace yourself. Unc's dying."

Present Day 2010

CHAPTER 53

HOUSTON, TEXAS

MIKE PULLED HIS BMW up beside Tonya's car the next morning. He pushed a button on the control panel and the window on the driver's side of his car effortlessly slid down.

Tonya had to lean over to the passenger side of her vehicle, grab hold of the old-fashioned window crank, and with much effort, manually roll her window down. "What's up?" she asked, somewhat out of breath.

"I won't be home until late tonight. But if you need anything, Jeeves or Granny P—"

"I'll be fine, Michael. I'm a big girl."

"You talk to your mom yet?"

"Yes, I did. Apparently, she already knew I was here."

"I told you people in this family talk. Could have been, anybody."

"I get it."

"Telling her, was it as bad as you thought it would be?"

"Not really. She seemed hurt that I didn't tell her about my new job. Indifferent about my breakup with Ted. And..."

"And what?"

"Over the moon that I was staying here with you. She said that as long as I'm here, she knows that you'll take care of me."

"She's right. One more thing, we need to talk about your car."

"What about it?"

"My neighbors are complaining. Your car is terrorizing their pets."

"That's ridiculous, your nearest neighbor is literately miles away."

"I know, right? That should tell you something."

"Whatever, Beauty just needs a new muffler."

"I think we can both agree that she needs a lot more than that."

"Goodbye, Michael. Crack all you want, but I am not getting rid of my car."

Tonya cranked her window up and drove off. Leaving a plume of smoke in her absence.

CHAPTER 54

Mike returned home late that evening only to discover that Tonya still hadn't returned home from work herself. After he telephoned her office, then her cell, he called Bella. Bella confirmed that no, she hadn't seen or heard from her.

"Maybe she's still at the school."

"Naw, I tried her office. She didn't pick up."

"She mentioned something about her phone not holding a charge lately. She probably stopped by the bookstore or something on her way home from work and lost track of time. I'm sure she's fine, Mike."

"Yeah, maybe you're right." Mike's cell phone buzzed. "Bella, I got another call. I'll holler at you later." Mike answered the call, not bothering to look at the number.

Selena's silky voice purred through the line. "Hey stranger, I've been trying to get a hold of you all week. I'm glad you finally answered your phone."

"Hey babe, I'm in the middle of something. Let me hit you back, alright?"

"Oh, o-okay."

Mike ended the call and dialed Caesar.

Caesar answered on the first ring.

"What's up, Mike?"

"Tonya's not in yet."

Caesar blew out a sigh. "Could be car trouble. You gotta get her out of that thing."

"From your mouth to God's ears, man."

"You want me to send some of my guys out? They can drive her usual route."

"Let's give her a little more time. She needs a new phone, though. I want to be notified the moment she arrives."

SUMMER 1996

CHAPTER 55

DALLAS, TEXAS

HAROLD BEAMED PROUDLY AT Joshua and smashed his glass against Jack's. "I'd like to propose a toast to the 1996 number one draft pick of the year. I just want to say I knew this day would come. Didn't I tell you, baby? Didn't I always say that this kid had it in him?"

"You did. Said the same thing about Mikey, too." Jack said.

Harold raised his glass to Mike. "You see! I was right! Two number one draft picks. One family, in three years! I mean, we had to have something to do with that, right?"

Jack raised his glass in salute again. "We had everything to do with it!"

Joshua grinned, and Mike released a low chuckle. Dessert hadn't even been served and much to Melissa and Barbara's dismay, both of their husbands were well on their way to drunk.

"What can we say? We owe all our success to you two." Joshua said wryly.

"And the Lord, baby, never forget about the Lord." Barbara said as she piled collards onto her plate.

Melissa nodded, "That's right, never forget where your help comes from."

Mike met his mother's pale blue eyes. "We won't, Mom. I promise."

"Hey, Jack, what do you think about the two of us retiring from the cattle business and becoming consultants for the NBA? We certainly know how to pick 'em, don't we?"

Jack grinned, "That we do."

Barbara rolled her eyes. "Oh, for Heaven's sake, does anyone else have a toast they want to make? Tonya, sweetheart, what about you?"

Tonya, who had been silently pushing food around her plate the entire evening, appeared to be lost in thought.

"Tonya?"

"Yes?"

Harold addressed his daughter from across the table, "Your mother wants to know if you have a toast to make. To your godbrother."

Tonya stared at her father for a beat.

Mike, who was sitting next to her at the table, laid his hand on top of hers. "You alright, Blackbird?"

"I'm fine." Tonya said, sliding her hand from beneath his. "Actually, Daddy, I would like to make a toast."

"That's my girl!"

Tonya stood and lifted her glass toward Joshua. "To the one person in this whole family who loves me enough to tell me the truth."

Joshua muttered a curse under his breath.

"I mean, even the man who claims to love me and wants to spend the rest of his life with me didn't have the courage to tell me. He thinks I'm so fragile that at any minute I'm going to break—"

"Tonya, what are you—"

"I know, Mama."

Melissa adverted her eyes to the floor. Jack looked confused.

Harold's eyes flew to Joshua. "What in God's name did you do?"

"Uncle Jack. I take it from the look on your face that you didn't know, either. Well, welcome to the club."

Jack looked around the table at the now somber faces. "What club? Will someone tell me what the hell is going on?"

"Welcome to the-dad-is-dying-of-cancer-and-every-body-knew-it-but-us-club. I should get us some t-shirts."

Jack looked like the wind had been knocked out of him.

Mike reached for her, "Tonya."

She snatched away, upsetting her chair in the process. "Don't you dare touch me!"

"Blackbird, I know you're upset, but would you just calm down for a moment so we can talk about this?"

"You lied to me, Michael!"

"I didn't lie. We all sat around this table and heard the same thing. The exact same thing. I just didn't tell you what I suspected."

"Because you thought I couldn't handle it!"

"Because it wasn't mine to tell."

Tonya wiped angry tears from her eyes, "Yeah, well, like I said, I'm grateful that at least one person in this family loves me."

Harold slammed his fist down hard on the dining room table. "I asked you a question, boy. What did you do?!"

Joshua glared at his godfather. "I did what you should have done in the first place."

Bedlam broke out at the table as everyone began yelling at once. Amidst the commotion, Tonya slipped from the dining room. Before anyone ever realized it, she was gone.

CHAPTER 56

"SHE'S GONE."

"What do you mean, she's gone? This is a 200-acre property. She can't be gone."

"Are all the vehicles accounted for?"

"Yeah, but—"

"Then she couldn't have gotten too far, not on foot."

"We checked all of her hiding spots, Dad. Her pack is gone too."

Jack ran his hand through his golden hair and let out a string of expletives.

Melissa glared at her husband but said nothing.

Harold pointed his finger at Joshua. "If you would have kept your big mouth shut and stayed out of my business, none of this would have happened."

Joshua shook his head. "You mean if you would have told the truth instead of trying to baby her, none of this would have happened?"

Barbara's hand came down hard on the kitchen counter. "Stop it, you two! Please. Fighting is getting us absolutely nowhere. What's done is done. It's all water under the bridge. So, can we please just concentrate on finding my child?"

"Barb's right. We need to focus our energy right now on finding Tonya, not bickering with one another." Melissa said.

Jack stopped pacing to stare at Mike, who was leaning up against the wall. "Mikey, what about the security detail you hired to protect us?"

Harold slapped his hands together, "Of course, why didn't I think of that?"

Mike looked at his father first, and then at his uncle. "You mean the security detail that you've both been giving the slip to ever since day one? Now, all of a sudden, you expect them to keep track of somebody?"

Jack stuck his hands in his pockets and shrugged. "I mean, that's what you're paying them for, Mikey. It's their job to find her."

Mike scrubbed one large hand over his face and pushed himself off the wall. "You two are a piece of work. You know that?" He muttered, as he walked out of the house.

Jack looked around at the faces still in the room. "What? What did I do?"

"Nothing man, it's a great idea." Harold said. "I mean, like it or not, the boy's gotta admit he's completely wasting his money if they can't find her."

Barbara rolled her eyes. Melissa sighed, and Joshua got up and followed his brother out the back door.

"Joshie, where do you think you're going? You and your brother both need to get back here so we can discuss this!" Jack called to his back.

"Caesar, this is Mike, I need—"

"She's safe, man. Parker's been trailing her ever since she left the house. She hitched a ride with one of the neighbors."

Mike sat back in the chair, relieved. "Where is she now?"

"She boarded a bus headed to Houston about an hour ago. You want my guy to pick her up when she arrives?"

"Naw, tell him to hang back and be ghost. Just make sure she's safe."

"She'll never know he's there."

CHAPTER 57

Joshua awoke to the sound of the ringing cellphone on the night table beside him. Groggily, he reached for it. "What?"

"It's me."

Joshua sat up in bed, now completely awake. "Give me the address. I'll come get you."

"No, I'm fine. I just wanted you to know that I was safe."

Joshua scrubbed his hand across his morning stubble. "Where are you?"

"Back in Houston. I'm on a retreat with Carrie."

"Tonya, what the hell were you thinking? You can't just jet like this, no matter how pissed off you get."

"I'm sorry. I just needed to get away before I exploded. I thought you, of all people, would understand that."

"You know I do. That's why you called me. I also know that worrying about you can't be good for Unc's health right now. This is happening. You might as well get your head around it."

"Yeah, but I mean, what if it doesn't have to happen?"

Joshua sighed hard.

"You believe God loves us, right? I mean, Josh, even when we were kids, you've always had a closer connection with Him than the rest of us. Do you remember that time Moses Kaufman pushed me down and scraped my knee and you gave him a bloody nose in Sunday school?"

Joshua yawned. "Tonya, there have been so many incidences of me knocking dudes upside their head on your behalf. How do you expect me to remember that?"

"I don't see how you could forget this time. The whole family had to go to counseling with Pastor Freeland because of it. You got suspended from children's church for a month. Pastor Freeland called your behavior thuggish and ungodly. And you told him, 'That it didn't matter how many fights you got into, or how naughty you were. You said God wasn't a phony and a cheat like him, and that He loved you, no matter what you did. You said that if anyone was thuggish and ungodly around here, it was him.' We were nine. All the adults were so mortified by your answer. Mama, Daddy, Uncle Jack and Aunt Mel. I remember Daddy and Uncle Jack just standing there with their hands in their pockets, staring at their shoes. Mama and Aunt Mel saying nothing and Aunt Katie laughing. She laughed until tears rolled down her face. Then she collected herself and said the same thing she always said when you would say something that was spot on —"

"Spoken like a true prophet." Joshua finished quietly.

"Yeah, and not long after that, Pastor Freeland got kicked out, proven to be exactly what you said he was: a phony, a cheat and a thug."

"You know I'm not walking that walk right now, Tonya. So why you bringing this up?"

"Because if anybody knows God, Josh, I know you do. The theme of this retreat is God still performs miracles. I figured that if you believed that, well then maybe I could believe to. Does He, Josh? Does God still perform miracles?"

"He does."

"And He knows everything, right? He knows that this family doesn't work without Daddy. He knows that we still need him. That I still need him." Tonya's voice cracked and Joshua squeezed his eyes shut and fought back his own tears.

"Listen to me. This won't break you. Alright? He'll never give you more than you can bear."

"I'm going to ask God for a miracle, Josh. I'm going to ask God to save Daddy."

CHAPTER 58

HOUSTON, TEXAS, FOUR DAYS LATER

TONYA WALKED AROUND BACK to Mike's pool. He sat quietly in a lounge chair, staring out over the clear blue water. He had to have heard her approach; she was sure of it, but he never looked up and the expression on his face was, at best, unreadable.

"Hi." she said, because she didn't know any other way to start.

"How was the retreat?" Mike asked, still staring at the water.

"It was good. I got a chance to reconnect with me. I recommitted my life back to Christ. And the best news of all is..."

She was about to tell him the best news of all, and he still wasn't looking at her.

"I believe God is going to heal Daddy."

His eyes met hers. A shadow of pain flew across his face, but just as quickly as it appeared, it was gone. Hidden beneath his handsome chocolate mask. "Congratulations, Blackbird, it's good to have hope. I'm happy for you."

Tonya sat down beside him. "I'm glad you feel that way, because some things about our relationship need to change. Michael, I can't—I mean, we can't continue our relationship the same way that it's been. The sexual part at least has to end. It's outside of God's law. And it's just that I'm asking God to do something for me. To heal my daddy, and I certainly can't be living outside of His law while I'm asking Him to do it."

Mike nodded, "I get it."

Tonya's face relaxed. "You do?"

"Yeah. You gotta do what you gotta do. Anything is worth it. Especially if you think it'll save Unc."

"Yeah, I thought so too."

"I'm happy for you, Blackbird. But just so we're clear, this is a deal breaker for me."

Tonya's face clouded with confusion. "It's a deal breaker for you because I don't want to have sex again until we are married?"

"Oh, just until we're married?" He said, like he had misunderstood her, but that now with this new piece of intel he had a greater understanding.

"Yeah, no, this is not forever, Michael. Just until we stand before God and make it official."

But his next question told her he hadn't misunderstood at all.

"So, when's the wedding, Tonya? I mean, since you're deciding everything for us. Did you come up with a wedding date too?"

"I figured that would be the furthest thing from either of our minds right now. What with Daddy not out of the woods yet."

"Right."

"What does that mean, Michael?"

"It means you don't get to decide for me. It means I'm not about to be that dude with the good girl back home, sleeping with everything that moves on the road. That ain't me. I won't let you turn me into a cliché."

"You won't let me turn you into a cliché? I don't—" a sob she wouldn't dare release got stuck in her throat. Tonya took a deep breath and began again.

"I don't understand. Could you please just tell me whatever it is you are trying to say?"

"I'm saying we're done, Tonya."

Present Day 2010

CHAPTER 59

HOUSTON, TEXAS, 11PM

THE TWO GUARDS POSTED at the mouth of Mike's property watched the old jalopy turn onto the service road and inch its way along the path.

"That's her, call it in."

The newest member of Mike's security team spoke discreetly into the tiny radio attached to the lapel of his jacket. "Main Squeeze safe and headed towards the big house. Copy."

Caesar's clipped, no nonsense tone came back through the radio. "Copy."

Tonya slowed the car upon seeing the guards and cranked her window down. Unless there was a big event happening at the house, there were almost never guards stationed at the first checkpoint.

"Hey, Ryan, you guys are here late. Putting in a little overtime?"

"Something like that." No need to tell her that Caesar had ordered the entire security team back to campus with the understanding that they would not be relieved of duty until she had been safely found.

"How's your semester going?"

"Pretty good. Thanks for asking."

Tonya stuck her hand out the window to the guard standing beside Ryan. "I know, Ryan, and I know you've worked here for a while now, but I don't think I've ever officially been introduced to you."

"I've been here for going on seven years now, Dr. Malone. Name's Ben."

"Please call me Tonya, Ben, and it's a pleasure to meet you."

"Pleasure's all mine."

"So, do you guys need to check my ID or something?" Tonya said, reaching for her wallet.

"That won't be necessary. Just go on through."

"That's what I'm talking about, beautiful, kind, and smart. I don't mind working the overnight shift for the likes of her." Ben said, once Tonya had driven through the checkpoint. "She's nothing like the Barracuda."

Ryan looked at Ben quizzically. "The who?"

"You know, Dracula."

Ryan stared blankly at his partner.

"Come on Ryan, The She Bear? Weavezilla?"

"Ben, are those codenames? Because I've never seen them in the system." Ryan pulled out a small tablet and began typing something on the screen.

"What are you doing?"

"I'm doing a system search for Weavezilla."

Ben rolled his eyes. "Geez, why do I always get stuck with the new guys? You won't find that in the system, dummy. Do you seriously think we would go on record referring to the boss's lady as Weavezilla? Dracula, The She Bear, Barracuda, are more like descriptors, okay?" Ben thumped Ryan hard in the chest. "By the way, never use unofficial names with anyone outside the team."

"I won't." Ryan said quickly.

"I tell you what, type in the official codename: Side Chick. Anyone the boss is dating that has access to his estate will be listed under the code Side Chick. Ryan typed in the codename, which in his estimation wasn't that much more respectful than the colorful descriptors Ben had already used to describe the woman. A picture of a woman who resembled the former model, Tyra Banks, popped up on the screen. Ryan studied the photo in front of him. "Are you kidding me? She's gorgeous."

Ben chuckled, "You really haven't met the boss's girl yet, have you?"

Ryan shook his head. "No, I haven't. The whole team was called back to campus for Ms. Malone. I just assumed that she was—"

"The boss's main squeeze?"

"Yeah."

"She is. It's an always and forever type of thing. Don't ask. The only thing you need to know is that Side Chick is the new girl. Hang on to your nuts. You'll meet her real soon."

CHAPTER 60

CAESAR WAS STATIONED AT the guard booth when Tonya pulled up to the final checkpoint that evening. Tonya smiled up at him. "Caesar."

"Squeeze."

"Looks like everyone's working late tonight. Shouldn't you be on a hot date or something?"

"I was on a date, Squeeze, and she was smoking hot. But then somebody didn't come home like she was supposed to, or at least make a call to say she was gonna be late so, I had to cut my evening short."

Tonya's mouth dropped open. "I'm so sorry. I didn't mean to ruin your evening. I was working late and then I got caught in traffic—"

"Say no more, Squeeze. It's okay."

"Is he—"

Caesar nodded. He held his fingers out about an inch. "I was this close to sending a search and rescue team to come find you."

"I've been living on my own for so long, I'm just not use to checking in with people."

"You'd make my job a lot easier if you'd get used to it. But, if you can't, old habits being hard to break and all, I can always set you up with a car and a security detail."

Tonya shook her head, "No, next time I'll call. I promise."

Mike was standing in the driveway, arms folded across his chest, when Tonya drove up.

Tonya smiled extra brightly when she got out of the car. "Don't tell me Granny P held dinner for me again. Boy, you guys must be starving."

"Where were you?"

"There was an accident on the freeway. I've been stuck in traffic for the last three hours."

"You couldn't call?"

"My cellphone hasn't been holding a charge lately. It died."

"Don't you have a car charger?"

"I do, but the charging port in my car is broken."

Mike squeezed the bridge of his nose. "Father, give me strength." He muttered under his breath.

"Michael, I saw the extra security tonight. Did something happen while I was gone? Are Bella and the children okay?"

"Nobody knew where you were, Tonya. You got me calling all over creation looking for you. You're out there on the road in that deathtrap." Mike reached into his pocket and pulled out a cellphone.

Tonya stared down at it.

"Woman, you better take this phone and don't you dare fight me on this."

"Fine." Tonya huffed. She snatched the phone.

"And unless you want a search and rescue team to drop out of the sky, you had damn well better answer it when I call you. Everyone's numbers are programed into it. Next time call." Mike growled.

"Okay."

"I need to know that you are safe at all times, Tonya."

"Okay."

"I'm not playing with you."

"I said okay!"

Mike turned and stalked off towards the main house, muttering under his breath.

Not even a full minute later, the cellphone he had given her rung in her pocket. Tonya, who was unlocking the front door, fumbled to answer it.

"What?!" she screamed. "Oh, hi, Mama. Sorry, I thought you were Michael."

"And why in the world would you be yelling at that gorgeous man?"

"He gets on my last nerve. Acting like he's my daddy."

"He's right, Tonya. It's almost midnight. You should have called."

"My phone died."

"Well, it's a good thing he got you a new one. What kind of phone did you get?"

Tonya looked down at the phone in her hand. "This says it's a Universe or something."

"Wow, I read about those phones. I didn't think the technology was available in the states. Heads of state have been kidnaped, and the Universe was the phone that saved them."

Tonya rolled her eyes. *Great.* "Did he seriously call Dallas to tell my mommy on me?"

"He called to give me your new cell phone number. I could hear the worry in his voice, so I asked him about it. Tonya, do us all a favor, and let that man take care of you."

CHAPTER 61

Pearl was sitting at the kitchen table drinking a cup of tea when Mike stalked back into the mansion that evening.

"Tonya back yet?"

"And driving me crazy."

"Car trouble?"

"Traffic."

"Well, thank the Lord she made it home in one piece."

Mike scrubbed one large hand across his face. Joshua had been right. On a fundamental level, Mike was not even remotely cool with her driving around in that thing she called a car.

"You know what the worst part about all of this is? Besides the 70 plus vehicles that I own, all in proper working condition that she could drive, she's got a perfectly good truck custom made for her, just sitting in the garage collecting dust. She won't even drive it. She's so damn passive aggressive. I swear she's doing this to spite me. And what if she gets into an accident on the road with that thing? Then what?"

Pearl patted the seat next to her. "Baby, come sit down before you wear a hole in the floor or, worst yet, bust a blood vessel."

Mike took a seat beside her. Pearl rose and grabbed a mug from the counter. She poured Mike some tea, then waited for him to take the first sip.

"Sometimes the people we love act like they ain't got the sense God gave a billy goat. That's why the Bible says that true love covers a multitude of sins. Now that's what you got to do whether she likes it or not, you've got to cover her."

"Granny P, that's all I've been trying to do."

"Did I ever tell you about my late husband, Earl, and his drinking?"

"First I'm hearing about it. You and Marcus always speak fondly of Earl."

"Well, he was what you would call a weekend alcoholic. Course, Marcus don't know nothing about that side of Earl. He got himself together long before Marcus came along, but when we first started out together, that drinking was something awful. Earl was a Monday thru Friday working man and a Friday night through Sunday night drunk. Now there was a whole lot wrong with that picture, but the main problem I had was that Earl was the breadwinner. And there were a few times that his weekend binging affected his ability to show up to work. I couldn't have my husband's addiction see us thrown outdoors, so I needed to see a turnaround and I needed it to come quick. So, I started praying and God answered me quickly. A little bitty miracle started happening in our home every weekend. It wasn't a water being turned into wine sort of thing, but it was still big stuff to me. Earl would get all cleaned up, ready for a night out on the town with the boys, and wouldn't you know it? That car wouldn't start. Wouldn't even turn over. It stayed parked on that curb outside of our house for the entire weekend. We'd even have to walk to the grocery store. But, come Monday morning, time for work, that same car would start up just fine. I'd say, 'You know, Earl, the Lord must have kept you from some danger in those streets.' And he'd look at me and say, "I guess so, baby. I guess so."

Pearl patted Mike's arm. "I prayed, and God met me in my hour of need with a miracle. Maybe you ought to pray too."

Mike leaned in close to Pearl. "Miracle my eye. Spill the beans, woman. What did you do?"

"I told you, I prayed. And the Lord spoke a word to me. He said, 'Pearl, go outside and remove that distributor cap.'"

CHAPTER 62

Mike was sitting in his office at Home Court Advantage, with Joshua going over some documents, when Vernice knocked once, then stuck her head inside the door.

"It's your mechanic on the line."

"Thanks Mother B. Put him through." Mike pushed the speaker button when he heard the call ring in his office. "Jupiter, what's up? You got good news for me?"

"Mike, Mike, you're killin' me, man! I can't do nothing with this."

"Come on, man, she loves that thing. Can't you pimp-my-ride-it or something?"

"Mike, are you kidding me? Rust has eaten away forty percent of the exterior. Not five percent. Forty percent of the car is gone. I can't pimp-my-ride something that doesn't exist. And don't get me started on the nightmare happening underneath that hood. It definitely won't pass an emissions test if she's ever pulled over. I did find out why it stopped running, though. Somebody removed the distributor cap."

"Alright, man, junk it. I'll break the news to her."

Joshua grinned at his brother when he ended the call.

Mike smirked. "What?"

"Congratulations. I see you figured out a way to get Tonya out of that hideous car."

"I don't know what you're talkin' about, Josh. Tonya's car wouldn't start this morning. I called my mechanic, end of story."

Joshua's face suddenly grew serious. "How is Selena adjusting to all of this?"

"All of what, Josh?"

"Tonya being back. Everything that will inevitably bring. She asked about you at church last Sunday."

Mike studied the documents in front of him. "What'd you tell her?"

"That you had a lot on your plate and that you would call her when you got a chance. Come on, bro. You know I had your back. But you will have to tell her something at some point."

"Tonya and I are friends, Josh. There's nothing to tell."

Joshua lifted his eyebrow. "Nothing but a conveniently missing distributor cap. Now me, I would have just set the thing on fire and told her to drive the Range Rover or walk if she couldn't deal with it."

A small smile turned the corners of Mike's lips. "Naw, that's what the old you would have done."

"I'm pretty sure new me would have done it that way, too. There are still a few things that make my blood boil. At the top of that list is Bella being reckless with her safety. But I gotta admit, your approach does away with all the yelling, the finger pointing, and the tears."

Mike leaned back in his chair. "Exactly. Cause at the end of the day, she's gotta feel empowered."

Joshua grinned. "I'm all for that. Even when my woman doesn't really have a choice, I still want her to *feel* empowered."

Bella finished her once a week two-hour shift in Serenity's classroom as a parent helper. After which, she stopped by Tonya's office to see if she was available for lunch.

"We can take my car." Tonya said, as the two women walked out of the school into the parking lot.

"Uh—no, that's okay. I can drive. Joshua's not happy about you driving around town in that thing. He'd crap a brick if he knew I got in there with you."

"Relax, Bella. Beauty went into cardiac arrest this morning."

Bella snorted out a laugh. She put her hand to her mouth when Tonya glared at her. "I'm sorry. I know how much she means to you."

"Mike has his mechanic trying to revive her as we speak. In the meantime, I'm driving the Range Rover again."

"You loved your Range Rover, remember? Heck, I loved your Range Rover."

"I know, but I feel like it represents the old me. You know? Who I used to be."

"So Beasty—"

"Beauty." Tonya corrected.

Bella cleared her throat. "I mean, Beauty represents the new you? Come on, Tonya. I know that man hurt you. I know he broke your heart, but an old broke down Honda Civic is no were near the real you. Let it go." Bella pointed to the gleam coming from the fender. "I mean, look at this car. You wouldn't even know it was 20 years old. It looks like it just rolled right off the showroom floor."

Tonya frowned at that statement, and Bella continued quickly. "B-but it's old too. Look at it this way, this car is older than Jabari."

"Yes, but Beauty is older than me." Tonya popped the automatic locks on her truck, and she and Bella climbed in.

Bella looked over at the speedometer. "500 miles? Are you kidding? Your Range Rover only has 500 miles on it!"

"I didn't get to drive it that often."

"She's vintage." Bella said, rubbing her hand along the soft leather interior.

Tonya sighed, "If Michael has anything to say about it, this is as vintage as I'm going to get."

"How do you have Bluetooth? Bluetooth wasn't even out when Jabari was born." Bella said, when Tonya's cellphone rang through the truck's speaker system.

Tonya rolled her eyes, "Of course I have Bluetooth, Bella, it's a bullet-proof car." Tonya pushed the talk button on her dashboard. "Hello, Michael."

Mike's deep voice filled the interior of the car. "I'm sorry, baby, but she's gone."

Tonya gasped. "Beauty's gone?"

"Yeah, she's gone."

Tonya turned to look at Bella, who looked like she was trying desperately not to laugh. "Don't. You. Dare."

"What?"

"Nothing, sorry. Bella's in the car with me."

"Yeah, Josh is here too."

"Do you think we should get a second opinion?"

This time, Tonya could hear Joshua's laughter in the background.

"Hold on a second," Mike muttered a rebuke to his brother and came back to the line. "Jupiter's the best in the business, babe. If he says she's gone, then... I'm sorry. I know how much she meant to you. Did you need to see her one last time?"

Tonya sighed, "No. I'm good. I think I'd rather remember her the way she was."

"Alright, I'll see you tonight."

By the time Mike and Tonya had disconnected their call, Joshua and Bella were both choking with laughter.

CHAPTER 63

Mike's eyes did a complete head to toe scan of Tonya when she entered the kitchen the next morning.

"Good morning. Where is everyone?"

"Granny P stayed at Hope House last night and Marcus left for school early this morning."

Tonya's lips turned down into a slight frown. "I didn't get a chance to say goodbye."

"He's got a girl. My guess is he'll be back before the week is out."

"Ah, young love. Who cooked this morning, Jeeves?"

Mike took a sip of his orange juice. His eyes never leaving her face. "Yep."

"Everything looks and smells amazing. I love it when Jeeves cooks." Tonya lifted the lids to the warming platters on the kitchen island and arranged the different food items on her plate.

Mike studied her as she moved around the large center island. When she finished, Tonya sat down at the breakfast table. She lowered her head, said a quiet blessing over her food, then dug in. She looked up a few minutes later when she felt Mike's eyes on her. Tonya swiped at her face self-consciously. "Do I have food on my face?"

"Nah, I'm just trying to figure out something."

"Well, whatever it is, why don't you just ask me?"

"Okay. Is your entire wardrobe black, or are you trying to disappear?"

"I'm not disappearing."

"You are. Right in front of me."

"I just left in a hurry. I couldn't take everything, so I just took the essentials. Jeeves offered to send for my things last month when I got here. I just haven't had time to..."

His knowing stare made the words die in her throat. Tonya cleared her throat and began again. "Michael, it's really not a big deal."

Mike raised an eyebrow. "No?" He stood up from the table, grabbed her hand, and pulled her down the hall to a large floor-length mirror. Mike positioned Tonya in front of the mirror and stood behind her. "What happened to that pretty little Blackbird I used to know?"

He ran a finger down the side of her face and Tonya felt a slight shiver run down her back. "Where are all your beautiful markings? The colorful bangles you used to wear on your wrist. When was the last time you put a flower in your hair?" Mike dropped his hand abruptly to his side. "Don't let him steal you. That would be the worst crime of all."

Tonya met Mike's eyes in the mirror. "Okay, you're right. I'll go out and get some new things as soon as I get my next check."

"No, we do this today." Mike pulled his phone out of the inside breast pocket of the tailor-made suit he wore. "Mother B, I need you to move some things around for me. I won't be in today. For anything essential, I'll be available by phone."

Mike ended the call and handed Tonya his phone. "Your turn."

Tonya sighed. She took the phone and dialed the number to her office and pressed zero. "Hey, Debra. It's Tonya, just calling to let you know that I won't be in today. I'm fine. Just some personal business I have to attend to." Tonya ended the call and stared up at Mike. "Happy now?"

"Not yet. Let's go."

CHAPTER 64

"If I'm going to pay you back—"

"You don't have to pay me back."

"If I'm going to pay you back, we have to go somewhere that I can afford."

Mike sighed, "Fine. What did you have in mine?"

"Goodwill."

Mike shook his head. "Naw, I don't get down like that. Besides, that's what's wrong with society now. Here you are a professional, trying to shop at Goodwill. What about all the poor, single mothers who can't afford to go anyplace else? You're buying up all the halfway decent stuff from them. Pretty selfish if you think about it, Blackbird."

"So, you support President Obama when he says that those who can afford more should pay more?"

"I do."

"I never thought of shopping second hand as buying all the cute stuff up from single moms."

"Just let me handle this, alright? I got just the place in mind for you. They'll hook you up, head to toe. They even got this dude there that is supposed to be like a hair whisperer or something."

Tonya ran her hand through her hair, which was pulled back into a tight bun. "What's wrong with my hair?"

Mike said nothing. He just reached over and flipped the passenger side visor mirror down in front of her.

CHAPTER 65

Mike drove Tonya to a beautiful, upscale boutique in downtown Houston.

"Oh, my Lord! It's the Man of Steel!" one customer gushed when Mike and Tonya walked through the shop door. Always gracious and kind to his fans, Mike took a couple of pictures and signed a few autographs before a sales associate came and ushered the small crowd that had formed around them out the front door.

"This is the real star today." Mike said, pulling Tonya forward, when the store manager came out to personally greet them. "Rosalyn, I'd like for you to meet a very dear friend of mine, Tonya Malone. I know you book out pretty far in advance. I didn't make an appointment, but I was hoping you could fit this beautiful lady in for the works today."

The older woman made a tsking sound as she called for a sales associate by the name of Amy. The same associate who Tonya had seen ushering Michael's fans out of the shop just moments before.

"Amy, the door, please." Rosalyn said.

Amy flipped the open sign in the window to closed and then locked the front door.

Rosalyn grabbed Mike's hand. "Mike, you are so much more than a client to me. You are family. Anytime you grace our doors, it is a blessing to us all. You never need an appointment. For you, we clear our books." Rosalyn turned her attention to Tonya. "Ms. Malone, it is a pleasure to have you in our store. Please follow me."

Tonya was fawned over and catered to like royalty by the salespeople. She tried on a variety of outfits in every style and for every occasion imaginable, while Michael handled business from his tablet and cellphone. Whenever Tonya emerged from the dressing room, he'd give her either a thumbs up or a thumbs down on a particular selection.

"I'll tell you what. Hit me back when the initial findings are in. Yeah, I'll have my phone on all day." Mike shook his head when Tonya emerged from the dressing room.

"It's a cocktail dress, Michael. I need at least one."

Mike held his hand over the mouthpiece. "No more black." He said and went back to his conversation.

"Much better." He said when she emerged from the dressing room wearing the same little dress, this time in white.

Tonya wandered over to a rack of bracelets in an array of colors. "How much are these?" Tonya asked the hovering shop assistant.

"$150."

"For a set of how many?"

"That's $150 each, ma'am." The shop assistant explained.

Mike looked up from his phone conversation and caught Tonya eyeing the bracelets. "Remember the poor, Blackbird."

"I am. That's why I refuse to spend $150 on a bracelet. That ain't right." Tonya shook her head and walked back into the dressing room.

"She'll take two in every color." Mike said to the sales assistant. "Just wrap them and stick them in the bottom of the bag."

After a spa treatment and a catered lunch, Tonya sat in the chair of the stylist, Jon Claude. The one Michael had referred to as the hair whisperer. Jon Claude released Tonya's hair from the simple black hair tie she had used to hold her bun in place.

"You've never had a perm." More a statement than a question.

"No, never." Tonya confirmed.

"Oh my, a virgin. So rare these days. What a treat."

Mike walked into the salon at that moment. "We gonna keep it like that too, playa."

Jon Claude rolled his eyes. "I was talking about the hair."

"Me too." Mike winked at Tonya.

Jon Claude spun Tonya's chair around and examined her from head to toe. "We wouldn't dream of putting chemicals in this hair. You are sheer beauty in motion."

Mike watched Tonya blush, as if this was new information to her. Once again, he contemplated hunting Ted down and doing him bodily damage.

"Thank you." Tonya said quietly.

"But the hair, it has seen better days. I can tell you've been through a deeply personal trauma."

Tonya stared at Jon Claude through the mirror. "You can tell all of that by looking at my hair."

"The hair, it never lies." Jon Claude spoke to one of the stylists gathered around, watching him work. "Bring, Ms. Malone, a glass of Perrier, please." To Tonya he said, "You're not drinking enough water. Your ends are split. We're going to have to take two inches off. I can tell by your curl pattern that your hair yearns to be free, to be in its natural state. You've been forcing it to be straight when it longs for curly. You, my dear, have been lying to yourself and everyone around you."

Tonya froze.

"You've been sparforming, and you are not a conformist."

Mike's eyes sparkled with laughter. "Preach."

"Does he have to be here?" Tonya said, glaring up at Mike.

Mike held his hands up in surrender. "I'll wait outside."

As if waiting in the wings for her cue, a pert blonde walked over to Mike. "Mr. Dutton, can I interest you in a manicure while you wait?"

Tonya quickly swallowed a sliver of jealousy when Michael followed the pretty attendant into the adjacent room.

Forty-five minutes later, she emerged from the hair whisperer's chair feeling like her old self and looking like a million bucks. Tonya smiled at the natural, riotous curls that hung freely around her shoulders and back.

Jon Claude presented her to Rosalyn, who selected a pretty floral dress from the outfits Tonya and Mike had chosen that day, along with matching shoes and a hand clutch. "You will wear this home. Your other items will arrive at your residence by car today."

When Tonya emerged from the dressing room for the last time, Rosalyn beamed at Tonya and clutched her hands to her chest. "If our friend is not already in love, and I suspect he is, he will fall madly in love the moment he sees you."

Tonya blushed deeply. She thanked Rosalyn, took Jon Claude's offered arm and allowed him to lead her back into the lounge area where Mike was waiting for her.

CHAPTER 66

RYAN WATCHED THE RED corvette drive up to the gate. The beautiful woman in the dark sunglasses handed her ID to him without so much as a word. Ryan looked at her ID card and checked the expected visitor's log for the day. "Good afternoon, Ms. Mason. How can I help you?"

"You can open the gate and let me in."

"Ah... do you have an appointment?"

Selena snatched her glasses off. "What is your name?"

"Ryan, ma'am."

"Well, Ryan, I'm here to see my boyfriend, who also happens to be your boss, Mike Dutton."

"I understand, ma'am, but I'm afraid he's not here at the moment."

"That's fine. I'll just wait for him inside the mansion."

Ryan's cheeks colored. "I'm afraid that's not possible, either."

Selena stared at Ryan. "Not possible. What do you mean?" Ryan stepped out of the guard booth and showed her the log. "What I mean is that every morning we receive a log of visitors who have been granted access into the mansion for that day.

I'd really like to help you out, Ms. Mason, but in order for me to let you through these gates, your name has to be on this list. As you can see, it's not here."

"Listen to me, Ryan. I don't care about your stupid list. I need to see my man today. If you want to keep this job, you had better open this gate and make that happen."

CHAPTER 67

"Mike stood when he saw Tonya enter the lounge area.

"So, what do you think?" Jon Claude said. "She is lovely, no?"

"Just like the girl I always remembered."

Mike tore his eyes away from Tonya long enough to address Jon Claude. "What's the verdict?"

"I need to see her once every two weeks, at the very least. Weekly would be optimum."

Mike nodded. "Weekly it is then."

Tonya looked back and forth between Mike and Jon Claude, "Wait, every week for how long?"

"Six months."

Mike shook Jon Claude's hand and led Tonya out of the shop with a hand pressed to the small of her back.

"Michael, today was an amazing experience." Tonya said once they had settled themselves into the car.

"I'm glad you enjoyed it."

"You tricked me, by the way. The moment Amy locked the front door, I knew I was way out of my league. I know I said I would pay you back on Friday, but I'm thinking I might need a payment plan."

"How about you say, 'thank you and I say you're welcome' and we count that as payment enough?"

"Thank you."

"You're welcome."

"Still, Michael, I can't come here every week to get my hair done. Especially not by Jon Claude."

"You not feeling him for some reason?"

"He was great. I got the feeling that it was a huge honor having him do my hair, the way all the other stylists stood around watching him work on me. One of the salesgirls confirmed it before we left. Did you know that Jon Claude doesn't do hair, he just consults?"

Amusement sparkled in his eyes. "So what's the problem, Blackbird?"

"Well, even if I could afford it, which we both know I can't, I don't have time to be up in the salon every week."

Mike started the car and backed up out of the parking space. "It's a good thing he's coming to you, then."

CHAPTER 68

MIKE AND TONYA RETURNED home that afternoon to find the front gate strangely, un-manned. Mike entered the override code that would allow them entrance onto his property. As the car rounded the long curving drive, they could see and hear the commotion coming from the main house. Pearl, Selena, and Ryan, the gate operator, stood outside the front door in the middle of a very heated exchange.

"What's going on?" Mike said, as he stepped out of the car and effectively silenced everyone with the sound of his voice.

Ryan, the gate operator, was the first one to speak. "I received a call from one of the staff members about a disturbance at the main house. I came to check it out, sir."

"I'll take it from here, Ryan. Get back to your post."

Selena glared at Pearl. "She won't let me inside the house."

"I told her you weren't here and that she should come back later."

"And I told her that since I was already here, I should just wait for you inside."

"Why are you here, Selena?" Mike asked.

"Why am I here?" Selena flashed an angry look at Mike, then locked eyes with Tonya, who had also gotten out of the car and was now standing beside him. "Why is she here?"

"Because she belongs here."

"If she belongs here, then where do I belong, Mike?"

Silence.

"Wow. I see." Selena turned to leave, brushing past him quickly.

Mike looked up towards heaven and released a heavy sigh. "Wait."

Selena stopped dead in her tracks. Mike held out a hand towards her. She took it and allowed him to pull her towards him.

"This is my fault. I should have properly introduced the two of you years ago. Tonya, I want you to meet Selena, my girlfriend. Selena, I want you to meet Tonya, my oldest and dearest friend in the world. When I said she belonged here, what I should have said was that she lives here. Tonya moved back home to Houston last month. She's staying in the cottage here on my estate. Tonya, Granny P, can the two of you go inside, please? I'd like to speak to Selena privately."

Tonya smiled, "Sure, no problem. Nice to officially meet you, Selena." She said as she extended her hand.

Selena folded her arms across her chest and rolled her eyes.

Tonya shrugged and followed Pearl into the house. Pearl closed the massive front door behind them. "Let me guess, Sister Satan?" Tonya said once the two of them were on the other side of the door.

"Live and in the flesh, baby. Come on, we can monitor the situation from the family room."

CHAPTER 69

Pearl turned the television to the home security station. From there she pulled up camera one, which recorded activity at the front door. An image of Mike and Selena came up on the screen.

"We got visuals. Now, let's see if we can get sound."

"No wait, we shouldn't." Tonya said.

"Don't you want to hear what they are saying?"

"Yes, of course I do, but Michael asked to speak to her privately. The right thing to do would be to respect that." Tonya said, losing more of her moral conviction by the second.

"That's the problem with your generation. Everybody's worried about doing the right thing, not enough folk willing to do the God thing."

"Grandma Pearl, how can spying on a private conversation between two people be godly?"

"Read your Bible." Pearl turned up the sound. "The Bible says watch as well as pray."

"What's up, Selena? We don't do this."

Selena bit her bottom lip and tapped her foot agitatedly against the pavement. "You're living with the woman that you asked to marry you?"

"This is not about her. This is about us. How we function. We don't invade each other's space. I don't come to your spot unannounced. You certainly don't have the right to roll up on mine."

"I haven't spoken to you in an entire month!"

"Lower your voice."

Selena took a deep breath. She attempted to modulate her tone. "You don't return my phone calls. When I do get you on the line, you're rushing me off. So, sorry to 'roll up on you' as you say. I just thought I'd check and see for myself if we were still in a relationship."

"Don't. I've always been upfront with you."

"Really, Mike? Because I didn't know you were living with another woman."

"Tonya's family."

"You let her stay in the cottage!"

"For the last time, Selena, lower your voice."

Selena had learned early in their relationship that Mike's will was iron clad. If he decided on a topic, he could never be swayed. She had also discovered that the hero inside of Mike hated to see any woman cry. If they weren't seeing eye to eye on a matter, Selena's tears would usually cause him to capitulate. The merciless tone he was using with her right now told her she was clearly fighting a losing battle. So, right on cue, she began to cry. Selena used the base of her palm to wipe her tears away.

Mike removed a white handkerchief from the inside breast pocket of his suit and handed it to her. For a moment, it looked like he was offering a flag of surrender. The next words out of his mouth told her he wasn't ready to surrender at all.

"The condo doesn't suit you anymore?"

"You know I love my condo. And I am very thankful that you bought it for me. It's just... you know what, Mike, never mind." Selena used the handkerchief to dab at her eyes and let her voice taper off.

"Whatever you have to say, you need to get it off your chest now. I won't have this conversation with you again."

Selena wrapped her arms around herself and bit back a cry. "You told me it wasn't available. When I asked, you wouldn't even consider the idea of me staying on your property. But now that she's back, suddenly the cottage is available again."

"You and I are dating. Tonya and I are not. End of story." Mike stepped towards her, closing the gap between them. "Baby, Tonya is here to stay. So, the sooner you get used to that idea, the better off we'll both be. This won't work if you don't trust me."

Selena nodded. A lone tear rolled down her cheek, and Mike wiped it away with the pad of his thumb.

"I'm sorry. I- shouldn't have come. I'll leave."

Mike nodded.

"When can I see you again?"

"I'll call you."

Selena walked towards the convertible parked in the driveway.

"Selena?"

She turned to face him.

"Don't let this happen again. Next time you won't get in."

She nodded, climbed into the car and drove off.

CHAPTER 70

Pearl clicked the television off. "He'll be walking through the door any minute. Just act like we are having a normal conversation."

Tonya bit her lip and stared at the blank television screen. "He bought her a condo."

"Don't whisper. Whispering implies that we were listening. I said act normal."

"This must be really serious. In all the years I've known him, Michael has dated a lot of women, but he's never bought any of them property before."

Pearl rolled her eyes, "Please, he bought that little red corvette she drove up out of here in too. He buys things for people all the time. The neighbor boy that lives down the street turned sixteen and Mike bought him a car. And I'mma tell you why he bought that condo. Cause her little sneaky behind kept making hints about the cottage. I'm not worried about Sister Satan. Anyone with a pair of eyes can see she's on her way out the door. Who I'm worried about right now is Ryan. I just wished the servants hadn't called down to the gate and gotten him involved in this. But Jeeves wasn't here, and

Michael has told them repeatedly that they are not to bother Jeeves during his days off. When they heard Selena acting a fool, they probably didn't know what else to do. Now the boy is going to lose his job over this for sure."

"Why? he couldn't have predicted how she would behave!"

"Shh, Tonya acting normal means not yelling either."

"Ryan is working his way through college. He can't get fired over this."

"I agree and I hope you're right, but Mike is real particular about that gate."

Mike's footsteps could be heard echoing on the marble tile as he walked towards them. "Pull Ryan's P file and call down to the gate and tell him I want to see him in my office immediately." Mike said, speaking to one of the house servants.

"Yes sir, Mr. Dutton."

Pearl shot Tonya a quick look as if to say, *see, I told you so.*

"Granny P, you good?"

Pearl and Tonya looked up to see Mike standing in the doorway.

"I'm fine, baby. Just sitting here shooting the breeze with our favorite girl." Pearl said, patting Tonya on her knee.

"Blackbird, you alright?"

"Yes, but if my being here is going to cause problems in your relationship, Michael, I can leave."

Mike smirked, "Please, she better fall back. This is my house. You being here isn't up for discussion."

Tonya shrugged, "Still, I don't expect you to turn your whole life upside down for me."

"Too late for all of that, Blackbird. In fact, you're about 35 years too late." Mike turned to leave.

Tonya followed him into the hallway, "Michael, wait."

Mike stopped in his tracks, took a deep breath, and looked up at the ceiling.

"Ryan is ex-military and the first generation in his family to go to college. He needs this job. So, whatever you do, please don't fire him."

CHAPTER 71

RYAN SAT ACROSS THE desk from his boss, Mike Dutton, for what seemed like an eternity. Usually, the big boss never got involved with employee related stuff. Martin Jeeves, the property manager or Caesar, the head of security, usually handled that. But today was a most unusual day. Today, neither Caesar nor Martin was onsite. Both men had flown out that morning to attend the home-going service for a fallen war buddy.

My first day flying solo at the gate and I totally screw it up.

Other than the grandfather clock standing proudly in the corner of the room, the boss's office was deafeningly silent. This only fueled Ryan's anxiety more. If Caesar were here, he'd be screaming at the top of his lungs, tearing Ryan a new butthole right now, and although not preferable per se, it was at the very least familiar. Actually, given a choice between the ex-ballplayer's infamous calm, and Caesar's tearing him a new one, Ryan would prefer Caesar any day. At least with Caesar, a guy knew where he stood. And Ryan didn't know how this meeting with Mike Dutton would turn out right now.

"How do you think this happened, Ryan?"

Ryan cleared his throat. "Sir?"

"If we know where the system broke down, we can repair the problem."

"Ms. Mason is on the pre-approval list, so when she insisted I grant her entrance, given your um... relationship, I-I thought it would be better to let her through than to let a scene ensue at the gate."

"But she doesn't live here, does she? And she is not a member of my immediate family."

"No, sir."

"In fact, she has no business with anyone else who lives here besides me. My family doesn't even like her, Ryan. At best, they tolerate her, and from what I understand, my staff isn't too fond of her either. What is it you guys at the gate call her?"

Ryan turned beet red. "Sir?"

"Her code name, Ryan."

Ryan could rattle off a hundred different unofficial code names. The question was, which of these names would get him fired?

"Ms. Mason hasn't been given an official code name per se, sir. We use a general girlfriend code for anyone in your life that occupies her position."

"Which is?"

"Side Chick."

The boss smiled a smile that didn't quite reach his eyes, "Side Chick. Of course."

Mike leaned back in his chair and absentmindedly played with a paperweight on his desk. He knew that his security team had dubbed Tonya, Main Squeeze, years ago. So in their minds, anyone else who came along would automatically be regulated to the position of the side chick. It didn't help that Tonya had an excellent rapport with his entire staff. They loved her, and the feeling was mutual. She had no qualms about advocating for anyone of them. Thus the reason he was sitting here talking with Ryan, breaking his own damn rules, instead of firing the young man for what would usually be an immediate termination offense. *Lord, the things I will do for this woman.*

"Mr. Dutton, I denied her entry at first. It's' just that Ms. Mason was very unhappy about my decision. She insisted that if I wanted to keep my job that I should open the gate."

"How old are you, Ryan?"

"Twenty-four, sir."

"Have you ever seen Ms. Mason's signature at the bottom of one of your checks?"

"No sir, I have not."

"So that logic doesn't make any sense, does it?"

"No sir, it doesn't."

"It's crazy talk, right? For all you know, she could be crazy."

Mike sat the paper weight back down and pinned the young man with his eyes.

"Have you ever dated a beautiful woman and then found out after the fact that she was crazy, Ryan?"

"Once or twice, sir."

"So, explain to me why you would allow a crazy talking woman with the code name side chick up into my house?"

"I-I failed sir."

"You're damn right you failed. Your number one priority is to protect the people who live inside my gates. Not to make my visitors happy, man."

"I take full responsibility for what happened today, sir."

"Good. Make sure it doesn't happen again."

Ryan blinked. "You mean... I'm not fired?"

"You can thank Ms. Malone for that. But Ryan, you should know, I won't be this gracious in the future."

"It won't happen again, sir. I promise."

"Get back to your post."

CHAPTER 72

Marcus groaned and slid down the wall of Tonya's dance studio. "I cannot believe this is so hard."

Tonya stretched her leg out effortlessly on the balance bar that extended across the length of her home studio. "Trust me, it will pay off in the end. Besides, this is exactly the kind of stamina you'll need if you are serious about playing in the NBA."

One of the things she loved most about her cottage was the professional grade dance studio Michael had installed for her when he'd first moved in. It was the one thing she missed the most while living in New York. Well, that and her wrap-around porch with the old-fashioned swing. And her clawfoot tub. Actually, there had been a lot of things that she had missed about her cottage. There had been a ballet school in Manhattan that Tonya used to visit and workout in from time to time, but she'd have to take the train all the way across town just to get there. Nothing was like having her very own studio. It was a dancer's dream.

"Why don't you rest for ten and we go for another round of twenty?" Tonya said as she walked over to the mini fridge and handed Marcus a bottle of water.

"Thanks."

"Let's see if you'll be thanking me after this final round."

Marcus laughed, "No, seriously, thank you for doing this. You offering to workout with me like this is pretty cool."

"I've been helping the men in this family succeed in the NBA for a very long time. Might as well use my skills to help the next generation."

Marcus stared down at his water bottle. "So, is that how you really see me? As family?"

"Of course. Why—"

"I mean, it's no big deal. It's just that you're the only one who didn't put in your two cents that night when we were talking about the draft. I'm just wondering why you abstained."

Tonya took a seat on the floor next to Marcus. "Marcus, have you ever heard the saying it takes a village to raise a child?"

"Yeah."

"Well, my folks and your dad's folks, they actually lived by that creed. When we got rewarded, it was the greatest thing ever because it was like getting quadruple the reward. But when one of us got into trouble, that wasn't so hot. We each had to answer to two sets of parents. Auntie Mel and Uncle Jack and Harold and Barbara."

"That's how my dad and Unc get down every day."

"Well, they learned from the best. I just felt like this decision was hard enough for you without adding one more voting adult to your village."

"I appreciate that, and I'd still like to know your thoughts."

"Well, in that case, I think your dad is right. But a better question is, why do you want to rush this?"

"It's like this, him raising me, taking me in, that totally changed his life. I'm an adult now. I kind of feel like he should have the right to be free."

Tonya shrugged. "Who says he wants to be free?"

"His lady sure would like him to be free."

You ain't never lied. Tonya resisted the urge to jump up in the air and slap the young man a high-five. His 'lady' would like for Michael to be free of the whole lot of them. That was for sure. Instead, Tonya mentally put her therapist cap on and asked the young man another question.

"Why do you think that is?"

Marcus shrugged. "I think she feels like he gives too many parts of himself away and she's afraid of losing him."

"I think you're right. I take it you've been watching her for a while now. Now I want you to watch him. Your dad loves you very much. There is nothing in this world that could ever make him turn his back on his family. Believe that. I also think that you have a keen sense of discernment. If you decide to stay in school, I think you should consider majoring in psychology."

"Seriously?"

Tonya nodded, "Seriously, you really get people."

Marcus leaned over and kissed her cheek. "Thanks."

"Like I said, let's see if you'll be thanking me twenty minutes from now. Come on, let's do this. Your ten minutes is up."

CHAPTER 73

MIKE FOUND PEARL AND Tonya in the cottage, sitting on the sofa watching a movie when he returned home. Mike dropped a quick kiss on Pearl's cheek and plopped down onto the sofa next to Tonya.

Her beautiful natural curls had been back and in full effect ever since her weekly appointments with Jon Claude had begun. Tonight, she had piled the riotous curls up into a messy top knot. She wore baggy flannel pajamas and a pair of outrageously pink, furry house shoes. Mike's thoughts circled back momentarily to the hip hugging, low cut dress Selena had worn tonight with the sexy red bottom heels.

It was the first time he'd seen her since her impromptu visit to the mansion, and Mike knew from the moment he'd laid eyes on her that Selena had declared a quiet war. She had wanted to put something on his mind, something that when he closed his eyes tonight, he wouldn't be able to forget.

Mike curled a tendril of Tonya's hair around his finger and chuckled softly to himself. Selena had come dressed for war, Tonya was dressed for movie night. Definitely not trying for sexy, and yet everything about her was completely alluring. She smelled amazing. Grounded like the lavender and vanilla scent she always wore. It was a scent he would always associate with home.

Her eyes found his. "What's so funny?"

"Nothing, Blackbird. I was wondering where everybody was tonight. I came back to an empty house."

"Well, Marcus had a date, and you were on a date, so Grandma Pearl and I decided to have a movie night."

Mike picked up the DVD case on the coffee table. "Chick flick, huh?"

"Yep."

"I'm surprised you didn't call Bella. She loves this kind of stuff."

"We thought about it, but then we decided only single ladies allowed. Isn't that right, Grandma Pearl?"

"That's right."

Mike lifted Tonya's feet up off the floor and removed her hot pink, furry slippers. "I believe I owe you a foot massage."

Tonya smiled. "I won't complain, but why?"

"For whatever you said to Marcus. He's staying in school. He wants to major in psychology."

Pearl threw both hands up in the air. "Praise, Jesus!"

Mike began slowly massaging one of her tiny feet in his large hands. "When he told me he was going to major in psychology, I knew my number one girl had to have a hand in that."

Tonya threw her head back and sighed. "All I did was tell him the truth. That feels incredible, by the way."

"Oh, before I forget, Selena wants to host a little get together at the house next weekend. She'd like to make dinner for the two of you. Her way of apologizing for her behavior."

Pearl looked at Tonya, then Mike, "She wanna cook... here?"

"That's what she said."

Pearl paused the movie. She pulled the glasses hanging from the chain around her neck up onto her face and peered intently into Mike's eyes. "Son, you didn't walk away from your drink tonight, did you?"

Tonya burst into a fit of giggles.

"Come on, Granny P, cut her some slack."

"No way, baby. You're doing enough of that for all of us."

Mike tickled Tonya's feet, "And you, you wanna tell me what you find so funny about this?"

Tonya squealed, "The thought of you being Roofied!"

Mike smirked. "I see I walked into a room full of comedians tonight. Seriously, Blackbird, you gonna come to this little dinner party or not?"

"I'll pass, but tell her thanks for the fake apology, though."

"Blackbird."

"I keep telling you, Michael, I'm just a tenant. Feel free to totally exclude me from your family festivities. I don't eat everybody's cooking, no way."

"I don't blame you, baby," Pearl chirped, "That's how you find yourself in a coma somewhere, with the saints of God standing over your hospital bed trying to call you back from the dark side."

"Come on, Blackbird, not even for me?"

Tonya pulled her feet off of his lap. "I'm not going to the dark side for anybody, Michael."

"You can't listen to—" Mike shot a look over at Pearl. "You see what you started?"

Pearl shrugged, "Hey, if the murder weapon fits you can't acquit."

"Okay, fine. If it means that much to you, we can all have dinner together, Michael."

His handsome face broke out into a grin.

"On one condition. I do the cooking."

"Hey now, I like that idea. I'll help you in any way I can." Pearl said.

"I think I can deal with that condition, Blackbird. You know, it's been a long time since you've last cooked for me."

Tonya picked up the remote control and un-paused the movie again. She settled her feet back onto his lap. "Um, hum, don't ever say I never did anything for you."

CHAPTER 74

Marcus found his dad inside one of the large walk-in closets of the master bedroom. "Dad, I'm out. I'mma bout to go get Lisa."

Mike, who was changing out of the suit he'd worn that day to work, set his sterling silver cuff links down on the dresser and looked at his son. "Marcus, be polite. Don't call. Don't honk. Get out of the car, walk up to the front door and get her like a gentleman."

"Come on, Dad. I ain't no buster. I got this."

"Oh, you got this, huh?"

"Yeah."

"And if her dad invites you into his office for a private sidebar?"

"I should... run for the hills, right?"

Mike chuckled, "That depends. How much do you like this girl?"

Marcus took a seat on the changing bench and looked up at his dad. "I think she could be the one. Wifey."

Mike slipped on a pair of jeans and a clean t-shirt and allowed his son's words to sink in. He pulled a pair of kicks off the shoe rack and sat down on the changing bench next to Marcus.

"She feels the same way about you?"

"Yeah."

"Then get ready to have that conversation with her pops."

"You think I should tell him my intentions towards Lisa?"

"You won't get a chance to tell him anything. Just look him in the eyes and remain respectful, even if he tries to come for you. Most importantly, remember who you are. You're not that kid growing up in New Orleans without a father anymore."

Mike laced up his tennis shoes and stood up from the bench. He held his hand out to Marcus and pulled him up, too. "Who are you, Marcus?"

"I'm the son of Kal-EL."

Mike pulled the younger man in for their customary handshake and embrace. "You know it, baby. Don't you ever forget it." Mike released his son. "Did you extend the invitation for dinner tonight to her folks?"

"Yes, I did. Lisa's mom told me to thank you for the invite, but they had a charity function to attend. I'm thinking tonight would have been a little too casual for their taste, anyway. I mean, Lisa's cool, but her moms and pops are kind of high-brow."

Mike raised an eyebrow and nodded. "We'll have to do it up right next time and invite them over. What does her father do for a living?"

"Dad, seriously?"

"What?"

"We really gon do this? Caesar has already done a full background check on Lisa's dad. You already know that he's a Methodist preacher. I'm guessing you probably know more about Lisa's dad than Lisa's mom does."

A small smile played at the corner of Mike's lips. "Touché. If you plan on your girl being a regular around here, make sure you set it up with the guys at the gate."

CHAPTER 75

Twenty minutes later, when Marcus pulled up to the front gate, Davos, one of the guards, handed him a tablet. "I hear you got a girl, bro. What's her name?"

"Lisa Davenport."

"You got a picture?"

"Yeah, let me check." Marcus reached for his phone. He pulled up a picture of Lisa.

"She's smoking hot, homey."

"Can you send that to me?"

"For what?"

"I'm not going to put it under my pillow, man. It's for the system. So we don't have to card her every time she comes through."

"Yeah, alright. Cool."

Davos handed Marcus a tablet. "I also need you to fill out this intake form." Marcus looked at the first question on the screen: relationship to resident, family member or significant other. With his finger, Marcus marked the box that said significant other. Another drop down box appeared along with the words: main girl, side girl, flavor of the month, flavor of the week, one-night stand, and psycho ex—do not admit this person onto the property under any circumstance.

Marcus looked up at Davos.

"And don't worry, she can be upgraded or downgraded whenever you like."

"Dude, are you kidding?"

"Do you know how many times we've had to downgrade someone for your dad?"

Marcus handed the tablet back to Davos, "Y'all acting like Lisa is the first girl I've brought around here. I ain't never had to do all of this before. I don't see why it's necessary now."

"You were just a kid then, Marcus. Now you're twenty-one. You're a grown man who is going to be dating fully grown women. And I don't have to tell you, my friend, but fully grown women come with their own set of problems. Think of it like this: you want the staff to treat her with the appropriate amount of respect when she rolls through, right? You don't want them treating your side girl like she's your main girl, do you?"

"She's my only girl, Davos."

"Well, you should have led with that, man. Trust me, that makes our jobs a lot easier. We'll give her a full access pass."

CHAPTER 76

WHEN TONYA GOT HOME from work that evening, she made a beeline back to her cottage where she showered quickly and changed into a pair of jeans and a t-shirt. After she had groomed herself, she walked along the cobblestone path that led from her place to the mansion. She was coming through the front door just as Mike was descending the long mahogany wood staircase. Like their guest who would be in attendance tonight, he was also dressed casually in jeans and a t-shirt.

"You ready for tonight?"

"Almost. I put my ducks on early this morning and Bella, Maggie, and Grandma Pearl will be here any minute to help me with the sides."

"You need anything from me? A last-minute run to the store or something?"

"That's very considerate of you, Michael, but I've got everything I need for now. Thanks."

"Alright, Blackbird, I'll be in my study till Walter and Josh get here. Holler if you need me."

CHAPTER 77

MARCUS PULLED HIS BMW truck over to the side of the road when he noticed his girlfriend looking like she wanted to bolt from the vehicle. They had just driven onto his father's property, but the closer they got to the mansion, the more agitated she appeared.

"Hey, don't be nervous. I told you, my family is going to love you. Alright?"

"I feel really, really, underdressed right now."

"You got on jeans and I got on jeans. I told you dinner is casual tonight. You look great."

"You think I should have brought a gift?"

"Nah, bae, you the gift." Marcus' eyes raked lazily over her form, causing a blush to rise to her cheeks.

"That's sweet of you to say, but I should have brought some flowers, or tea."

"Tea?"

"Yeah, I read somewhere that rich people really like tea. Can we stop at the store, please?"

"Baby, we're already here. We're not turning around for tea. If you want tea, I'll make you a cup as soon as we get inside. Any kind of tea you want, I promise."

"I don't want tea. I just want your family to like me."

"Then just be yourself. My family hates fakes."

Another look of panic shot through Lisa's eyes. "Really?"

"More than anything. So just be the girl I fell in love with, alright? I survived your dad."

"I'm really sorry about that, by the way. The whole cow and milk analogy. I have no idea where he was going with that."

Marcus snorted, "I did. But it's all good. I'm sure I'll be having a similar conversation one day with the dude who wants to date my daughter. But for real, though, you have nothing to worry about. My folks are way more laid back than your Pops. Nobody's going to clean a gun while they ask you about your position on abstinence. Now, my Grandma, she'll just flat out ask you, so be ready for that, but she won't be holding a gun while she does."

Lisa's honey colored skin flushed with embarrassment. "I'm so sorry. I still can't believe Daddy did that. And it makes absolutely no sense. Him and Mama are going to the gala tonight. Why would he be cleaning his hunting rifle?"

"Just trying to scare me, baby." Marcus leaned in and tucked a lock of her hair behind her ear. "Good thing I don't scare easy." He kissed Lisa softly on the lips. "When we go inside, I'mma introduce you to everybody. You can have the standard get-to-know-a-little-bit-about-you conversation, then the two of us can go hang out somewhere privately until dinner. How does that sound?"

"Great." Lisa blew out a deep breath. "What should I call everyone?"

"Call my grandma, Ms. Pearl. But for everyone else, they'll want you to address them by their first names.

"Your dad is the Man of Steel, your uncle is Bad Boy Joshua Keys, and I'm supposed to call them by their first names?"

"That's right. Mike and Joshua."

"But your uncle is a pastor now, shouldn't I—"

Marcus shook his head. "At home, no titles."

"You're right, your folks are way more laid back than mine. My parents will probably want you to call them Mr. and Mrs. Davenport, even after we are married."

"We'll cross that bridge when we come to it. For now, just remember, no pics, no autographs."

"I wouldn't, ever. I get that your family really values their privacy."

Marcus smiled over at her. "Then we're good." He motioned to the guard walking toward them. "We've been out here for so long he thinks there's a problem."

Marcus slid down the driver's side window.

"Is everything alright, Mr. Dutton? Can I be of some assistance to you, sir?"

Marcus smirked at the guard. "Dude, cut it out. She's already nervous enough."

The guard laughed, "Hey, man, we saw you on the monitors. You were out here for so long, I had to come make sure this pretty little lady wasn't trying to jack you. I'm Davos, by the way." Davos said, waving at Lisa.

"I'm Lisa, Davos. Nice to meet you."

"Welcome, to Dutton House, Lisa. Is this your first time on the property?"

"Yes."

"Well, we're very glad to have you. They're going to ask you for your driver's license at the intake office, but once you're in our system, you won't have to show it again."

"Thank you."

Marcus put the car in drive and Davos spoke into the speaker clipped to his vest. "Son of Kal-El coming through."

Marcus rolled up the window and drove down the path leading to the main gate.

Lisa looked at Marcus. "Was that one of the codenames you told me about?"

"Yeah."

"So who is Kal-EL?"

"Superman."

"Oh, I see. Since your dad is the Man of Steel, that must make you the Son of Kal-EL."

"You got it."

CHAPTER 78

THE PLAN HAD BEEN for Marcus to introduce Lisa quickly to his folks and take off for some place quiet until dinner. But his dad, his uncle and Walter Trendale were currently trying to rope him into a game of pool. His Grandma, Aunt Bella, Tonya and Maggie Trendale were trying to whisk Lisa off to, he had no idea where.

"We got this Marcus. You hang out here with the guys. Lisa will be fine with us." That was his Aunt Bella speaking.

Interestingly enough, neither his Aunt Bella nor his Grandma Pearl had given Lisa the stink eye. Those two, especially, made it abundantly clear when they didn't like someone. Thus the reason Marcus hadn't bothered to bring too many of the women he dated home in the past. Marcus could count on both Tonya and Maggie Trendale to be polite and kind, but the immediate acceptance from his aunt and grandma had been a welcomed surprise.

"Uh, wait a second, y'all." Marcus said to the women who were attempting to hurry Lisa from the room. He pulled Lisa to the side. "You good with this? This isn't what we planned."

Lisa's eyes danced with joy. "Are you kidding? This is exactly what I asked God for." she whispered. "I can't wait to get to know all the women who know and love you."

Marcus leaned in and kissed her then, and in that moment, he didn't care that his family was watching.

CHAPTER 79

"THAT'S A MIGHTY FINE woman you got on your arm this evening, Marcus." Walter said as he leaned over the pool table and made his shot.

Marcus grinned, "I know."

"Looks like she's got your nose wide open, too." Joshua said. "What's her family like?"

Marcus blew out a breath, "Over the top protective. Lisa is an only child, and she's not exactly what you would call street smart, but her mom still refers to herself as a stay-at-home-mother and Lisa is twenty-one. And her dad, he's a pastor, but that dude is nuts."

"I take it ya'll had that sidebar." Mike said.

"Yeah, me, him, and his gun."

Joshua stood up straight. "He threatened you?"

"I don't even know, Unc. It was so subtle, I'm still trying to figure it out."

Mike stared at his son. "What do you mean, you're still trying to figure it out? What did he say?"

When Marcus arrived at the Davenport home that evening, Lisa's mom answered the door.

"Marcus, good to see you again. Come inside. Lisa will be out in just a moment. She's getting dressed."

Mr. Davenport, who was standing behind his wife, immediately ushered Marcus into his study. "Can I get you anything to drink?" the older man said as he closed the door.

"I'm fine. Thank you, sir." Marcus eyed the rifle that sat on top of the large oak desk in the center of the room. He couldn't help but notice that the barrel of the gun was pointed directly at his chest.

Mr. Davenport took a seat behind the desk and motioned to the chair in front of him. "Have a seat, Marcus. It's not loaded. As a man of the cloth, I don't believe in violence, but I do enjoy a little big game hunting for sport every now and again. I was cleaning my rifle before you got here. Do you hunt, Marcus?"

"No, sir. I don't. I've seen too many gunshot wounds in my old neighborhood growing up. I'm not a fan of gun violence of any sort."

"That's right. Lisa told me that. Yours is a rags-to-riches tale. You've cleaned up so nicely, I forget you come from the other side of the tracks."

Marcus didn't know what to say to that, so he said nothing at all. He just met Mr. Davenport's gaze head on.

Davenport picked up the rifle and ran a cloth along the length of the barrel. "We have that in common, you and I. I was adopted by cousins on my mother's side of the family. The Davenports of Atlanta. Don't know if you've heard of them. They are a very influential family of black Methodist preachers. I clean up nicely too, but make no mistake, I cut my teeth in the mean streets of North Philly."

And Marcus translated that to mean: *Don't let this collar fool you, boy. I ain't no punk.*

"Marcus, did Lisa ever tell you about our family's close connection with Dr. Martin Luther King?"

"No sir, she never mentioned it."

"The Davenports of Atlanta traveled in the same circle as the Kings. Dexter King, and I grew up together. We were boyhood friends. Martin, Dexter's father, preached non-violence, and he owned a lot of guns. Did you know that, Marcus?"

"I knew he preached non- violence, sir. Wasn't aware that he owned any guns."

"Dr. King had so many guns that if you came to the King house, wanted to sit down on the sofa and have a chat with the family, he would have to clear a seat for you. You see Marcus, Dr. King preached non-violence, and he believed in it in theory, but if someone were to come into his house and attack his woman or his children, all that non-violence s#@t would go out the door. You understand what I'm trying to tell you, Marcus?"

"Yes sir, loud and clear."

Walter snorted. "Hell yeah, that was a threat."

Joshua shook his head. "Naw, he told you the truth. I can't be mad at the man for that."

Walter rubbed the back of his neck. "My girls are eleven, so I ain't got to worry about that yet. But in a few more years, when these young thunder cats come sniffing around, I might have a couple of sidebars while holding a gun my damn self."

Joshua pointed his pool stick at Marcus. "Exactly. Especially if the mama is fine, and the girl looks like her mama. Who Lisa look like?"

Marcus chuckled, "Her moms, for sure."

Mike clasped Marcus on the shoulder. "Sounds like you held your own, though. I'm proud of you."

Joshua leaned over the pool table and prepared to take his shot. "I'm proud of you, too. For a moment there when you said gun, I thought I was gon have to come out of retirement. But the more I think about it, I kind of like this girl's pops."

CHAPTER 80

In the kitchen, the women busied themselves preparing a Friday night feast of epic proportions. Pearl peeled sweet potatoes for the sweet potato whip. Maggie Trendale shucked the corn. Lisa snapped peas. Bella kneaded dough for her famous slap-your-mama-cinnamon-rolls, and Tonya busied herself making her world's famous goat cheese mac and cheese.

The women, who were busy talking and laughing while they worked, grew silent the moment Selena walked into the kitchen.

"Hey, I just came to see if anybody needed my help."

"You can help snap them peas." Pearl said, nodding to the bowl on the table that Lisa was working on.

"Actually, I'm not that great of a cook, but I'm excellent at taste testing. It smells wonderful in here, by the way."

"Explain to me how you were planning on having this pass-the-peace-pipe-meal if you don't even cook?" Bella said.

"The plan was to give the servants my menu because that's something else I do very well, delegating." Selena looked around the kitchen expectantly. "Where are the servants? Other than the guards at the gate, I haven't seen anyone in uniform all evening."

"It's Friday, Selena. Most of the staff have the night off." Tonya said.

"I've been here for plenty of parties on the weekends. Whenever there's a gathering at the house, Mike always requires the staff to work."

"Since this is just supposed to be a small gathering of family and friends, I asked Michael to honor their day off. Is there something in particular that you need? Anything I can help you with?" Tonya said.

"Well, no, but... who is going to serve the food?"

"Child, please." Maggie Trendale muttered. Pearl sucked her teeth. And Tonya unconsciously slipped into using what Bella referred to as her therapist voice, and what Michael and Joshua called her, I'm-speaking-to-an-absolute-idiot-right-now-voice.

"Well, for starters, Selena, since there are just a few of us, we are going to be eating in one of the smaller dining rooms. The plan is to set all the food out on platters. That way, everyone can self-select what they would like to eat and serve themselves." Tonya wiped her hands on the apron she was wearing. "If you'd still like to help, you can choose the dishes and service ware and set the table."

"Yeah, I don't think so. Like I said, I'm good at supervising and taste-testing. That's what I bring to the table. Cooking, at least in the kitchen, is really not my thing."

Pearl sat the knife down hard on the cutting board. "Lord, Jesus, please come take this wheel!"

Tonya cleared her throat. "As you can see, Selena, we are still in the middle of preparing the meal, so neither of your skill sets is of particular use to us right now."

Selena tossed her hair over her shoulder.

"Okay, well, in that case, I guess I'll go see what the guys are up to."

"Yeah, you do that, homey." Bella said, glaring at her departing back.

CHAPTER 81

Mike looked up from the pool table to see Selena standing in the doorway of the game room. "Hey, baby, what's up?"

"Would you mind terribly if I stayed in here and watched you guys play?"

"Not terribly. But the whole point of this little gathering in the first place was so you could bury the hatchet with the ladies. Shouldn't you be in the kitchen making peace with them?"

"I tried, but Tonya said, and this is pretty much a direct quote, that she didn't need my kind of help."

Pearl took a deep breath and turned her attention to Lisa. "Now that Sister Satan is gone, we can get on with polite conversation. You're very pretty, Lisa. I like your spirit."

"Thank you, Ms. Pearl."

"Oh, no need to thank me. It's true. The fact that he brought you home in the first place tells me that my grandson really cares for you. How do you feel about him?"

"The feeling is mutual. I care for Marcus deeply. We've only been dating officially now for about six months or so, but in that time, we've gotten very close."

"And when you say close, exactly how close do you mean? Holding hands close, swapping spit close, or rubbing body parts together close?"

Tonya gasped.

"Pearl, you talking about polite conversation? That question is nowhere near polite." Maggie said.

Bella shook her head. "Plead the fifth, Lisa. Plead the fifth."

Lisa wiped her hands on the dishtowel in front of her. "No, it's okay, really. This is the abstinence talk, right? Marcus prepared me for this." Lisa held out her left hand to Pearl and showed her the pink diamond. "My daddy gave me this when I turned twelve. It's a promise ring. It will remain on my finger until my husband replaces it with a wedding ring. So, to answer your question, Ms. Pearl, Marcus and I hold hands, and we do swap spit. But the rubbing of body parts together is exclusively reserved for the man who replaces this promise ring."

Mike had just missed his shot when he felt his cellphone vibrating. He set the cue stick down on the edge of the table and pulled his phone from his pocket. "Caesar, what's up?"

"You asked for eyes but not ears on the women this afternoon."

"Yeah." Mike glanced over at Selena, knowing that a fight couldn't have broken out, seeing as the source of contention was right here in the room with him.

"Take a look at camera three."

"Marcus, turn to station three." Mike called over his shoulder.

Marcus grabbed the remote and flipped to station three. An image of the storage room right off the kitchen came up on the screen. Tonya had dragged a dining room chair into the storage room. She set two boxes on top of the chair and was now attempting to climb up onto her makeshift ladder.

Joshua stared up at the screen. "That's at least a twelve- foot drop. What in the hell does she think she's doing?"

"I figured you could get to her a lot quicker than I could." Caesar said.

"Good looking out." Mike ended the call and darted from the room.

CHAPTER 82

Jeeves, Mike's Steward of the House, and Mike both ran into the dining room from different directions.

"Mademoiselle, please come down from there at once!"

"I've got her, Jeeves." Mike said as he lifted Tonya up into his powerful arms.

"Mademoiselle, you must never do that again. It is very dangerous."

"I was looking for the dishes with the Dutton House crest on them."

"If you need something, you must remember to press the call button."

"But it's your day off, and I didn't want to disturb you."

"Mademoiselle, if you were to fall and injure yourself, it would not only cause me great lament but also as the manager of this fine estate, it would be my personal duty to see to your care."

"Let me translate that for you, Jeeves." Mike said. "A three hour wait with you in the emergency room tonight would ruin everybody's day off."

"Thank you, sir. I will attend to the plates. They are no longer housed here. We use them mostly for large state dinners, so I had them moved to the formal dining room." Jeeves turned and exited the room.

Tonya bit her lip. "I guess I should have probably checked the other dining room first."

Mike frowned down at her. "I'm right down the hall. Josh, Marcus, Walter, all right down the hall. What were you thinking?"

"That I didn't want to disturb you and your company."

Mike studied Tonya for a beat. He knew she wasn't referring to either Josh or Walter as his company. One because Walter and Maggie were darn near family, and two, because of the way she had just rolled her eyes and drew out the word, company.

When Selena first proposed this little dinner party, Mike's Holy Ghost indicator light had flashed BAD IDEA, in big bold letters across his heart. But Selena had been so geeked about it. And she was right; he hadn't made her a priority since Tonya's return. And it was just a party to clear the air between his two best girls, right? How bad could it be? Staring into Tonya's big, brown, accusatory eyes right now, Mike realized just how bad of an idea this really was.

"That was a foolish and reckless move, Blackbird. You're neither one of those things. So, you want to tell me what's going on?"

"How did Jeeves even know what I was doing in the first place?"

"My guess is that he saw the whole thing play out on the security camera upstairs, just like Caesar did before he notified me."

Tonya folded her arms across her chest, "You have Caesar monitoring me?"

"It's a party. We have unknown factors inside the house tonight. Caesar is monitoring everybody."

"Well, it wasn't reckless. I weighted the boxes down. I wasn't going to fall. Besides, I do that all the time at my place."

Mike's face clouded with anger. "Well, don't. If you need something that you can't reach, call me."

Tonya shook her head. "What if you're not around, Michael? What if it's the middle of the night and you're on a hot date? I'm just supposed to what? Wait forever? How long am I supposed to wait for you to come along and do what I can clearly figure out for myself?"

Mike stared up at the ceiling and released a heavy sigh. Painfully aware that they weren't even arguing about the boxes on top of the chair anymore. This fight wasn't even about Selena. This fight, the one they were having right now, was about any woman at any time who would dare to stand in the place where only she belonged. Mike spoke to the voice activated camera on the wall above their heads and disabled the feed. "Camera off." He walked towards Tonya, closing the gap between them, forcing her back up against the wall. She blinked rapidly, like a deer caught in headlights, as Mike placed two large hands against the wall and caged her in. He leaned in close, close enough to catch a whiff of the alluring lavender and vanilla scent that he loved, close enough to kiss her. He was just about to do that... kiss her, but he stopped himself short because his Holy Ghost indicator light was telling him that kissing her right now with his girlfriend down the hall would be a very bad idea. Mike bit down hard on his bottom lip instead.

"Let me repeat myself, since we seem to have some sort of communication problem. I don't care what time of the day or night it is. I don't care who I'm with. If you need something, anything at all that's outside of your reach, I'll come running to you. I don't care if I'm married, in the bed, about to do the wild thang with my wife. If you need something, anything at all, and it's not within your reach, you call me. I'll come running to you. No. More. Standing. On. Boxes. Is that clear enough for you, Blackbird?"

Tonya's face flushed. "Yes, crystal."

"And do we ever have to have this conversation again?"

Tonya shook her head, "No. Message received."

Mike's eyes roamed lazily over her form, causing her to squirm beneath his gaze. "I'm starving. Is that food ready yet?"

"Um, yeah, I just, I need to set everything out on the table."

Mike released the cage that had been his arms. "Good, me and the guys will help you."

CHAPTER 94

Tonya and Mike entered the smaller family size dining room and found the table already set. The place cards on the table, along with the linen napkins folded to perfection, said that Jeeves had already determined everyone's seating arrangements. Mike called the guys from the game room and everyone made quick work of going back and forth to the kitchen and getting the food out on the dining room table.

Joshua walked into the kitchen and lifted the casserole dish out of Tonya's hand. "You sure this is going to be enough?" he said, staring at the bubbly brown crust of her world-famous mac and cheese.

"Should be. There are two more casserole dishes like this one in the warming oven."

"And?"

"And, since I know it's one of your favorites, I already set aside a pan for you and Bella to take home."

Joshua dropped a quick kiss on her cheek. "My girl. By the way, how are your sparring lessons going?"

Tonya resisted the urge to roll her eyes. "Barely tolerable."

"Good. That means it's hard. I saw the footage of your little climbing expedition in the storage room a few moments ago. I'mma forgo the lecture this time, since you made me my personal pan of mac and cheese, but you need to remember that you aren't twelve anymore."

"Got it, Josh, no more standing on boxes."

Joshua strolled towards the kitchen door. "My girl."

"Hey, Josh? If I throw in a pan of sweet potato whip and duck legs, can we consider lessons with Caesar over and done with?"

"Nope. Sparring lessons will continue until I receive a report back from Caesar saying that you know how to properly throw a punch."

CHAPTER 84

Selena sat at the dinner table that night thinking of all the ways this evening had already gone drastically wrong. It was supposed to be a dinner party thrown by *her*, in honor and acceptance of her man's *best friend*. She, the girlfriend, was supposed to have been the bigger person. But Selena had been outmaneuvered. As it had turned out, Miss Goody Two Shoes wasn't so naïve after all. She had boot ganged Selena's party. Now, Selena had been cast in the role of interloper, while Tonya played the part of the altruistic friend. And that stunt she had pulled in the storage room, standing on top of boxes, causing Mike to have to run to her rescue—*pure genius*. Mike had literally taken off from the game room in a sprint. What she wanted to say, really, really, really, wanted to say, as she and the others stood by watching the silent video feed of Mike in the storage room rescuing Tonya, was, 'turn the daggone volume up!' But before she could figure out a way to say this, without appearing insecure or worst yet, crazy, the screen went blank. Now, thinking of Mike and Tonya alone in the storage room together was making her blood boil.

The dinner conversation had flip-flopped five times already, from academics to sports, then back to academics again. Neither topic particularly interested Selena. Everyone seemed overjoyed that the boy, Marcus, had finally decided on a major. This, of course, made absolutely no sense to Selena. It wasn't like the boy *needed* college. Mike had adopted him, and until she gave him some legitimate heirs of his own, Marcus was the sole heir to Mike Dutton's fortune. Marcus's girlfriend, a cute but mousy girl-next-door-type named Lisa, talked about her passion for International Children's Law. Her and Miss-Goody-Two-Shoes practically monopolized the conversation with that topic for the entire night. Apparently, Tonya had spent some time overseas working against the illegal trafficking of children and unfair child labor laws. *Blah, Blah, Blah, Blah.*

Selena ate her duck and whipped sweet potatoes in silence. All the men around the table took turns praising the women effusively for the delicious food. They even praised Little Miss Goody Two Shoes Junior, Lisa, and all the girl had done really was snap a few string beans.

Mike looked over at Selena expectantly, willing her silently to offer the women some words of praise as well. But the only words she could muster were a variation of the same thought she had been turning over in her head since the TV screen in the game room went blank. *Why is this girl here, and where on earth is her man?*

"Tonya, how's your fiancé? It must be hard for him with you moving back to Houston."

An awkward silence fell across the dinner table.

Selena looked around the room. "I didn't say anything wrong, did I?"

"Ted and I broke up, Selena."

Selena blinked hard. "What? No! You can't. I mean... I'm so sorry for your loss."

"Don't be. I'm good." Tonya said with a thin smile.

"Wow, you two were together for so long. Was it a mutual decision to part ways?"

"I'd rather not talk about it right now, Selena. Especially at dinner. If you don't mind?"

"Of course. I get it. I didn't mean to pry. It's just that Mike and I have been together for a long time too, but when it comes to you, his best friend in the universe, sometimes I feel completely out of the loop."

Tonya's watch dog, Bella, didn't miss the opportunity to clap back.

"Ever think that maybe you don't know because you don't need to know? Personal info is just that, personal." Bella said.

Joshua shifted in his chair and grunted.

Selena ignored Bella and pressed on. "All I'm saying is—"

That's when Mike cut her off. "You asked. She said she didn't want to talk about it. So just leave it at that, baby."

Selena looked at Tonya, then over at Bella, who was smugly staring back. *Yep, pure genius. Nicely played witches.*

CHAPTER 85

Joshua stood in the master bathroom brushing his teeth next to a silent and obviously angry Bella, who was also preparing herself for bed. He was tired, and he did not know why his wife was upset, but the two of them had made a commitment to each other five years ago at their vow renewal ceremony to never go to bed harboring anger towards each other. With a wife as strong willed and stubborn as Bella was, that sometimes meant the occasional sleepless night, nevertheless, they'd kept this vow. Joshua rinsed his mouth and dried his face. He walked over and stood behind his brooding wife in the mirror. Placing his hands on her hips, he dropped a soft kiss on the contour of her jaw. "You haven't said two words since we left my brother's this evening. You want to talk about it?" He murmured.

"She is such a heifer."

Joshua breathed a hard sigh of relief and dropped his head to her shoulder. "Oh good, for a minute there I thought you were mad at me."

Bella's eyes met his in the mirror. "You don't mind my being angry with Selena?"

"I don't particularly like you being angry, period, baby. But if you are angry, better her than me."

"Did you see how she continually tried to front Tonya off at dinner tonight? 'For someone who doesn't live here, you sure know where a lot of things belong.'" Bella mocked, in an almost perfect imitation of Selena. "And if she would have brought that douchebag Ted's name up one more time, I swear I was going to jump across that table and pull her larynx out of her throat."

Joshua turned his wife around and pulled her into his arms. "Naw, see, that's exactly what we don't do anymore, PDA."

Bella rolled her eyes. "I don't know what you're talking about, Josh. We do PDA all the time."

"Public displays of affection, yeah, but not public displays of aggression. Baby, you can't pull that woman's larynx out of her throat."

Bella pouted, "Why not?"

Joshua ran his finger across her lips. "Because you're a new creature in Christ and the old Bella has passed away."

"You're right. I am a new creature in Christ, but Josh, trust and believe, I still ride hard for my family, though."

"I know." Joshua said as he kissed her lips softly, "That's one of the things I love best about you."

Bella's eyes lit up. "What if I snatch her larynx out real quick and then repent afterwards?"

Joshua frowned. "You can't repent if the action is premeditated, baby. You'd have to pre-pent."

Bella chewed her bottom lip. "Yeah, I guess you're right."

"You know I'm right." Joshua stared down at his wife. "I want you to stay out of this, okay?"

"Okay." she said quickly. Too quickly.

"Bella, I'm serious. We've got enough drama in our own lives. Let them find their own way. If Mike and Tonya are meant to be together, then—"

"How can you say that? Selena is not right for him, in no form, shape, or fashion. Josh, didn't you see the two of them together tonight?"

"I did."

"Tonya is the wife of his youth. Those two are a perfect fit. How could you not see that?"

"Okay, what I see is that if we continue this conversation, you and me are about to be in a full-blown argument over somebody else's life. I love my brother. I love my sister. I want God's best for them both. You know this. But you and me fighting over their problems, that ain't the vision. I'm tired, Bella. All I want to do right now is to go to bed and make love to my wife. You feel me?"

"Yes, I do and I want that too, but—"

"But nothing. If you really believe that they are meant to be together, then pray about it, Bella. Prayer still works."

CHAPTER 86

AT 6 AM THE next morning, Serenity climbed out of her bed and padded down the hall to her parents' bedroom. She opened the door to the master suite and climbed up onto the enormous four-poster bed, injecting herself into the small space between her parents. In her sleep, Bella shifted to accommodate their daughter.

Serenity turned to her father, her head laying against his pillow, "Morning, Daddy."

Joshua didn't open his eyes, but a smile played across his lips, "Morning, Wildflower."

"Guess what today is, Daddy?"

"Saturday."

"Guess what else today is?"

"What?"

"It's Suri Day."

Silence.

"Did you hear me, Daddy? I said it's Suri Day."

One eye popped open. "My Suri Day or Uncle Mike's Suri Day?" Joshua asked groggily.

"Uncle Mike's Suri Day."

"Oh, good."

"Don't you like Suri Day anymore, Daddy?"

Joshua pulled Serenity close and kissed the top of her head. "I love Suri Day, baby. I invented it, remember?" He yawned. "I'm just glad I didn't forget."

Bella rolled over, pulled the covers up over her head, and groaned in protest. Just like with every other Suri Day, Serenity was up at the crack of dawn.

"Today we are going to go to *House of Bounce*, and *Pizza Time*."

"Sounds like fun."

"I think I'm going to let Auntie Tonya come with us this time."

"I thought you had a-no-mommy-no- girlfriends- allowed rule."

"I'm going to make an objection."

"You mean an exception."

"Yeah." Serenity lowered her voice to what she thought was a whisper, "Mommy can't go anymore cause she's always saying 'no' and 'too much'. No candy, too much sugar, no pizza, too much cheese."

Bella's muffled voice came from under the cover. "You realize I can hear you, right?"

Joshua chuckled, "It wasn't just Mommy, you didn't like it much when Ms. Selena came along either, remember?"

Serenity slapped her palm against her forehead. "Ugh, she was the worst!" Serenity was quiet for a while. In the silence, Joshua drifted back to sleep.

"Daddy?"

"Huh?"

"Is Auntie Tonya Uncle Mike's girlfriend?"

"I don't think anybody really knows the answer to that question, baby, including your Uncle Mike."

"I hope she is. I like her so much better than Sister Satan."

"Who?"

"Sister Satan." Serenity said, clearly exasperated that her daddy wasn't following along in the conversation.

Bella yanked the cover from over her head. "Okay, that's enough talking to Daddy this morning. Suri, why don't you go back to your room and pick out what you're going to wear for Suri Day?"

Joshua sat up in bed, now fully awake. "Let her answer my question first, Bella. Who are you talking about, Suri?"

"Ms. Selena."

"Why would you call her that? That's not very nice."

Serenity's face dropped. She stared down at the sheet, sensing the subtle change in her daddy's mood.

"Serenity, look at me. Why would you say something like that?"

"I don't like it when you're mad at me."

"I'm not mad. I'm just trying to understand why you would call her that."

Serenity shrugged. "Everybody calls her that."

"Oh, boy." Bella muttered.

Joshua stared at Bella over Serenity's head. "Everybody like who? Mommy?"

Serenity looked back and forth between her parents. "No Daddy, Mommy wouldn't say that. Mommy calls her, 'that fake heifer.'"

"Yeah, not really helping, baby." Bella said, shrinking beneath Joshua's gaze.

"Auntie Katie, Granny P, and Grandma Mel call her Sister Satan."

"My mom calls her that?" Joshua asked incredulously.

"Un huh, but you can't tell them I told, Daddy. If they know I know who they're talking about, nobody will ever say anything interesting around me again. Can I go pick out my outfit for Suri Day now, please?"

CHAPTER 87

Selena reached across the bed and grabbed the ringing phone. She smiled when she heard Mike's deep, melodious voice on the other end of the receiver. She couldn't remember the last time she'd had the pleasure of hearing his voice two days in a row. Whenever it had been, it had definitely been before Tonya's return.

"Hey, beautiful, you ready for tennis?"

Oh crap, she had forgotten about that. They had made plans to meet for tennis weeks ago, the night he'd taken her out for dinner. "Can I have an hour?"

"Sorry, babe. I've got a tight schedule this morning. It's Suri Day."

"Of course. How could I forget?" Selena said, trying to mask the venom in her voice. "I must have overslept."

"We can always hook up later, if you're tired."

"No. I stayed up late last night preparing a legal brief for my boss. Are you kidding me? I've been looking forward to this all week. I don't want to cancel. I can be ready in ten. You wanna call and I'll just come down?"

"Alright, baby, see you in ten."

Selena ended the call. She rolled over in bed and let out a string of curses at the man with the purple hair and tattoos running up and down his arms, neck and face. She snatched the pillow from underneath his head and beat him with it. "You slept over? Get up, now! My boyfriend is on his way. He will kill you if he finds you here!"

CHAPTER 88

Tonya looked at Michael and Serenity standing on her front porch. "I am very honored to be invited, because I know that Suri Days are very important. It's your special time to hang out with your uncle and your dad. I wouldn't want to impose."

"You won't if you can follow the rules." Serenity said.

"Okay, what are the rules?"

Serenity looked up at her uncle, who was holding her tiny hand in his much larger one.

"What happens on Suri Day stays on Suri Day." Mike said.

Serenity nodded her head in agreement, "We don't talk about it ever. I get to say whatever I want with no judging."

"That's fair. I can agree to that. Are there anymore rules?"

"Just one more. It's a pretty hard one for adults. Mommy has a real hard time with this one. That's why she can't come to Suri Day anymore. I get to eat whatever I want even if it makes me sick. Some things are worth the tummy ache."

"Okay, it's your stomach."

Tonya, Mike and Serenity spent the whole day at House of Bounce. They even took a break and got their hands stamped, went for lunch and came back. At lunch, Mike ordered a cheeseburger and fries. Tonya ordered a Cobb salad, and Serenity declared in a voice that said she dared Tonya to object, that she would have a large plate of fries and a triple decker banana split sundae. "I'll have my dessert first, please." Serenity said sweetly to the server.

Serenity was so exhausted she could barely walk to the car when they left the House of Bounce that evening.

"I had a great time with you today." Tonya said as she assisted Serenity into her booster seat. "I'd like to have my own Suri Day someday soon."

Serenity yawned. "I gotta look at my schedule. Maybe I can figure out a way to add you in." She yawned again. "Can you drop me off first, Uncle Mike? I'm so sleepy."

"You got it, baby."

And just like that, Serenity was out like a light. Twenty minutes later, Mike carried a sleeping Serenity to the Keys front door and handed her off to Joshua. Tonya followed behind him carrying the gigantic bag of toys and stuff animals Mike had won for Serenity at the House of Bounce.

"So, how was everything?" Bella said as she took the bag from Tonya.

Tonya grinned sheepishly at her friend. "I'm so sorry, Bella, but I'm not at liberty to say. Suri rules."

"Girl, don't tell me you've gone and drank the Kool-Aid too?"

"I can't help it, Bella. I mixed it, poured it and drank it. She's so frigging adorable."

Mike and Joshua both laughed, and Bella shook her head.

On the ride back to the mansion, Mike couldn't help but compare the day that he and Tonya had just spent with Serenity to the one and only time Selena had tagged along on a Suri Day. Whereas today could be filed in the category of unprecedented success. The latter could be filed under epic failure. Tonya loved children. It was clear in everything she did, and they loved her too. Selena barely tolerated children. She had made it clear that she was in it for the long haul, that she wanted forever; but there was no way he could even conceive of forever with a woman who loved him and only tolerated his family.

Mike glanced over at Tonya. "You were great with her today. Thank you."

Tonya gave him a stank eye. Mike resisted the urge to laugh.

"You can't thank me. Suri is my niece, and goddaughter too."

"I know."

"Even if she wasn't, it's pretty hard not to fall in love with her. She's such an amazing child." Tonya stared out the window at the passing landscape. "I hate that I've missed so much time with her and the boys."

"Well, you're here now. No better time like the present to catch up. FYI, she doesn't always order like that. I think she just did it to test you."

"Did I pass?"

Mike chuckled, "For a minute there, you looked like you wanted to arm wrestle that ice cream sundae spoon out of her hand, but, yeah, you passed."

CHAPTER 89

MIKE, TONYA, JOSHUA, AND Bella had just been seated at their table when Selena approached them in the restaurant.

"Well, don't the four of you look cozy?"

Bella rolled her eyes.

Mike rose from his seat next to Tonya at the table and kissed Selena on the cheek. "I thought you had a work thing tonight?"

"We did, or at least we thought we did. The client was a no show." The man standing beside Selena said.

"This is Alvin, my co-worker. Alvin meet my boyfriend, Mike Dutton. His brother, Joshua Keys. Joshua's better half, Bella. And Tonya is... what shall I call you? An old family friend?"

Alvin pulled Bella's hand to his lips and kissed it. "I've watched your wedding at least a dozen times."

"Why?" Joshua said.

Alvin grinned. "My daughter considers it a cult classic. She thinks Bella is more beautiful than all the Disney princesses put together. I'll have to tell her you are even more lovely in person."

"That's sweet. Please, tell her thank you for me." Bella said, extricating her hand from Alvin's and returning it to her own lap.

Alvin turned to Tonya and reached out his hand. "Tonya, I feel like I already know you. Lena has told me so much about you."

"I don't see how that's possible when she knows nothing about me." Tonya said.

"I just told him you were single." Selena added quickly.

"Yes, but she left out the part about you being breathtakingly beautiful."

Tonya smiled at the man, pumped his weak hand and, like Bella, she also returned her hand to her lap.

Alvin turned his attention to Mike and Joshua, who were both now studying him with stony faces. Alvin bowed low. "The Man of Steel needs no introduction, neither does the legendary Bad Boy Joshua Keys. It's truly an honor to meet you both. I'm humbled to be in the presence of such greatness."

Silence.

"Maybe your client is just running late. You should go check." Bella said.

"Trust me, beautiful, this guy is a no show. And we were so looking forward to eating here, weren't we, Lena? On the salary they pay us, we certainly couldn't afford to eat here. Our boss is very cheap."

Selena nodded. "I've been sipping water for over an hour. I'm practically starving."

"Tell you what, my man, why don't you and Selena stay and enjoy the food? I'm sure you have some business to discuss. Let your server know your meal is on me." Mike said.

"Wow, that's very generous of you."

"Actually, we're done for the evening. Do you mind if we just join you?" Selena said.

Mike's gaze landed on Tonya first, then Bella. "Blackbird?"

"I don't mind."

"Bella, baby, you cool?"

"Sure." Bella said tightly. "The more the merrier."

Selena beamed. "That's the spirit, Bella." She flagged a server. "Can you add two more chairs to this round table over here, please?"

"Right away, ma'am."

"I'm going to sit by my man. And Alvin, how about you squeeze in between Tonya and Bella?"

"It would be my pleasure to sit between these two lovely queens." Alvin said, giving Tonya the once over.

Joshua slid Bella's chair closer to him. He lifted the hair off her shoulders and planted a kiss at the base of her neck.

Bella tilted her head backwards and stared into his eyes. "What?"

"Be nice."

"Why?"

Joshua leaned in close and whispered something that only she could hear. Bella grinned. "You should have led with that. I'll be on my best behavior."

Alvin stared at Joshua and Bella. "Now that's exactly what I want, what the two of you have, an enduring, timeless love. Tonya, what about you?"

Tonya, who was clearly not following along in the conversation, looked up at Alvin. "What?"

"Are you looking for love?"

"Not particularly, no."

"Tonya just had a breakup." Selena explained.

"Which we aren't going to talk about tonight." Mike added firmly.

"This is so serendipitous. I did not know you guys were eating here." Selena said.

Bella opened her mouth, then closed it quickly when Joshua tugged on a lock of her hair.

"I thought I mentioned our dinner plans to you the other night?" Mike said.

Selena shook her head. "Nope, or at least I don't remember if you did."

"So, Tonya, what's your story? Where are you from?"

"Nothing to tell. I was born and raised in Dallas. Went to school in New York, recently moved for my job. That's me in a nutshell."

"Tonya's being modest." Selena said. "I doubt your life could fit into a nutshell. Tonya moved to Houston after a horrible breakup."

"Which we aren't talking about tonight." Mike said again.

Alvin nodded, "I agree. We should steer our conversation to much happier topics. I, for one, would much rather hear about this beautiful angel sitting beside me than the fool who couldn't appreciate her."

Tonya placed her palms on the table. "Okay. Wow."

Mike stared at Alvin for a beat.

"I'm going to the restroom." Tonya announced, "Bella, you want—"

"I'm right behind you."

"You two know what you want to order?" Joshua asked.

Bella and Tonya both shook their heads.

"Actually, I have something in mind for the both of you. Let me do the honors." Mike said.

"Ooh, can you order for me too?" Selena said.

"Of course. I got you."

Selena kissed Mike's cheek and stood up from the table. "Thank you. Ladies, wait up. I'm coming with you."

Mike watched as the women walked away from the table. Then he turned his attention to Alvin. "I'mma tell you this one time and one time only, bruh, fall back."

"Excuse me?"

"You heard my brother, man. You coming on way too strong and the lady obviously isn't feeling you. Pump your breaks." Joshua said.

"No disrespect, fellas. This is just the way I do it. When I see something I want, especially a beautiful lady. I go for it."

The server appeared at the table. "I see the ladies have left. Do you need a little more time, sirs, before you order?"

"No, let's get this circus over and done with." Joshua said.

Ten minutes later, the server arrived and began setting the steaming hot plates of food onto the table.

"Grilled sea bass for the lady." He said, setting the plate down in front of Tonya. The server looked at Mike. "Absolutely no onions or scallions in the sauce. We also prepared her meal on a separate grill in the back, so there would be no chance of contamination."

"Thank you, Michael. This looks delicious." Tonya said.

The server set a plate down in front of Bella. "Seafood medley for you, ma'am."

"This smells amazing." Bella said. "Thank you, Mike."

Mike winked at Bella. "I knew you'd like it."

"And the lobster risotto for you, ma'am." The server said as he set the hot, steaming plate in front of Selena.

"Lena, I thought you were allergic to shellfish?" Alvin said.

Selena frowned down at her plate. "Yeah, deadly."

"Sorry, my bad. I was on a seafood kick tonight. Totally forgot about that. Take that back and make her a chicken and mushroom risotto, please." Mike told the server.

"No problem, sir. That's an excellent choice. I will have that right out."

Bella stared at Selena. "Can I ask you why you would choose to come to a seafood restaurant if you're deadly allergic to shellfish?"

"Well, I think I already told you, Bella, we came here to meet a client."

"You did. I just thought you'd give us an honest answer this time."

Mike cleared his throat. "Josh, bless the food, please." Joshua did. The server returned with Selena's food and everyone ate in uncomfortable silence for the rest of the meal.

"Tonya, would you mind terribly if I take you home tonight?" Alvin said.

Tonya's head snapped up. "What?"

"I'm asking if I can drive you back to your place tonight. You know, give these two lovebirds a little privacy. It's just that day in and day out. I have to listen to Lena complain about how busy her boyfriend is. How she never gets to hang out with him these days since his best friend has come back to town. So,

I figured, I could drop you by your place. We could talk, get to know each other a little better."

"That sounds like a plan to me." Selena said quickly.

"Not to me, it doesn't." Tonya said. "Josh, can you drop me off on your way home?"

Joshua fixed his glare on Alvin. "You know I got you."

Mike was glaring at Alvin, too. "Nah, Tonya's riding with me. Everybody's going home tonight the same way they came."

Tonya gathered her purse and rose from the table. "I'll be outside."

"I'm right behind you." Bella said. She grabbed her purse, shot a nasty look at Selena, and followed Tonya out of the restaurant.

Joshua met his brother's eyes across the table.

"You breezy, bro?"

"Like a Sunday morning, Josh."

Joshua nodded. "I'll go handle the bill then. See you outside."

"I don't get it, man. You have this gorgeous woman sitting beside you. All she wants to do is spend a little time with you. If she were mine—"

Mike stared into Selena's now teary eyes. "But she's not yours. Are you, Selena?"

Alvin looked at Selena and then back at Mike again. "Hey, no. Come on, man. Don't be ridiculous. Selena wants you. I want Tonya."

Mike stood and dropped two hundred dollars on the table for the server. "You're way out of your league, son. You should quit while you can still walk out of here on your own steam."

Alvin stood. Selena tugged unsuccessfully at Alvin's coat sleeve, trying to get him to sit back down.

"If Tonya's just a friend like you claim, you won't have a problem with me shooting my shot."

"Like I said, you better fall back, fool. Tonya is mine." Mike growled.

Selena's head whipped back around to stare at Mike. "She's your what?"

Mike stared down at Selena as if seeing her for the first time. "I don't like games, *Lena*. You and I will talk later."

CHAPTER 90

WHEN MIKE EXITED THE restaurant, he didn't say one word. He nodded to Joshua and Bella, tipped the valet, placed one large hand on the small of Tonya's back and led her to the waiting car. Tonya stared out the window as Michael raced down the freeway. His anger was so tangible it was like a third passenger in the vehicle. Still, she knew him well enough to keep quiet. He needed to talk. She hoped he would, but words from her at this point would be combustible. Like the striking of a match in the presence of gasoline.

So, she did the same thing she used to do when they were children. Quietly waited for him to initiate the conversation. While she waited, Tonya prayed. Because when Michael got angry, really, really, angry, the worst thing in the world was for him to go silent. Silence meant he was imploding.

"I'm sorry about tonight. You shouldn't have had to deal with that." Mike said after a good twenty minutes into their drive. "I'mma cancel her."

Tonya released a breath she didn't even realize she'd been holding. "Michael, you don't call off a five-year relationship because of one bad night. I think you should sleep on this. In the morning, you'll see things differently."

"Do you even know how close I came to catching a case tonight?"

"Over that guy? No, he was so not worth it. He was annoying. And he didn't understand the concept of boundaries but—"

Mike hit the steering wheel. "Exactly. No boundaries."

"Yeah, but didn't he kind of remind you of a black Stuart, though?"

Tonya was obviously trying to lighten the mood. She couldn't have known it, but bringing up Stuart, their idiot childhood neighbor, who had put Bella on Joshua's barely tame horse, Lady, and almost gotten her killed, was not the thing Mike needed to lighten the mood. It only served to remind him of another time that he'd been angry enough to do bodily harm to someone.

Mike stared at her in the moonlight. "If I would have given into the impulse to hit him just once, I don't think I could have stopped myself. I could have killed that man, Tonya. And for what? Because I didn't like the way he stepped to you? What are we doing here, Blackbird?"

She wasn't anywhere near ready to answer that question, so the only thing left for Tonya to do was to avoid and redirect.

Tonya laid a soothing hand on Mike's wrist. At least she hoped it was soothing. "Let's forget about Alvin for a second, okay? Because seriously, Michael, he is a non-factor. Not worth catching a case over, not worth going to jail over."

"Prison."

"Yeah, Stuart 2.0, definitely not worth all of that. I think the real problem here is that your girlfriend feels threatened by me. She went to great lengths just to 'accidentally' bump into us at that restaurant tonight."

"I told you, it's handled. She's canceled."

"Michael, before you do that, I think you should try to see the situation from her point of view. Don't forget, I know what it's like to star in the role of insecure girlfriend when it comes to you."

The large metal gates opened for them automatically as Mike drove onto his property. "When did you join Selena's fan club?"

"Oh, trust and believe, I am not a fan. But I don't want to be the cause of your breakup, either. Promise me you'll sleep on it?"

Mike remained quiet as he followed the long, winding road that cut through his property. He pulled up in front of Tonya's cottage, killed the engine, walked around to the passenger side and got her door. When she got out of the car, Tonya spoke again. "Michael—"

"I heard you."

CHAPTER 91

SELENA AND ALVIN LAID in bed together naked, passing a joint back and forth. Alvin took a pull and blew out a plume of smoke. "Breaking those two up is going to be a lot harder than you think. He knows we're together, by the way."

"They're not together." Selena took one last pull from the joint. She deposited it into the astray on the bedside table and straddled Alvin. "And we're not together."

"What's the safe word tonight?"

"Mike Dutton."

Alvin pushed her back onto the bed and stood up. "I'm going home."

"Alvin, wait."

"You think you gon call your punk a@$ man's name while you're in bed with me?"

"I was kidding, Alvin. Come back."

Alvin sat on the edge of the bed and stared into Selena's glossy eyes.

She crawled over to him on all fours. "I'm sorry, alright? I'm high. It was a joke. You can choose the safe word."

Alvin gripped her chin hard. "Tonya." He hissed. "That's the safe word. When I'm choking and screwing you within an inch of your life, that's the name you'll invoke from now on."

Selena yanked her face from his grip. "Fine, I'll play your little game for one night but—"

"That's the safe word from now on. You'll play my way from here on out or we won't play anymore. You want these twelve inches, right?"

Selena nodded her head slowly.

"That won't work, and you know it. I'm an officer of the court. I need to hear your verbal consent."

Selena mumbled a yes under her breath.

"Louder, sweetheart, so that the camera can hear you."

Selena's gaze flew frantically around the room.

Alvin laughed, "Relax, just getting you back for that Mike Dutton crack. Trust me, when I record us, we'll both know and enjoy it."

Alvin adjusted himself against the headboard. He grunted loudly as Selena impaled herself on top of him. "So, if we're not together? What do you call this?"

Selena picked up the discarded tie Alvin had worn to dinner that evening and began securing his right hand to the headboard. "I call this scratching an itch."

"Your girl wasn't feeling me at all tonight. Not even a little. It's not normal for a heterosexual woman to resist my charms. Not unless she already has a man. Even if she does have a man." Alvin ran his free hand up and down Selena's spine as he grinned devilishly up at her, "You see, you can't resist me."

"Shut up and choke me."

CHAPTER 103

Two weeks later

Selena made the drive to Home Court Advantage and walked the all too familiar route to Mike's office. When his secretary had called her to set up this meeting, Selena had immediately suggested that they meet over lunch, but Vernice had politely explained that the only time Mike had available was a Wednesday morning slot, and even then, all he could spare to give her was a thirty-minute block of time. "I received her messages," is what Vernice said he had said. "Let her know I can meet with her early next week."

So here she was, bright and early, standing in front of his secretary's desk at 8:30 in the frigging morning for her thirty-minute time slot.

"Good morning, Vernice."

"Hello Selena, you can go right on back. He's expecting you."

Mike was sitting at his desk, staring out the large floor to ceiling window that gave an unobstructed view of the Houston skyline. Selena rapped lightly on the open door before entering the room.

"Close the door behind you." Mike said, still staring out the window. Selena noted he didn't rise from his seat to greet her with a kiss like he normally would have.

"The last time I was summoned here, I was fired from Home Court. So, what's up, Mike? Am I being fired?" It probably wasn't the best idea to start off being argumentative with him right out of the gate, but she had been blowing up his cell with her desperate entreaties and the best he could do was to have his secretary pencil her in for thirty minutes of his time. Naw, this was some grade A bull —

Mike nodded to one of the chairs on the other side of his large desk. "Have a seat."

Selena glanced over at the large leather sectional in front of the fireplace. At least when they had fired her, he'd invited her over to the sofa and sat down beside her.

Selena plopped down into the chair. "What's this about?"

"After that little stunt you pulled at the restaurant, I think we need to take a break."

"I see, so I am being fired."

"Let's call it a break."

"So, what does this mean? Are we still exclusive or are we seeing other people? Help me understand, Mike."

"It means you are free to do whatever you like."

"And you can do whatever you like too, right?"

Mike stared at her quietly.

"I see. It always comes back to her."

"No, you don't see. That's the problem. This has nothing to do with Tonya, and everything to do with you and me. If anything, it's because of Tonya that I'm not completely done with you. She thought you might be feeling insecure because of our friendship and that I should try to see this from your perspective."

"She's right, I am completely insecure. I see less and less of you every day while the woman you asked to marry you sees you every day. Because she lives with you."

"You should think of this break as a time of introspection. Ask yourself some hard questions, like why do I want to be with a man I clearly don't trust?"

"Mike, I do trust you. It's just ..." Selena covered her face with her hands and began to sob. "I thought I saw a future with you. I thought we were ready to go to the next level."

Mike rose from his chair and walked over to the floor length window. "Definitely not ready for all of that."

Selena grabbed a Kleenex from the box ontop of his desk and dabbed her eyes. "I can see that now. But my point is, I thought we were. At least I did until she showed up."

"I told you from day one, my family was the most important thing in the world to me. You said you understood that. If there is ever going to be an us, you need to accept every part of me."

He said some other things too, things that, honestly, Selena couldn't remember if she'd tried. She was just so numb.

When Selena left Home Court Advantage thirty minutes later, she could hardly drive because of the tears. Real tears. She felt like someone had punched her in the gut. And the worst part about it was that she hadn't expected anything remotely like this. Instead of heading for work, Selena jumped on the expressway and headed to her cousin's apartment. When Leslie didn't answer the door, Selena used the spare key she had given her in case of emergencies. She let herself into the apartment because this was definitely an emergency. Selena sat down on Leslie's couch, rocking, crying, and moaning, until she fell into a fitful sleep.

CHAPTER 93

LESLIE ARRIVED BACK AT her apartment to find her cousin passed out on her couch. She carried her groceries into the kitchen and returned to the living room to wake Selena. Leslie called her name several times, no answer. She even tried shaking her awake. Finally, after a full two minutes of yelling her name and smacking her face, Selena opened her eyes. Leslie could see that they were red and puffy from crying.

"Hey, cuz, what's up? Why are you here in the middle of the day like this?"

Silence.

"Talk to me. What happened?"

"I lost him, Les. I lost everything. Mike broke up with me."

Damn. The hero? Leslie had expected this from the Bad Boy, but had her simple-minded cousin really lost the hero? "I don't understand. What happened? I thought y'all was about to tie the knot."

"Tonya happened. He says it's not her, but I know it is."

Selena began rocking back and forth, moaning. She knocked her head repeatedly against the back of the couch. "I've lost everything. All our plans they're g-g-gone."

"Calm down, cuz. It's not over, okay? You've invested five years into this relationship, it ain't over. We gon get that man. You hear me? We gon get that man."

"I lose everything if I lose him, Les. Everything."

"You haven't lost anything yet. Just hold on. This is nothing. Nothing a little magic can't fix."

FALL, 1996

CHAPTER 94

DALLAS, TEXAS

"Tonya, what in the world is this?"

"Carrot, beet, and celery juice. It'll boost your immune system. Now drink up."

"Don't you have classes or something? Why are you here in the middle of the week?"

"I told you, Daddy. All my classes are scheduled on Monday, Tuesday and Wednesday. That means I will be here every Thursday until you make a full recovery. So, stop your bellyaching and drink."

"I spoke to Jack earlier today. Mikey's coming home this weekend, too."

"Daddy, I don't want to talk about Michael."

"It's been six months. How long you planning on ignoring that man? We're all getting mighty tired of watching you sit across the dinner table and pretend like you don't see or hear him. It's not his fault, you know. I'm the one who told him not to tell you."

"I said I don't want to talk about this right now."

"And I don't want you hovering all the time, but we don't always get what we want. Do we? He was following my wishes, Tonya."

"Drink, Daddy."

Harold downed the purple juice and wiped his mouth. "This is disgusting."

"More disgusting than gin?"

Barbara walked into the kitchen carrying a load of laundry and caught the tail end of the conversation. She sat the basket down on the kitchen counter. "She's got a point there."

"Will it give me a buzz afterwards?" Harold said, teasing his wife and daughter. Neither one of them had been pleased with the fact that he had continued to drink after his diagnosis. Harold had stopped for a while, but once he'd realized that he was indeed dying, he figured that well, there were so few pleasures left in this short life of his. Gin might as well be one of them.

"Your cells will buzz with life. Daddy, I'm asking God for a miracle for us. But we have to do our part too. This is us doing our part to keep you healthy."

Tonya unplugged the juicer and begin to disassemble it. She took it to the sink to wash it. Barbara took the clean dishtowels out of the laundry basket and placed them inside the kitchen drawer. Her eyes met Harold's one last time before she picked up the basket and walked silently out of the room.

Harold squeezed his eyes shut and prepared to have the hardest conversation of his life. A conversation that was harder than dying of cancer. Cancer was a cakewalk next to having to tell his little girl that he wouldn't be there when she graduated from college. That he wouldn't be the one to walk her down the aisle on her wedding day. That the only time he'd meet his grandchildren was when he'd see them in glory.

"Tonya, come here for a minute."

"Just let me wash this, Daddy. If I don't get it now, the beet juice will stain the juicer."

Why did she have to be such a believer? How come she just couldn't be like everybody else and figure this s@#t out on her own? See the handwriting on the wall?

Because you raised her that way. He thought, in answer to his own question. Forget about whether the glass was half full or half empty, Harold kept Tonya's glass brimming to the top, bubbling over with possibilities her entire life. To protect her innocence, he had let her be naïve in the world for far too long. The girl had actually believed in Santa Claus until she was twelve years old. It was Joshua who had broken the news to her then, the same one who had ripped the band-aid off now. Looking at his daughter, who was genuinely worried about staining a juicer that didn't have a skunk's chance in hell of saving his life, he realized his godson was right. *Damn. Joshua was right.*

"Just let it be for a minute, alright? Let me talk to you. I need to tell you something..." *I need to tell you I'm dying.*

Tonya sighed hard, removed the rubber gloves, and turned to face her father.

Harold patted the chair beside him. "Please, come sit down."

Tonya walked over and sat in the seat beside her dad.

Harold reached out and took her smaller hands in his. He studied her hands for a moment, and just like when she was a baby, he marveled that something so tiny and so perfect could come from him. "You always did have beautiful hands. Doctor hands. Promise me you'll become a doctor no matter what. If you marry Mike, you can take the last name Dutton, but if you marry some other buster, you keep my name: Malone."

Tonya rolled her eyes. "Daddy, just let me clean it off—"

"I won't be there when you graduate, but Jack will be there, and Mike will be too. And Jack, I already worked it out with Jack. He's going to give you away on your wedding day."

"Daddy, no. You just have to have faith. We have to believe."

"I know you've renewed your commitment to Christ, and that's a good thing. You're going to need Him now more than ever when I'm gone. But, baby, I've made my peace with this."

Large beads of sweat dotted his forehead, and the room was spinning out of control. Doing the hard thing was... even harder than he'd expected.

Tonya snatched her hands from Harold's.

"Hear me out, baby girl, please." Harold's words suddenly became thick as molasses.

"No. I won't. It's not God's will for you to be sick."

"Maybe not kiddo, but that doesn't change the fact that I am."

"I won't accept that."

"You have to."

"I can't and I won't!" She stood up abruptly, upsetting her chair in the process.

Harold stood up too, but he felt like he was moving in slow motion. "I should have prepared you a long time ago." He leaned against the table to steady himself. "But I was just trying to protect you."

"Daddy? Daddy!!!!!!"

Tonya ran towards her father. She tried to reach him before his body hit the floor, but it was too late. Harold was gone.

CHAPTER 95

HAROLD OPENED HIS EYES to find himself lying in a hospital bed, a million tubes coming out of his body and a room full of people staring down at him. He took in the faces around the room. Barb and Tonya were here, of course. Jack and Melissa also, as he had expected. But damn it, so were his godsons. Mike wasn't due in until Saturday night, and Joshua had no business being here whatsoever. He may have been the number one draft pick of the season, but this was his rookie year. He needed to get his a%$ back to New Orleans pronto. Harold was just about to tell him this when he heard his sister's voice.

"His eyes are open, but he's not saying nothing. You sure this ain't a stroke?"

Holy mother of God. Katie was here. She was supposed to be in the south of France.

"How long have I been out?" Harold said, with a voice that felt like sandpaper.

"Thank God. Baby, don't talk yet. Let me get you some water." Barbara quickly poured him a cup of water from the pitcher that was beside the bed.

Harold drank the offered water and adjusted himself in the hospital bed to an upright position. "How long?"

"Three days." Jack said.

Harold's gaze landed on Katie. "You took an international flight all the way back from France, a trip you've been saving up for an entire year. I can't tell you how incredibly stupid that was. But I will tell you this, I am not paying for your return ticket." Harold's gaze landed on Joshua, "And you, what the hell are you doing here?"

"Yep, good to see you too, Unc." Joshua said dryly.

"It's your goddamn rookie year, man. You ain't got time for this s#$t! You've got something to prove out there on that court!"

Mike shook his head. "Wow, man. Did you not just hear my dad say that you've been in a coma for the past three days? Where did you think we'd all be?"

"Exactly!" Katie exclaimed. "And did I ask you to pay for my return ticket, you ungrateful jackass?"

"Don't worry about the ticket, Aunt Katie. I got you. First class." Joshua said as he glared at his uncle.

Harold pointed his finger at Joshua, "Oh, Mr. Big Spender here. First class. You should be getting ready for your first game."

"As long as you are in this bed, I don't give a damn about that game."

"Oh, so you don't give a damn, huh? Well, that's just great! Great! You hear this, Jack? We've been working toward this moment his entire life, but he doesn't give a damn!"

"Stop it! Harold, please! I called them. They're all here because I called them."

Harold stared at his wife and the tears that were rolling down her cheeks. "Barb, why would you do that? Katie on her dream vacation. Joshua just starting his dream career. Baby, why —"

"Because the doctor didn't know if you would wake up." Barbara said, choking back a sob.

Melissa, Katie and Tonya moved quickly to Barbara. The three of them wrapping her in a tight hug.

Tonya cooed encouragement to her mother. "No matter what anybody says, Mama, we can't give up hope. Okay?"

"The doc thought we should all be here to say our good-byes." Jack said to Harold.

Harold stared at his wife's back, "Well, he's wrong. I'm not dying today."

"That's the spirit, Daddy." Tonya said, wiping tears from her own eyes.

There was a soft knock on the door, and then the doctor stepped into the room.

"Mr. Malone, you're awake. If I could ask you good folks to step outside for a moment, I'd like to—"

"Whatever you got to say, doc. You can say in front of them. This is my family. No point in keeping secrets now." Harold looked over at Tonya. "I've kept this secret long enough."

The doctor nodded solemnly. "Very well. The cancer has spread to your brain, that's why you passed out. Now that you're awake, I'm going to keep you one more night for observation, but if there is another episode..."

"Spit it out, doctor." Katie said impatiently. "What happens if he has another episode?"

"If you go into cardiac arrest again, I'll need to know whether you want us to resuscitate you."

"What kind of question is that? Of course you resuscitate him. You do everything in your f-#$% power to resuscitate him."

Everyone in the room stared at Tonya.

Harold laughed. "Jack, you hear that?"

"Sure did."

"My daughter just dropped her first f bomb. Sure glad I got the chance to hear that before I died."

"What kind of doctor are you?" Tonya said, the agitation clearly building in her voice. "Why would you even ask such a question?"

Mike started towards her. "Blackbird." Tonya held her hand up to stop him. "Stay away from me."

"I hate to state the obvious, Ms. Malone, but your father is dying. My only goal right now is to keep him comfortable.

Were he to go into cardiac arrest, saving his life could cause unnecessary damage to his organs. I see on my chart here that he is an organ donor. We'd like to preserve his organs the best that we can."

Tonya lunged for the doctor's neck.

"No, you don't." Joshua said, catching Tonya around the waist and lifting her up off the floor.

Barbara gasped. "I'm so sorry, doctor. Please forgive my daughter. This is very hard on all of us. She's not herself today."

Katie glared at the doctor. "You really need to work on your bedside manner."

"Joshua, let me go!"

"Not until he leaves, and you calm down."

"Doctor, please leave. If we need anything else, we know how to reach you." Melissa said curtly.

"Of course, I am sorry. I wish I had better news. But on the bright side, lives will be saved because of Mr. Malone's generous organ donations."

Katie grabbed her purse and moved towards the doctor.

Jack caught Katie's arm. "I think you'd better go, doc. Otherwise, you'll be the one needing that transplant list."

The doctor left the room without another word, closing the door with a soft click.

Barbara looked at both her sister-in-law and her daughter. "What is wrong with you two?"

"I couldn't help it. He got on my last nerve." Katie muttered.

"He got on my nerves too, Katie, but we can't be bailing you out of jail right now. And Tonya, I don't know what in the world has gotten into you. Cussing and carrying on. This is not the way a young Christian woman is supposed to behave."

Harold laughed, a deep belly laugh. Laughed so hard tears rolled down his face.

"Unc, you alright?" Mike said.

"Man, I feel great. That was the best half time show I've ever seen in my life. Katie reaching for her purse like she's getting ready to shank the man. Joshua, of all people, having to hold somebody back."

"Glad we could all provide a little deathbed humor for you." Joshua said, still holding onto Tonya.

"Well, you heard the doctor. I'm dying. So, let's get these goodbyes out of the way."

"Let me go. I refuse to stand around and listen to this." Joshua released her and Tonya pushed past Mike and made a beeline for the door.

"Tonya, wait —"

"Let her go, Mike. She'll be alright. I want to talk to you and Joshua both."

Jack clasped Mike on the shoulder, "Your mother and I will see to Tonya." Jack and Melissa both followed Tonya out the door.

"Barb, the papers for the insurance company are in the top drawer of my study. I increased the coverage on the ranch. After I'm gone, there should be enough money for you to pay the ranch off free and clear and finish paying for Tonya's schooling. Plus, you have my pension, so you should never have to work another day in your life. I took care of everything."

Barbara leaned over and kissed the inside palm of Harold's hand. "We don't have to talk about this right now, dear heart. Let's just enjoy each other. Enjoy our family."

We gotta talk about it now, baby. I'm not leaving this hospital bed alive. This is my last hurrah. But I don't want you to cry. What I want is for you to take some of that leftover insurance money after you pay off the ranch and Tonya's school. I want you to take that money and spend some time traveling the world with Katie. Harold smiled at his sister. "Barb, you know as well as I do that somebody's gotta keep an eye on Katie." Katie leaned in and kissed Harold's cheek. "Kiss Mama and Daddy when you get to Heaven for me."

Barbara wiped the fresh tears from her eyes. "I'm going to step outside for a bit. I need some air."

Katie nodded. "I'm right behind you."

The door closed softly behind them, and Harold caught the look of anguish on Joshua's face. "I'm not dying today, son. I

will see you play in the NBA. I promise you that. I love you."
Harold said gruffly.

Joshua leaned down and pressed his forehead against
Harold's for a moment before quickly darting from the room.

Harold closed his eyes, trying to get his emotions in check.
When he opened them again, he saw silent tears rolling down
Mike's face. Harold watched Mike's tears in quiet amazement.
In all the years he had known this boy, had helped raised this
boy, had loved this boy, Harold could honestly say he had never
once seen him cry. When Mike was twelve, he'd taken a tumble
off the barn roof and broken his leg. It had to have hurt like
hell, especially since they'd had to reset the bone on site. Still,
Mike didn't cry. Not one tear. His birth mother, a drug addict,
desperate for her next fix, had sold him to an undercover cop
once. That had to have hurt like hell too, but even then, the boy
didn't cry. For Mike to be standing here in this moment like
this, Harold knew he was witnessing an incredibly powerful
thing.

"Do you still love my daughter? Still want her hand in marriage?"

"Yes, sir."

Harold reached out, he grabbed Mike's hand and pulled him
into an embrace. "I give you my blessing, son. You look after
our girl for me. Even if she doesn't want you to. She's going to
lose her way for a while. Our little birdie is going to forget how
to fly. You help her, Mike. Help her find her wings."

CHAPTER 96

Tonya pushed the sofa in the family waiting room away from the wall, looking for a wall socket. She pulled her juicer, the plunger, and the veggie catch bin from her duffle bag. Along with an assortment of fresh fruits and vegetables, a catch container for the juice, and a roll of paper towels. Tonya laid the fruits and vegetables out on the paper towel and made quick work of preparing the produce to go into the juicer. She flipped the on switch, and the juicer came to life with a loud roar. She dropped the first carrot down the shoot, then an apple. So consumed was she with her task, Tonya didn't see or hear the nursing attendant who had entered the room.

"Excuse me, ma'am? Ma'am?" The attendant tapped Tonya on the shoulder. "Ma'am?!"

Tonya flipped the switch on the juicer to the off position. "Yes, how can I help you?"

"Ma'am, this is a hospital. You can't blend or whatever it is that you're doing in here."

"It's not a blender, it's a juicer. My father is a patient in this hospital, and he needs the nutrients in this juice to repair his cells."

"I'm sorry, ma'am, but we can't allow you to do that here."

"Why not?"

"Well, because it's against hospital policy."

Tonya stood up, tucked a tendril of hair behind her ear and read the attendant's name tag. "Fine, go get it, Molly."

The attendant stared at her blankly. "Get what?"

"Go get your policy. Show me where it says I can't supply fresh juice for my father on the last days of his life. Especially since his joke of a doctor who practices here has decided not to treat him anymore. Go ahead, get your policy and show me."

The woman's face filled with pity, which only enraged Tonya more.

"I know this must be a hard time for you. If you need someone to talk to, I can call a social worker."

"You don't know sh#%t Molly. Don't patronize me. Just show me the policy!"

"Ma'am, if you continue to be aggressive, I'm going to have to call security."

"Aggressive? Seriously, Molly, you want to go there?! What are you going to tell them, that I stabbed you with a carrot?!"

Mike, who had just left Harold's hospital room, followed the sound of Tonya's elevated voice down the hall. "Hey, hey, what's going on here?"

"She can't blend in here. And if she doesn't stop, I'm going to be forced to call security."

"It's a juicer, you idiot! Not a blender. And I'm doing what the very incompetent staff at this hospital refuses to do! That's save my father's life!"

"Can I talk to you for a sec?" Mike said. Ignoring Tonya and focusing his attention on the attendant.

"Sure."

The woman followed him over to a corner of the room. Mike stuck his hand out to her. "Hi, Molly, is it?"

"Yes." She shook his hand.

"My name is Mike Dutton."

Molly smiled sheepishly up at him, "I know who you are. I'm a fan."

"Thanks for being a fan, Molly. I'm really sorry about this. Her dad is in the ICU right now and my whole family is having a very difficult time accepting his prognosis. So, if you could do me a favor and just hold off on calling security, I promise I'll handle this."

"Alright, Mr. Dutton."

Mike watched Molly walk out of the lounge area. He turned his attention back to Tonya. Tonya had turned the juicer back on and was now frantically jamming more fruits and vegetables down the shoot. Mike walked over to the sofa, unplugged the cord from the wall, then picked Tonya up and carried her out of the large sliding exit doors into the hospital parking lot.

Tonya flailed and screamed like a wounded animal. Trying unsuccessfully to break free from Mike's embrace.

"Blackbird, stop."

"Let me go, Michael!"

"I can't do that, baby. Not until you calm down. When you calm down, I'll let go, alright? But you have to calm down."

Tonya stopped struggling in his arms, and Mike set her down on the pavement.

"I'm sorry, alright? I'm sorry that you're hurting right now. I'm sorry I can't take the pain away."

"No! I don't need you! I don't need you and I don't want you! Why are you here, Michael? I don't need you! I don't need any of you doubting Thomases." Tonya spat. Then she took off running like the wind.

Present Day 2010

CHAPTER 97

HOUSTON, TEXAS, SUNDAY MORNING

EVERY SUNDAY SINCE HER return, Michael would look across the table at Tonya and ask her how she felt about church that morning. Tonya would say that she still wasn't feeling it. He'd tell her to change clothes and meet him outside. And the two of them would spend Sunday morning, worshiping some place quiet, outdoors, and alone. This morning, Tonya decided to skip their usual preamble. She showed up to breakfast wearing a jogging suit and a pair of kicks.

"If you're looking for Mike, he left for service nearly an hour ago. You're welcome to join me if you'd like. I like to attend the morning Bible study, but that doesn't start for another forty minutes. You still have time to get dressed." Pearl said.

Tonya smiled brightly, trying her best to hide the humongous sense of disappointment that had settled over her.

Her rational mind understood that he had not stood her up. They'd never pre-planned these spontaneous outings. So how could he have stood her up? So why was she feeling so ... *heartbroken?*

Tonya mentally shook herself. She felt it, just as plain as day: a spirit of heaviness, a spirit of rejection, and a spirit of abandonment. All trying to bum-rush her at once, and wrestle her to the ground. And for what? Because Michael decided to go to church this morning?

Tonya mentally chastised herself. *Come on, get it together girlfriend, we are not that chick.*

Tonya knew heartbreak, and this wasn't it. Heartbreak was what she felt when she had come to him, three days before she was due to leave for the mission field, and he told her they couldn't be together anymore. That he had a date with one of his stand-ins. She had ended the sexual nature of their relationship six months prior to that, and how had he dealt with it? The Negro had stand-ins. Stand-ins. That was heartbreak.

But why was she even thinking about any of that right now? Something that happened over a decade ago. He didn't stand her up for another woman this morning. He went to church. They weren't even a couple anymore. He had a girlfriend. Partly because of her, yes, but he still had a girlfriend.

At that moment, Tonya decided it was a good thing that Michael was a no show. She definitely needed some time alone. She needed to go somewhere and have a little talk with Jesus because her feelings were far too feral, far too intense for the situation at hand.

The only thing Michael was guilty of was following his normal routine.

But, if he had decided to do something other than our usual routine, couldn't he have at least told me?

Maybe what Michael was really guilty of was taking her words to heart. She had told him, when she had arrived, not to rearrange his life.

Perhaps he had finally decided that she had been right all along. Maybe he'd concluded for himself that Tonya just wasn't worth it.

Tonya leaned over and kissed Pearl on the cheek, "Thanks for the offer, Grandma Pearl, but you go on without me. I'm going to hang back and worship on my own."

CHAPTER 98

SELENA AWOKE THAT SAME Sunday morning to find three dolls lying on top of Leslie's makeshift altar. Two dolls—one male and one female — were bound with chains. The other doll, a female barbie, lay at the far end of the altar alone.

"What's all this?"

"I told you, I got you, cousin. It's a separation spell."

"Don't we need a make-him-love-me-and-never-let-me-go-spell?"

"All rolled together into one. Once we break the agreement between your man and Ms. Goody, then we can activate the next stage of the spell. There is just one thing you'll have to do in order for the magic in the binding spell to take root. You'll have to sleep with him."

Selena shook her head. "I told you, it won't work. He made some type of vow to the Lord when he got saved, and according to him, he'll remain abstinent till the day he's married."

"Look, cuz, you've had a major setback. And that's discouraging. I get it, but I'm doing my part. Now you've got to do yours. Don't forget why we are doing this. Don't forget what's at stake."

"I haven't."

"Good. Then you figure out a way to make him break that vow."

Author's Note

Yes, I know, I did it again. I left our hero and heroine swinging from a metaphorical cliff. When I began this journey with the characters of Mike and Tonya, many moons ago, I wholeheartedly believed that their story could be told in one volume, but as the characters started to reveal themselves and the novel swelled to almost 600 pages, I realized that wasn't true. Please check out the completion of Mike and Tonya's story in Flight of the Blackbird Part II. Available for purchase today. Yes, today! You don't have to wait for the next book in the series this time.

If you are coming to this series for the first time, go back and read the first three books of the Redemption Price series: *Passing Through Waters, Opening the Floodgates* and *The Fire This Time*. It's not required reading to enjoy Mike and Tonya's story, but it will make for a much fuller reading experience.

If you've enjoyed reading this book, tell a friend and go online and write a review. Professionally, reviews go a long way to helping independent authors increase their book sales. Personally, because so much of what we do as writers is done in isolation, reviews encourage us and lift our spirits and let us know you value what we do. So, whether it's long and eloquent or short and sweet, please take a moment and leave a review.

FYI, I love connecting with readers, even if it's just to gossip about my characters like they are real people. Please drop me a line at doingbusinesswithgod@gmail.com Better yet, send me a photo of you and your book. Let me know your favorite part. Blessings to you and your household. Until we meet again.

Sincerely,

Catrina J. Sparkman

1.   Discuss the role of fathers and fatherhood? How does this theme play out in this story? What attributes make up a good father? Tell how you think the presence (or lack of) father figures play out in each of the characters' lives? One of the father's in the book, Lisa's dad, pulls out his gun while having a 'talk' with Marcus. What do you think about this display of Fatherhood?

2.   Discuss Tonya's actions in the story. What do her actions reveal about her character?
   a.   Holding on to her car Beauty?
   b.   Refusing Mike's help?
   c.   Choosing to wear black everyday?
   d.   Not wanting her family to know she had returned to Houston?

3.   The characters Selena and Shannon appear to both be holding space in the lives of men who don't see them as, 'the one'. Discuss this concept of being a placeholder? How does a person know whether they are a 'placeholder' or a 'main squeeze'? How are Selena and Shannon alike? How are they different? What traits (if any) can you identify in Selena and Shannon that would make their romantic partners handle them in this way?

4.   Joshua and Bella have a conversation in the book about his treatment of Serenity versus his treatment of his sons? Discuss Joshua's position, do you agree or disagree? Why? Should both males and females be able to set boundaries and have them respected? Should there be a greater concern for women in our society today to be able to set and demand respect for their boundaries?

5.   Tonya returns to Houston after her break up with a man she believes was 'the one.' Reflect upon a time when you experienced a hurt or a setback that turned out ultimately for your good?

6.   Leslie attempts a separation spell, but in order for the magic to take root, she tells Selena that she needs Mike to break his vow. Discuss whether or not you think the magic portrayed in this story is real. If magic is real, can it ever be successfully used against a Christian? Tell why you think it would be necessary for Mike to break his covenant with God?

7. Discuss Mike's actions towards Selena. Does he genuinely care for her? Why or why not? As a Christian man, is he responsible to handle her in a certain type of way? If so, in what way? Does he fail or succeed?

Catrina J. Sparkman is a playwright and author of multiple works of fiction and non-fiction. She is a graduate of the University of Wisconsin Madison with a Bachelor of Arts in English, Creative Writing and Masters in African American studies. She is a content writer, a theatrical consultant, workshop trainer, and public speaker for various national and international organizations. Catrina is the Artistic Director of the Creator's Cottage. As well as the founder and CEO of the Ironer's Press. She makes her home in Madison with her husband, Wes and their children.

Also By

Non-fiction:
Doing Business with God: An Everyday Guide to Prayer &
Journaling
Intimacy the Beginning of Authority
Divine Revelation for a Twitter Generation: Growing in the
Prophetic
Doing Battle with the Names of God
The Fourth Watch
Intercession 101: The Heartbeat of God
Wired for War
The Realm of Declaratory Grace

Fiction
Mother Love A Play
Redemption Price Series
Passing Through Waters
Opening the Floodgates
The Fire This Time

www.ingramcontent.com/pod-product-compliance
Lightning Source LLC
Chambersburg PA
CBHW051241210726
48287CB00002B/350